# HEART OF A KILLER

# What Reviewers Say About Yolanda Wallace's Work

**Tailor-Made**

"An enjoyable romance that hit several harder-to-find demographics in the lesbian romance market: a religiously observant protagonist, an interracial relationship, and a gender-nonconforming protagonist."
—Veronica Koven-Matasy, Librarian, Boston Public Library

"Wallace has proven to be a varied writer who crafts diverse characters in a wide range of settings, and this take on a simple, sweet, butch/femme love story really showcases her soft writing style and firm grasp of lesbian romance. This story reads easily and flows smoothly. It had me smiling from the first page"—*Love Bytes Reviews*

**True Colors**

"[In *True Colors*], Robby has three jobs, none of which is likely to endear her to the President or his advisors. As well as working in her friend's shop, she also writes a pseudonymous political blog and performs as a go-go dancer in a popular lesbian bar. When [the President's daughter] Taylor asks her on a date, Robby at first thinks only of the gossip she might pick up for her blog. As the two grow closer, however, Robby—as well as Taylor—has to work out how much, if any, of her life she is prepared to sacrifice for love. I really enjoyed this book. ...I definitely want to investigate this author's back catalogue as soon as I get some spare reading time."—*The Good, The Bad and The Unread*

**Divided Nation, United Hearts**

"I found myself totally immersed in the story of Wil Fredericks, a woman who runs away to join the Union army disguised as a man and meets the woman of her dreams. …Yolanda Wallace has managed to write a wonderful love story set against the worst of times. I loved it and highly recommend this book. Five stars!"
—*Kitty Kat's Book Review Blog*

"*Divided Nations, United Hearts* delivers on its promise."—*Just Love Reviews*

**24/7**

"This story is intense, exciting, a bit erotic, romantic and very, very good!!"—*Prism Book Alliance*

"Ms. Wallace as always delivers an entertaining read that is fun and well researched. Thrill seekers, this is your book."—*The Romantic Reader Blog*

**Break Point**

"Wallace captures the spirit of the time, from the changing attitudes of the Great Depression, to the terrifying oppression of the Third Reich, working in real events and people to construct a vibrant setting. The romance is strong…"—*Publishers Weekly*

"I adored this book. I'm not big into tennis but I cared about both of the main characters. I like that they both basically stuck to their morals to do the right thing rather than the thing that people were trying to make them do instead."—*Blow Pop's Book Reviews*

"[*Break Point*] is so full of suspense, gads I nearly bit my fingernails to the quick! The characters are so easy to care about. The near constant anxiety as I worried endlessly for Meike's life was almost too intense. It was interesting to see Helen grow and so painful to see what Meike was put through but when they were together it was such a relief!"—*Prism Book Alliance*

"*Break Point* is a heart wrenching story set at the height of WWII with a refreshing perspective—of Germans who do not endorse of the actions of Hitler and his henchmen and of an American being manipulated by an FBI agent for government purposes. This is countered with the love story of two people, who might be destined to find completion together, but first, they must overcome obstacles that sometimes seem impossible—a compelling tale of history and compassion, destiny and enduring love."—*Lambda Literary Review*

"If you are a sports fan this book will definitely appeal to you. ...[A] well written tale."—*The Romantic Reader Blog*

## The War Within

"*The War Within* has a masterpiece quality to it. It's a story of the heart told with heart—a story to be savored—and proof that you're never too old to find (or rediscover) true love."—*Lambda Literary Review*

## Murphy's Law

"Prepare to be thrilled by a love story filled with high adventure as they move toward an ending as turbulent as the weather on a Himalayan peak."—*Lambda Literary Review*

**Lucky Loser**

"Yolanda Wallace is a great writer. Her character work is strong, the story is compelling, and the pacing is so good that I found myself tearing through the book within a day and a half."—*The Lesbian Review*


**Rum Spring**

"The writing was possibly the best I've seen for the modern lesfic genre, and the premise and setting was intriguing. I would recommend this one."—*The Lesbrary*

Visit us at www.boldstrokesbooks.com

# By the Author

In Medias Res
Rum Spring
Lucky Loser
Month of Sundays
Murphy's Law
The War Within
Love's Bounty
Break Point
24/7
Divided Nation, United Hearts
True Colors
Tailor-Made
Pleasure Cruise
Comrade Cowgirl
Heart of a Killer

**Writing as Mason Dixon:**
Date with Destiny
Charm City
21 Questions

# HEART OF A KILLER

*by*

## Yolanda Wallace

2019

# HEART OF A KILLER

ISBN 13: 978-1-63555-547-9

This Trade Paperback Original Is Published By
Bold Strokes Books, Inc.
P.O. Box 249
Valley Falls, NY 12185

First Edition: October 2019

---

**Credits**
Editor: Cindy Cresap
Production Design: Susan Ramundo
Cover Design By Sheri (hindsightgraphics@gmail.com)

# Acknowledgments

My wife has a thing for action movies, so I've been exposed to dozens of lethal assassins over the years. All were good at what they did, though some seemed to take more pleasure in it than others. My titular killer, Santana Masters, was partially inspired by John Wick, the haunted hit man so memorably played by Keanu Reeves in an ongoing series of films, though (spoiler alert) no puppies are harmed in the pages that follow. I hope to spend more time with Santana in the future, but I will be sure to ask her permission first.

I would like to extend my continued gratitude to Radclyffe, Sandy, Cindy, and the rest of the Bold Strokes Books team for giving me and my fellow authors roots while allowing us to grow wings.

I would also like to thank the readers for their continued support. I love the fact that you are as excited about lesfic as I am. You are my inspiration, and I couldn't do what I do without you.

As always, I would like to thank Dita for continuing to indulge and, in most cases, fuel my fantasies.

# Dedication

To Dita,

You slay me.

## Prologue

Santana Masters was good at her job. Great, in fact. That didn't mean she had to like it. Every time she pulled the trigger, she felt a piece of herself die along with her victims. She hadn't chosen this life, but she had to keep living it until she finally repaid the debt she had incurred long ago.

She took a few deep breaths to slow her heart rate, peered through the scope on her rifle, and waited for her target to appear in her crosshairs. Jeong Park was a high-ranking cabinet official who had apparently reached the limits of his usefulness. The cash-strapped government of the rogue nation he called home had placed a seven-figure price tag on his head, and it was time for her to collect the bounty. She would receive only a small percentage of the payout. The rest would be deducted from what she owed. By her reckoning, that amount should have zeroed out years ago, but her handler seemed to think otherwise and, unfortunately, he had the last word. She had to keep going until he finally gave her permission to stop. If she didn't, she would lose everything she loved. Permanently this time.

By nature, her profession had a limited timeline. Its proponents could stay sharp for only so long before their skills started to erode. She had been in the game since she was fifteen years old. That was almost twenty years ago. How long would it be before a younger, more ruthless version of herself came along? How long would it be before she, like Park, would be considered extraneous? Before she became the target instead of the shooter. Probably sooner rather than later, but she didn't have time to think about that now.

"Take the shot and get out" was her mantra for a reason. It helped her stay focused and didn't leave any room for doubt. Hesitation could get her caught. Getting caught could get her killed. And despite how much she hated her life, she wasn't ready for it to end.

Unlike most targets, Park had made her job easy for her. A creature of habit, he never instructed his driver to take any alternate routes as they made their way around their nation's capital. He also stuck to the same daily schedule he had kept since his nephew had appointed him to his current office. The same nephew who was now paying to have him killed. Apparently, not all family squabbles could be solved sitting around the dinner table.

Today was Saturday, which meant Park would put in a cursory appearance at his office before spending the afternoon with his mistress, a member of the state-run media who was either about to become part of the story or part of the cover-up. Santana didn't plan on sticking around long enough to find out which.

She felt a surge of adrenaline course through her body when Park's limo pulled into view. She tamped down her emotions so her hands would remain steady. She had set up her sniper position more than half a mile from the apartment building Park's car was currently idling in front of. At that distance, the slightest deviation in her aim would alter the trajectory of her shot by several feet, not a few inches. Close-range kills were easier. Long-distance ones posed more of a challenge.

Syncing her breathing with the rhythm of her heartbeat, she waited for Park to exit the vehicle. The air was still, meaning she wouldn't have to make many adjustments to her shot She resisted aiming for where Park was now and anticipated where he would be in the time it would take for the projectile to hit home. She had been watching his comings and goings long enough that she didn't have to guess where he would move next. She already knew.

"Take the shot and get out."

Her breath puffed in the frigid air as she said the words. She had been lying prone on the nearly frozen ground for over an hour, but she no longer felt the cold. She pulled the trigger, waited for the burst of blood and gore that signaled she had hit her mark, then did what she did best: she disappeared.

She disassembled her rifle, collected the spent shell casing, and policed the area to make sure she had left no trace of her presence behind. She had already stashed a QBZ-95 near the demilitarized zone, allowing her benefactors an opportunity to blame either Chinese or South Korean operatives for the assassination. The bullpup-style automatic rifle fired a much smaller round than the military grade weapon she had used, but in certain parts of the world, the story was much more important than the facts.

No matter. The "truth" would sort itself out eventually. In the meantime, she had a plane to catch. She could finally allow herself to relax once she got to Japan. Tokyo, one of the most populous cities in the world, was a convenient place for her to get lost before she slipped back into the shadows while she waited for her next assignment.

In Tokyo, there were not only plenty of people but plenty of places to party. As soon as she made her way across the heavily fortified two-and-a-half-mile swath of land that lay between her and her getaway vehicle, she would find one. She had earned a chance to let her hair down, and she meant to take it.

## Chapter One

Brooke Vincent liked being the center of attention. Brooklyn DiVincenzo, on the other hand, did not. Brooke Vincent was a glamorous tech company CEO who had never encountered a party she couldn't crash. Brooklyn DiVincenzo was a geeky computer nerd whose idea of a perfect evening was sitting cross-legged on her couch in her favorite pj's while she wrote lines of code and ate a pint of chocolate chip cookie dough ice cream. Brooke Vincent was a sophisticated world traveler. Brooklyn DiVincenzo was the youngest member of a close-knit middle class family who hadn't been expected to acquire either the ways or the means to escape the confines of the New York borough for which she had been named.

As unlikely as it might seem to some, Brooke and Brooklyn were one and the same.

Brooklyn became Brooke whenever it was expedient. When she needed to deliver an energetic speech to motivate her employees or when she needed to make a few provocative statements on social media to get her company some much-needed press attention. As far as she was concerned, there was no such thing as bad publicity. Not as long as it accomplished her goal of raising her company's profile and its bottom line at the same time.

She was in Tokyo for a tech convention. Representatives from companies headquartered all around the world had convened to offer sneak peeks at some of the innovations they were working on, share a couple of drinks, and kick a few ideas around while they were at it.

Everyone was there. From the billion-dollar conglomerates whose success she hoped to mirror as well as the smaller companies with whom she often competed for contracts and employees. She and her team were holding their own, but she looked forward to the day when they could finally pull ahead of their peers instead of keeping pace with them.

These kinds of events were necessary but exhausting. Brooklyn had been on for three days now. Tonight was New Year's Eve, and she wanted to celebrate it as herself.

Her hotel was located in Tokyo's Shibuya district, which was illuminated by the bright lights that made the city seem like a cross between Times Square and the Vegas Strip. The four-star dwelling featured nine restaurants, an art gallery, and four bars.

In Japan, the New Year holiday, known as Shōgatsu, was traditionally a quiet, solemn affair. Many people returned to their hometowns to spend time with their families, share moments of quiet reflection, and make plans for the coming year. Western-style celebrations, complete with fireworks and countdown parties, were becoming more popular, however. A fact made obvious by the large number of people Brooklyn spotted wearing festive hats and sunglasses after she left the quiet confines of her hotel room.

Bypassing the rowdy dance clubs and karaoke bars, which were already crowded with revelers, she headed to the main bar on the hotel's top floor. The ten thousand yen cover charge, which converted to around ninety US dollars, entitled her to a welcome cocktail, all the sushi she could eat, a complimentary champagne toast when the clock struck midnight, and unlimited access to some of the best views in the city.

She snagged a cherry blossom martini from a passing waiter's tray and took a seat at a small table near the floor-to-ceiling window. A game show that was long on visuals and seemingly short on rules was playing on the flat-screen TV behind the bar. To her right lay the city of Tokyo in all its Technicolor glory. She sipped her drink while she watched dozens of digital ads assault her senses. Normally, she would have been overwhelmed by the visual overload, but the refreshing combination of sugar and alcohol in her cocktail provided the perfect counterpoint to the kinetic imagery.

She held up her glass, which was filled with sake, plum wine, cranberry juice, and a splash of soda.

"To all the people who said I would never reach this point. Look at me now."

She hadn't achieved all the goals she had set for herself, but she was well on her way. She had a foothold in the tech industry, she had a solid business plan, and she was starting to be noticed by all the right people. The next step would be taking her company public. It would most likely never be on par with the corporate giants like Apple and Microsoft, but she could dream.

"A woman as beautiful as you are shouldn't be drinking alone. May I join you?"

Brooklyn dragged her eyes away from the view. Her gaze came to rest on a short, sweaty man in a too-tight suit and an off-kilter tie. Though the night was relatively young, he had obviously already had one too many. His cheeks were dotted with color, making him look like one of the rag dolls Brooklyn had once possessed when she was younger.

"I'm fine on my own. Thanks."

The man moved closer instead of walking away. "Are you waiting for someone? If you are, I can keep you company until he arrives. If you aren't, lucky me."

Brooklyn hated persistent suitors. Some people simply couldn't understand the concept that no matter how politely it was worded, a refusal was still a refusal.

"You have to kiss someone at midnight," the man said with a smile even oilier than his product-drenched locks. "It might as well be me."

He pulled out the chair across from her. Before he could take a seat, a woman sporting an expensive haircut and an even more expensive designer suit placed a hand on his arm.

"I think the lady would like to be alone tonight. Why don't you take the hint and leave her that way?"

The woman's tone was measured, but her voice commanded attention. So did the rest of her. She was tall and broad-shouldered. Her fitted dress shirt hugged her trim form. And, God, was she gorgeous. She looked like a freaking matinee idol. Not one of the slew of interchangeable celebrities that currently dotted the entertainment landscape. More like a timeless classic from yesteryear.

Intrigued, Brooklyn waited to see how the scene taking place before her would play out. She hoped her unwanted admirer would take the hint because it would definitely suck to see her knight in shining armor end up falling on her sword.

"No offense," he said, "but I saw her first."

He tried to jerk his arm free, sloshing some of his drink on Brooklyn's table in the process. Still, the woman held on. Her smile was pleasant—charming, in fact—but the white-knuckled grip she held on the man's arm was anything but.

"Let's not allow this to get ugly, shall we?" the woman asked.

The man's defiant expression morphed into one of uncertainty then one of pain. "No problem." His voice was at least an octave higher than its previous pitch. Brooklyn smiled at its cartoon-like quality. She abhorred violence, but she had to admit she was a little turned on by the woman's effortless display of power. "She's all yours."

"I'm so glad we could reach an understanding."

The woman finally released her grip and the man slunk away, rubbing his arm as if trying to take away the pain.

The woman turned back to Brooklyn and gave a courtly bow. Drop-dead gorgeous and chivalrous to boot. So far, she was two for two. "I apologize for the disturbance."

"Totally not your fault. Thanks for interceding the way you did."

"It was the least I could do."

Modest, too. Make that three for three. "Do you make a habit out of rescuing damsels in distress?"

"You strike me as many things, but a damsel in distress certainly isn't one of them."

The woman's words seemed sincere, not a transparent attempt to stroke her ego as she tried to convince her to fall into bed. Not that she'd have to do much convincing. "Thank you for the compliment."

"More like a statement of fact." The woman held Brooklyn's gaze as she waited for her words to sink in. Damn, she was smooth. "Enjoy your evening."

The woman turned to leave. As much as Brooklyn wanted to enjoy the view as she watched her walk away, she didn't want to see her go. She held out a hand to stop her. "Will you allow me to buy you a drink to express my appreciation for your act of chivalry?"

The woman flashed that charming smile again. "If you're offering, I'm not about to turn down a free drink."

Brooklyn caught a roving waitress's eye. "What would you like?" she asked as the waitress made her way over to their table.

The woman claimed the seat across from Brooklyn. "Scotch. Neat. A twenty-year-old single malt if they have it. Twelve if they don't."

Classic. Understated. Brooklyn had no idea who this woman was, but she liked her style. Her dark hair was short and parted on one side, making her look like a distaff Cary Grant. She didn't have the legendary actor's English accent, but her bearing and mannerisms were just as suave as his had been on the silver screen.

"Thank you for the drink," the woman said after the waitress left to fill their order.

"I think my expense account can afford to take the hit."

The woman's smile turned playful. The first time during their brief time together that Brooklyn had seen her let her guard down. The stoic guardian angel thing had its merits, but this was a good look, too. "I won't tell your boss if you don't."

"Too late," Brooklyn said with a wink. "She already knows."

"The woman at the top of the food chain, huh?"

"Guilty as charged."

"Color me impressed. And thank you for confirming my suspicions about you."

"Who do I have to thank for coming to my rescue?"

The woman's gray eyes sparkled with a hint of mischievousness. "On a night like this in a setting like this, I find anonymity works best, don't you?"

If Brooklyn had thought the woman couldn't possibly get any more alluring, she had been woefully off the mark.

"I like a bit of mystery every now and then," she said, "but I have to call you something. How about Tall, Dark, and Handsome? Does that work?"

"TDH for short. What shall I call you?"

Brooklyn thought for a moment. She wanted to play the game TDH had drawn her into, but she didn't want to blurt out the first name that came to mind. Outside, a few flakes of snow had begun to fall, reminding her of a character in one of her favorite animated movies.

"You can call me Olaf."

"An inspired choice, I must say." TDH unleashed a throaty laugh as she extended her hand. "I'm pleased to meet you, Olaf." Even though Brooklyn could tell she was holding back, TDH's grip was strong. Almost crushing. No wonder her wannabe Romeo had run away with his proverbial tail tucked between his legs.

Brooklyn's father had taught her to appreciate the value of a good handshake. TDH's showed she had enough confidence in her own power not to be intimidated by someone else's.

"What would you like to drink to?" TDH asked after the waitress set a highball glass filled with Scotch on the table.

"The kindness of strangers," Brooklyn said without hesitation.

TDH gently tapped her sturdy glass against Brooklyn's more fragile one. "A worthy sentiment, to be sure."

"What brings you to Tokyo?"

Brooklyn thought the question was fairly innocuous, but TDH gave it careful consideration before she replied.

"I was on a business trip. Japan provided a convenient layover on my way home. I'm flying out tomorrow morning. I wasn't planning on meeting anyone tonight. I just didn't want to ring in the new year alone."

"Great minds think alike." Brooklyn felt lucky to have met someone who was on the same page. "Where's home?"

TDH waved a hand dismissively. "A tiny speck in the Pacific you've most likely never heard of. It's on the map, but you have to know what you're looking for to be able to find it."

"That sounds remote. I'm part of a large family and I live and work in New York City. I can't imagine not being surrounded by dozens of people at all times. On second thought, that sounds heavenly. Do you have room on your flight for one more?"

"I'm afraid I'll have to refer you to a travel agent for the answer to that question. Would you like to get something to eat? I hear this hotel makes a salmon roll that's to die for."

"Yes, let's."

The scrumptious buffet was the main reason Brooklyn had eschewed pajamas and room service for a little black dress and heels. After she and TDH made their way through the buffet line, they returned to their table and chatted amiably while they ate.

TDH asked more questions than she answered. By the time the clock neared midnight, Brooklyn felt certain her gorgeous protector knew much more about her than the other way around. Not that there was anything wrong with that. In fact, it gave her something to look forward to the next time they saw each other. If there was a next time.

"I'm sorry for monopolizing the conversation," she said. "I feel like I've spent the past two hours babbling about myself. You must think I'm the ultimate narcissist."

"Far from it. I've enjoyed having a chance to get to know you."

"I would love a chance to return the favor. I don't even know what you do for a living."

"Does it matter?"

"Where I'm from, your occupation defines you. When you strike up a conversation with someone, the first question usually isn't *What's your name?* but *Who do you work for?*"

"Then I suppose you could consider me a bit of a free agent."

"I suspected as much."

"Why do you say that?"

"You seem like someone who's used to calling her own shots."

"You're very perceptive." A small smile played across TDH's handsome face. "Remind me not to attempt to hide anything from you."

The comment could have been innocuous or it could have been an invitation for a return engagement. Not bothering to analyze TDH's words too carefully, Brooklyn dug a pen out of her clutch bag, wrote her cell phone number on a cocktail napkin, and slid the napkin across the table. Sharing her business card would have been easier, but she didn't want to break the rules TDH had established for what was turning out to be an incredibly sexy game.

"If you're ever in New York, dial that number and ask for Olaf."

TDH glanced at the napkin, then slipped it into the inside pocket of her suit jacket. "I'll do that."

As the crowd counted down the waning seconds to the new year, Brooklyn felt absurdly giddy. In that moment, everything was fraught with possibility. Even a chance meeting with a complete stranger.

When the countdown reached zero and couples all around them celebrated the moment with kisses ranging from chaste to passionate, Brooklyn ached to do the same. She didn't make a move in that direction, though, because she was fairly certain her breath reeked of wasabi and raw fish. She had spent the past two hours trying to make a good impression. She didn't want to sabotage all her hard work before she had a chance to make a lasting one.

She pressed her lips to TDH's cheek, then whispered in her ear. "Thank you once again for coming to my rescue. If we're fortunate enough to meet again, I hope it's under much more pleasant—and pleasurable—circumstances."

And if she had anything to say about it, it certainly would be.

## Chapter Two

Santana typically worked out wearing a sports bra and a pair of loose-fitting shorts. Aside from her bright yellow running shoes, today she had opted for all black. The sun felt good as it beat down on her bare shoulders, arms, and back. The light sheen of sweat on her skin helped keep her cool as she ran.

She glanced at her sports watch to check her progress. She had put in fifteen miles so far and had another five to go. She preferred shorter distances, but she often liked to test her limits. Sometimes, she simply wanted to enjoy the view. Today was one of those days.

The island nation of 'Ohe Sojukokoro was so small she could circle it during a long run. She had tried on many countries for size, but 'Ohe Sojukokoro was the only one that felt like home. Its name, composed of the Polynesian word for bamboo and the Yoruba word for cove, was as beautiful as the country itself. According to local folklore, its founding family was a native princess and an east African warrior who was swept out to sea and ended up shipwrecked on an island thousands of miles away from home.

Though she hadn't been born there, 'Ohe Sojukokoro spoke to her in a way no other place did. She and the country shared some of the same qualities, namely multicultural roots and a fiercely independent spirit. She had found it purely by accident when she had eavesdropped on a conversation between a couple of surfers in an airport bar while she waited out a layover between assignments. The moment she had touched down for the first time, she had known she would never leave. Not for good, anyway. Though work frequently called her away, she always came back. She always would.

She could be herself here, not one of the myriad of identities she assumed whenever the situation warranted. As she jogged past their places of business, the shopkeepers greeted her by name, making her feel like a local instead of a tourist.

"Slow down, my sistah," David Kahale said as she neared the Kon-Tiki Bar and Grill, the most popular restaurant on the island. "You're running like someone's chasing you."

Sometimes she felt that way, too. She had been trying to outrun her past practically since the day she was born. One day, she hoped to finally get ahead of it.

"Save me a seat at the bar for lunch," she said without breaking stride. "I'll be back as soon as I freshen up."

"I'll be sure to double whatever you order," David said. "After a workout like that, you're gonna need it."

"Thanks, David. You're a man after my own heart."

His hearty laugh propelled her on her way. She picked up her pace as she began the last phase of her run. The steep incline provided a serious test of her endurance. The first time she had tried to navigate the route, her spirit had been willing, but her rubbery legs and burning lungs had had other ideas. Now that failure served as motivation. That and the sprawling house that topped the hill.

No matter how tired she was when she reached this point, she always felt a rush of energy when her house came into view. On paper, she appeared to possess many things, but her house was the only thing that truly belonged to her. More like a fortress than a home, the five thousand square foot structure was filled with enough high-tech toys to keep her entertained and a state-of-the-art security system designed to keep her safe. Though she took pains to avoid drawing attention to herself, she wasn't foolish enough to think she didn't have enemies. She was smart enough, however, not to let them know where she laid her head at night.

She lived a solitary existence. Not because she wanted to. Because she had to. She longed to form a connection that was more than simply platonic, but her conscience wouldn't allow her to embark upon a serious relationship because she didn't know if she could keep her partner safe.

She checked her watch again, confirming that she was close to breaking her personal best time for the distance. Resisting the urge to grit her teeth, she forced her body to stay relaxed as she increased her rate of turnover. Legs churning, she reached her driveway thirty seconds faster than she ever had before.

She took a millisecond to celebrate her accomplishment, then began her recovery routine. She hydrated, stretched, then submerged herself in the hot tub. The warm water helped her muscles relax. She wished she could find something that had a similar effect on her mind, but she knew she wouldn't truly find peace until she finally earned her freedom. And perhaps not even then.

The chime of an incoming message drew her from her reverie. The sound filled her with dread every time she heard it. She hadn't expected to hear it so soon. She didn't usually receive another assignment so quickly after completing a previous one. She had thought she would have more time to try to forget about the odious task she had just carried out until she was compelled to perform another one.

She dried her hands on a nearby towel and reached for her laptop. After she opened the application, she read the details of the hit job.

"Apologies for the short notice," the message read, "but our client is anxious for results and would like the task to be performed as quickly as possible. Preferably within the next few days. To assist your efforts, we have already performed the necessary surveillance on the target, as you will see in the attached dossier."

She opened the accompanying file. The target was identified as twenty-eight-year-old Charlotte Evans, who worked in Manhattan but lived in Jersey City, New Jersey, where the cost of living was significantly lower than it was across the Hudson River. She wasn't a high-ranking political official like Santana's previous target. According to the brief profile included in the dossier, she was a mid-level executive for a tech company. That partially explained the relatively low fee. Despite the special measures that had been taken for the expedited request, the listed charge was only six figures instead of seven.

Santana didn't know what the woman had done to raise someone's ire enough to want her dead, but she didn't have time to sit around wondering why. Because of the security settings on the app, the post would be automatically deleted thirty minutes after she accessed it. That gave her just enough time to memorize all the necessary details before the information was erased from her computer's hard drive as well as the app's servers.

She scrolled through the series of photographs included in the folder and examined the risk. Charlotte shared a house with two other people in the Hamilton Park neighborhood. The area was part of Jersey City's historic district and was centered on a Victorian age park of the same name. The park hosted several family-friendly events throughout the year, including a weekly farmers market, an Easter egg hunt, a youth festival, and a Shakespeare festival. The neighborhood sounded like the perfect place to live—and a terrible place to carry out a professional hit.

Santana thought she would be better served carrying out the job in Manhattan. The number of potential witnesses would be exponentially higher, but the percentage of people who would be concentrating on something other than their own agendas would be far lower. And New York, like Tokyo, offered plenty of places to hide. Her handler must have reached the same conclusion because the message included the address of a place across from the target's office where she could set up shop.

She pressed the Confirm button, booked a flight to New York City, and headed inside. She needed to decide which identity to assume while she carried out the job she had just been assigned.

Peering into the retinal scanner, she unlocked the door to her ready room, the space where she housed the items that helped her ply her trade. Passports, driver's licenses, birth certificates, weapons, cash, and a dozen air-gapped computers that were highly prized and nearly impossible to hack. With the items in this room, she could become anyone she wanted to at any time.

She selected the passport she thought would offer the least amount of resistance when she attempted to make her way through

US Customs, then stepped into the walk-in closet to select the wardrobe to match her chosen identity.

As she stood in front of the shelves, racks, and drawers filled with clothes, she remembered when her wardrobe was limited to her school uniform, a few pairs of jeans, a couple of T-shirts, and the "nice" dress her mother begged her to wear on special occasions. How times had changed.

She had been raised by a single mom. The two of them hadn't had much in the small apartment they shared in the slums of Manila, but they'd had each other.

When Benjie Aquino, a local thief, offered her a chance to make some easy money, she had eagerly accepted the opportunity. Her mother was perpetually exhausted from working two and sometimes three jobs at a time in order to make ends meet, and Santana had been willing to do whatever she could to help out. She had accepted Benjie's offer, agreeing to serve as a lookout while he robbed a high-end jewelry store in Manila's main retail district. Her portion of the take had been negligible compared to his, but she had felt like a millionaire when she pocketed the money he gave her.

Her mother had cried when Santana presented her with the crumpled bills. Her tears of joy had turned into tears of sorrow after she pressed Santana for details about the money's origins. Santana and her mother had gotten into a heated argument. Too stubborn to apologize, Santana had packed what little belongings she had and run away. That impulsive act was the biggest mistake she had ever made, and she had been paying for it ever since.

She gathered the clothes she needed and packed them in a suitcase. Then she locked the ready room behind her and headed upstairs to take a shower. She often wondered what her life would be like if she had chosen to swallow her pride all those years ago rather than give in to it.

"That's the thing about hindsight," she said as the water washed over her. "It always comes too late."

She might not have been able to give her mother the life of luxury she had once thought she wanted, but she could still do the one thing that mattered most: keep her safe.

## Chapter Three

B rooklyn felt like she had lost her audience. Her staff was attentive during her presentation, during which she detailed her impressions of the conference she had attended in Tokyo, and they posed incisive questions when she asked for their input, but they seemed more interested in the freebies she had snagged from the overloaded swag tables than the presentation itself.

"What am I missing?" she asked Charlie Evans after the meeting came to an end.

Charlie was not only one of the most talented programmers on her staff. She was also her best friend and her favorite sounding board. Their impromptu pitch sessions often carried over to the next day. Some of her best ideas had come as a result of bouncing them off Charlie first. No matter what the subject, she could count on Charlie to be honest with her. Sometimes brutally.

"Just the obvious, that's all."

The answer might have been clear to Charlie, but Brooklyn wasn't seeing it. "Do you mind filling me in?"

Charlie, a caffeine addict of the highest order, popped a piece of hard candy with a soft espresso center into her mouth before she raked her hands through her hair. Like her eyes, her natural hair color was brown, but she preferred dyeing her locks a rotating rainbow of colors. This month's chosen hue was electric blue with frosted tips worthy of a lead singer of an eighties-era hair metal band. Somewhere, Brett Michaels must have been eating his heart out.

"You've stated more than once that this company is second to none," Charlie said. "Now none of the staff cares about what the competition's up to. All they want to know is what we're planning to do next. They don't want to tweak someone else's innovations. They want to come up with their own."

"If I read you correctly, you're saying I've done my job too well."

"I told you not to take all those motivational speaking classes, but when was the last time you bothered taking my advice? Oh, I remember." Charlie snapped her fingers. "When I suggested you should make a move on the hot blonde who was checking you out when you and I went to dinner last month."

"The one you ended up going home with instead of me because you were the one she had her eye on in the first place?"

Charlie flashed the devilish grin that had helped her charm her way into dozens of women's beds over the years. Brooklyn had always proved immune to her charms because, even from the beginning, she had suspected they would make better friends than lovers. As it turned out, they had made even better business associates. She wouldn't be where she was now without Charlie on her team, and she couldn't wait to see where they would eventually end up. Hopefully as rich as Steve Jobs and Bill Gates, but without the not-so-friendly rivalry.

"At least one of us got laid that night," Charlie said. "Speaking of which, what did you get up to in Tokyo when you weren't attending one boring panel after another?"

"The panels were informative, not boring."

"To-*may*-to. To-*mah*-to. You say informative. I say snoozefest. But I'm willing to play along. What did you do when you weren't being 'informed'?"

"Nothing. Why?"

"Because you look like you've swallowed a freaking glow stick. Given your aversion to small children and the various bodily fluids that leak from their assorted orifices, I think it's safe to say you're not knocked up. That means you must have met someone while you were away." Charlie propped her feet on her desk and locked her hands behind her head. "My roommates and I take turns making dinner. Russell's next up in the rotation. His lasagna sucks ass, so if it's all the same with you, I'd rather stick around here than head home. Spill. I'm dying to hear about Brooke Vincent's latest carnal adventures."

Charlie was well aware of the machinations Brooklyn often resorted to in order to help BDV Enterprises maintain a high social media profile. She had helped Brooklyn pull off some of the stunts. The rest Brooklyn had told her about over burgers and beers.

"She didn't have any."

"Really?" Charlie looked skeptical. "That's a first."

"It was a business trip, not a vacation."

"That's never stopped you before."

Brooklyn wasn't proud of some of the shenanigans she had pulled, but she knew the work she and her team put in was on par with or exceeded their peers.

"I wanted to try something different this time. I want our company to be taken seriously, not considered a flash in the pan."

"Substance over style. I can dig it." Charlie nodded in agreement. "Now tell me her name."

"Whose name?"

"The woman who's got you looking like the Cheshire Cat, provided he ditched the tacky stripes in favor of stylish little black dresses."

The office had emptied out after the meeting, leaving Brooklyn and Charlie alone. Brooklyn hadn't spoken to anyone about the mysterious woman she had met on New Year's Eve, but she hadn't been able to think about anything or anyone else in the interim. She grabbed a chair from a nearby desk, pulled it closer, and took a seat.

Charlie officially occupied the office next to hers, but she only used it when she wanted to have one-on-one conferences with members of her team. On a daily basis, she preferred to work in the open concept outer office so she could feel like part of the action instead of one step removed.

"I would tell you her name if I knew it," Brooklyn said, "but we were never formally introduced."

"Sorry. Try again. You're a classic oversharer, B. If someone asks you a question that requires a two-word response at most, you break into a seven-minute soliloquy. Do you honestly expect me to believe you bumped uglies with someone and didn't bother catching her name before you dropped trou?"

"We didn't have sex. We just talked. Well, flirted. Shamelessly, I might add."

"How did you meet?"

"I went for a drink in one of the hotel bars and she rescued me from a drunk businessman who didn't know how to take no for an answer. When I asked for her name, she said she preferred to remain anonymous."

"That could be shady or sexy, depending on your point of view. What did she look like?"

"Like Cary Grant and Bruno Mars had a baby and they dressed her in bespoke suits instead of onesies."

"Oh, my God, that's fucking hot. Did you get her phone number at least?"

"No, but I gave her mine. I told her if she's ever in town, she should dial the number and ask for Olaf."

"Ex-squeeze me?"

Brooklyn blushed as she remembered the code names they had agreed to answer to rather than revealing their real identities. "It's a long story."

"Then grab us a couple of beers from the break room and help me fill in the blanks. Or is that what she said?"

Brooklyn got up to retrieve the drinks. "Your lack of social graces is mind-boggling. You know I only keep you around because you're such a kick-ass programmer, right?"

"That and my winning personality."

Brooklyn waggled her hand back and forth as if she were weighing the odds. "That's subject to debate."

Charlie tossed a paper clip at her. The vast majority of their printouts were soft copies rather than hard in order to protect the environment, but Charlie kept a full cup of paper clips on her desk so she could have something to fiddle with while she worked.

Some people chewed their nails or squeezed stress balls. Charlie preferred twisting the tiny metal objects into various shapes. If she ever washed out as a programmer, which was highly unlikely given her vast array of skills, she could have a successful career making balloon animals.

"You love me and you know it," Charlie said.

"Unfortunately, you're right, but my therapist says I'm making tremendous progress."

"I'm happy to hear that. Now stop stalling and fetch those beers. My boss will kill me if I'm late to work tomorrow."

"Yeah, I hear she can be a real ballbreaker."

"Now that she's getting laid on the regular, I think her attitude might take a turn for the better."

Brooklyn conceded defeat, knowing this was an argument she couldn't win. One chaste kiss had fueled nearly a week of feverish fantasies. If she and TDH ever became intimate, she might never get any work done. Despite her lofty ambitions, she was willing to accept the tradeoff.

In the break room, she peered into the refrigerator. She kept a selection of beer and wine on hand for after-work get-togethers that often evolved into impromptu brainstorming sessions. Like some authors she knew, a few staffers' creative juices didn't start flowing until they'd had a drink or two. She didn't judge their creative process. She just reaped the benefits.

She grabbed a couple of craft beers and used a bottle opener to pop the tops. Then she looked for a pair of koozies to keep the beers cold while she and Charlie talked. She opted for two she had grabbed during the first industry gathering she had attended when she was an unpaid intern with big dreams and a pile of student loan debt. Her debt had gotten smaller over the years, but her dreams had continued to grow. Some days, she felt like a lottery ticket holder right before a multimillion dollar jackpot was drawn—filled with ideas for the future but devoid of the capital needed to make her ideas come true.

When she closed the cabinet, she heard what sounded like the tinkling of ice in a glass.

"Did you get started without me?" she asked, holding a bottle of beer in each hand.

Charlie was always quick with a retort so Brooklyn was surprised not to receive a response of some kind.

"I can think of only two things that leave you speechless: work and women. You've already shut your computer down so I know it's not work. Who am I about to be stood up for? Is it the barista from your favorite coffeehouse or the—"

The words died in Brooklyn's throat. Charlie was sitting exactly as she had left her. Her eyes were open and her lips were still curved into a smile, but a large bullet hole had blossomed in her forehead. Blood and bits of what looked like brain matter covered the laptop, the bowl of espresso-filled candy, and the container of paper clips on her desk.

The bottles of beer slipped from Brooklyn's grip as her body went numb. The noise the neoprene-covered bottles made when they hit the unforgiving linoleum floor was muffled by the sound of her scream.

# Chapter Four

Santana didn't know what had just happened. She'd had her target in sight for nearly an hour, but she hadn't been able to pull the trigger. At first, she couldn't risk taking the shot when the office was filled with potential witnesses. One or more of them might have been able to spot her before she was able to make her way off the roof and down to the sidewalk ten stories below.

Most of the other staffers had cleared out fifteen minutes ago, but the target had lingered to talk with one of her fellow employees. Because of the partially obstructed sightline from her vantage point, Santana hadn't been able to see with whom the target was conversing. All she had been treated to were glimpses of shapely legs here or an expressive hand there. When the figure had retreated completely from view, she had finally been able to make her move.

Only she hadn't been able to take the shot.

She had gone through all of her normal rituals, but something hadn't felt right. *She* hadn't felt right. Something about the interaction between Evans and the woman she was conversing with made her hesitate. Even though she couldn't see both of them clearly, she could sense the dynamic between them. A true, honest friendship she couldn't bring herself to end.

She had tried to tell herself that this hit was no different from the dozens of others she had performed. Her other targets had had friends and families, too. But none of her other targets had been as seemingly innocent as this one. She hadn't been their judge or jury, but she had certainly been their executioner. Tonight, she hadn't been able to bring herself to fulfill any of those roles.

She had decided to postpone the hit until another day. Until her thoughts weren't as jumbled as they were tonight. She had been about to abandon her position when she heard a shot ring out. A shot that she didn't take.

The sound had come from behind her. She had looked back just in time to see a furtive figure in the window of an abandoned warehouse. Though the spot was farther away from her vantage point, it was the perfect location for a sniper's nest. It offered a clear view of Charlotte Evans's office building and provided plenty of cover for whoever was lurking inside. The person who had just performed the job she couldn't bring herself to.

The shooter retreated. She started to chase after them, but she doubted she'd be able to catch up to them before they got lost in the crowd on the busy sidewalks down below.

"Shit."

She swung her rifle back toward the office building and peered through the telescopic scope. What she saw made her forget how to breathe.

The office of the tech company Charlotte Evans worked for— BDV Enterprises—was housed in what was once a piano factory. Most of the building's original fixtures remained intact, including the faded lettering on the weathered brick exterior. The windows and sleek interior design, however, were thoroughly modern. The place would have looked right at home on a spaceship in a sci-fi movie.

Evans had remained upright rather than falling face-forward on her desk, but Santana knew she was dead. No one could survive such a devastating head shot. But it wasn't the sight of Evans's lifeless body that stunned her. It was the realization that the woman Charlotte had been talking to was the same woman Santana had shared drinks with in Tokyo on New Year's Eve. The gorgeous woman with chestnut brown hair, hazel eyes, and a luminous smile. Santana had rescued the woman from an overly aggressive suitor, then chatted amiably with her over cocktails and sushi. When the clock had struck midnight and the woman had pressed a good-bye kiss to her cheek, Santana had felt like the prince being abandoned by Cinderella at the ball. Instead of a glass slipper, she'd had only a humorous nickname to remember her by.

"Olaf."

The word hung in the cold air like a plume of smoke, then slowly disappeared. Peering through the scope, Santana saw the woman scream. The sound, even though she couldn't hear it, pierced her to her core.

She wanted to go to her. To wrap her arms around her and tell her everything would be okay, but she knew none of her platitudes could possibly ease the pain—the fear—she saw on the woman's face.

She remained motionless—transfixed, actually—until she saw the woman reach for her cell phone. Based on typical response times in the area, police and paramedics would arrive within fifteen minutes. Rush hour traffic might delay them a bit, but not long enough for Santana to sit around wasting time staring at a woman she had met once and thought she would never see again.

Moving quickly but efficiently, she broke down her rifle and gathered her belongings. She took a second sweep to make sure she hadn't missed anything, then draped her duffel bag over her shoulder and headed for the door that had allowed her to access the roof. She closed the door behind her and walked down the hall, resisting the urge to run. In this situation, patience was not only a virtue, it was a requirement. Panicking could draw unwanted attention. Though she hadn't fired her weapon, she would have a hard time explaining what she was doing carrying it on the streets of New York City.

She forced herself to remain calm until she slipped into the stairwell. She opted not to take the elevator because she wanted to avoid as many security cameras as possible. Once inside the stairwell, she allowed herself to pick up the pace. Her gloved hands slid along the railing as she hurried down the first flight of stairs.

Her breathing was somewhat restricted by the balaclava covering her face, but she couldn't remove the covering without leaving DNA behind. Something as small as a strand of hair or a flake of skin could lead the authorities right to her. Even though she hadn't committed a crime tonight, she would have a hard time explaining what she was doing so close to the scene of one.

She decided to leave the mask in place until she was well away from the area. The weather was cold enough that she wasn't likely to be the only person wearing something to protect their face from the elements, meaning chances were good she wouldn't be remembered by other passersby.

She would get rid of the gun and her clothes once she reached her safe haven. The apartment she had rented in Central Park South belonged to Vilma Bautista, the fake identity she had assumed for this assignment. On paper, at least. Her handler was the place's true owner. He had purchased it in order to launder some of the proceeds from his criminal enterprises. She, or rather Vilma, was nothing more than a glorified squatter.

Vilma was a wealthy financier who was frequently away on business so her long absences weren't considered unusual. The building's staff was both accommodating and discreet, meaning they aimed to please and didn't ask questions. It was the ideal place for her to hide out, especially after a kill. All she had to do was get there.

She heard the distant wail of sirens when she finally reached the street. A blast of cold air hit her in the back, making the trickle of sweat slowly making its way down her spine feel like melting ice. She allowed herself to get caught up in the flow of foot traffic as she tried to put some distance between herself and the scene. Calling an Uber would have been faster, but she preferred to keep moving rather than stand still. She didn't have a cell phone on her anyway. She didn't want anyone to be able to track her movements as incoming or outgoing calls pinged off nearby cell towers.

She hailed a cab once she was about ten blocks away. She gave the driver the address of a building half a mile from her apartment, then made sure to pay in cash so there wouldn't be a digital trail of the transaction.

She tossed a few pieces of her rifle into Central Park Lake, the twenty-two acre body of water popular with nature lovers and fishermen alike. If someone managed to hook a piece of the assembly, they wouldn't be able to identify who owned the weapon. The serial number had originally been printed on the barrel of the gun, the only piece still in her possession. She had filed off the number years ago, and forensics experts would have an incredibly difficult time attempting to recover it after she dropped the remaining parts of her rifle in the trash compactor in her apartment building. As for the clothes she was wearing, she would launder them, then donate them to charity. Drop boxes had been set up all over the city so she shouldn't have trouble finding one.

She removed her gloves and uncovered her face when she was a few blocks away from her apartment. In this neighborhood, a masked figure was more likely to scream mugger than innocent citizen attempting to stay warm.

The doorman greeted her with a slight bow when she approached. "Welcome back, Ms. Bautista. Did you have a good workout?"

"It raised my heart rate, that's for sure."

"Very good. Enjoy the rest of your evening."

"I intend to. Thank you."

She rode the elevator to the top floor. When she reached her apartment, she wiped down the remaining pieces of her rifle, placed them in a plastic bag, and dropped the bag in the trash chute in the hallway.

After she returned to her penthouse, she locked the door behind her and sagged against it. She couldn't shake the image of Olaf's face. The expression of abject terror on her beautiful visage had been seared into her mind.

She buried her hands in her hair as she sank to the floor. Each assignment she had received had been impersonal, both in the planning and the execution. This one, however, was anything but. Though she didn't know Olaf's real name, the two of them had a connection, however tenuous. Had that connection been used against them, or was she reading more into the situation than was actually on the page?

None of it made sense. One night, she met a woman she found intriguing. Less than a week later, she was hired to kill someone in that woman's orbit. Who was the real target, Charlotte Evans or someone else? More importantly, who was pulling the strings?

Her cell phone rang before she could answer any of the questions racing through her mind. Her handler's number was listed on the display.

"What the fuck happened tonight?" she asked without bothering to say hello. "Why did you send me on an assignment when you had already given the job to someone else?"

"Call it an insurance policy," Winslow Townsend said coolly. "Lee always suspected you would balk at an assignment one day, and it turns out he was right. The price of this failure will be added to rather than deducted from the amount you owe me."

The news was disappointing but not as bad as Santana had expected. She had feared a far worse punishment. "Who did you turn to? Who made the order? Why did they want Charlotte Evans dead?"

In person, Winslow had an air of cultured refinement. He looked like an easy mark. Benjie and Santana had made that mistake once. That was how she had ended up under Winslow's thumb in the first place.

She and Benjie had used their contacts inside a posh Manila hotel to rob Winslow's room while he was in town to gamble in a luxury casino. Their accomplice must have panicked and given Winslow their names because Winslow and his men had showed up at Benjie's house before they'd even had time to inventory their loot. Winslow's men had pressed guns to their heads while Winslow held court in front of them.

"You took something valuable from me, Aquino," Winslow had said as she and Benjie cowered in fear. "Now I'm going to take something even more valuable from you."

Despite his faults, Benjie had been there for her when she needed him. He had cared for her. Guided her. Taught her how to survive. When it had appeared both their lives were on the line, he had offered his in exchange for hers. He had pleaded for Winslow to kill him and let her go, but Winslow had had something else in mind. Death wouldn't have suited his purposes anyway. As Santana soon discovered, it wasn't his usual MO. When someone wronged him, he liked to draw out their suffering, not exact swift retribution. He had returned home to Singapore and taken Santana with him. To explain her presence to anyone they might come across, he had passed her off as one of his maids' children. Then he had financed her education by hiring the best private tutors. He had also taught her how to kill. She wasn't the only person he had groomed in that manner. There were more like her in cities all around the world, but she was the one he turned to most often.

Even though she had shared a household with him throughout her formative years, she had never felt like she truly belonged. As his son Lee always took great pains to point out, she was an employee, not a member of the family.

The first night she had stayed in his mansion, Winslow had allowed the door to her room to remain unlocked. "Do you really think you can trust her?" Lee had asked as he and Winslow stood in the hallway.

"She won't go anywhere," Winslow had said. "All dogs are loyal to whoever gives them attention, and this little mongrel is starving for it."

"What if she tries to bite the hand that feeds her?"

"Then I won't hesitate to put her down. No one is irreplaceable, my son. Not even you."

Winslow let his cool, polished facade drop as he directed his wrath at her.

"Your job is not to ask why. Your job is to do whatever I tell you to do whenever I tell you to do it. Did you receive the photo of your mother I sent you? She's a bit long in the tooth for me, but she looks good for a woman of a certain age, don't you think?"

Each time Santana thought of turning on Winslow, he sent her evidence to show he had eyes on her mother and could have her taken out any time he wished. It had been so surreal for Santana to be a witness to her mother's life while being unable to take part in it. Even though the photos were not-so-thinly-veiled threats used to keep her in line, they also supplied Santana with a modicum of comfort. Because they let her know that her mother was still alive.

"If you defy me again," Winslow said, "I won't have someone put a bullet in your mother's head. I will have them put one in yours. Do we understand each other?"

Santana understood all too well. And it was obvious that if she wanted answers, she would have to find them herself.

## Chapter Five

Brooklyn couldn't stop shaking. Each time she thought she had finally managed to pull herself together, the tremors would start again. First her hands, then her arms. It didn't take long for the rest of her body to follow suit.

She still couldn't believe she would never hear Charlie's voice again. That she wouldn't be able to bounce ideas off of her, hear her laugh, be forced to sit through one of her famously long-winded stories, or be the willing butt of her jokes. How could someone who was as filled with life as Charlie was be dead? She couldn't wrap her head around it.

When a paramedic began to wheel a gurney past her, Brooklyn reached for the black body bag. She drew her shaking hand away before she could make contact. She didn't want to remember Charlie that way. She wanted to remember her as she was. As she always would be. Smart. Funny. Alive.

"Are we almost done here?" she asked as the paramedic wheeled Charlie's remains from the room. "I haven't called her parents yet. They need to know what happened."

The call would be the hardest she'd ever had to make. She had no idea how she would break the news to Charlie's parents that their only child was dead. For some things, there were just no words.

Paul Barnett, the police detective who had been bombarding her with questions for the past few hours, flipped his small notebook closed and stashed it in the inside pocket of his suit jacket.

"That's all the questions I have for now. My partner and I will be in touch if we need more information or have updates to provide."

He gestured toward the man who had introduced himself as Duncan Theroux. Like Barnett, Theroux was portly, balding, and appeared to be in his mid-fifties. While Brooklyn answered Barnett's questions, Theroux viewed the footage from the office security cameras. He had said he wanted to see if Charlie's murder had been captured, but Brooklyn suspected he was also trying to verify her version of events.

She hoped the brutal act that had taken Charlie's life was visible on the recording so the police could have all the evidence they needed to catch her killer. If it was, she didn't plan on watching the footage. Finding Charlie had been bad enough. Seeing how she had gotten that way would be unbearable.

"We'll also take care of notifying the deceased's next of kin," Barnett said. "I'm certain they'll have questions, and we'll definitely have a few for them as well. Perhaps they'll be able to give us something to go on."

Brooklyn was relieved he had volunteered to perform the odious chore of informing Charlie's parents. She also felt guilty for not being able to provide any valuable information. "I'm sorry I couldn't be of more help."

"Don't beat yourself up about it." The five o'clock stubble that had started to form bristled as Barnett ran a hand over his face. "You're in shock right now." He handed her a card with his name and contact information printed on it. "If you think of something that might be useful to the investigation, give me a call."

"I will."

"The crime techs will remain onsite for the rest of the night to gather evidence and take photographs. They should clear the scene sometime tomorrow."

Brooklyn shuddered as she thought about working in the same room where a murder had taken place. She tightened her grip on the thin, scratchy blanket someone had draped across her shoulders. At first, she hadn't noticed it was there. Now she didn't want to let it go.

"I'll contact my employees and tell them they can work remotely for the foreseeable future. I'll also get in touch with a counselor in case anyone has trouble dealing with their grief."

"That's a good idea. In the meantime, is there someone we can call? Someone who can look after you?"

Until a killer's bullet had brought her life to a premature end, Charlie had been the person Brooklyn called whenever she found herself in a jam. Her family had their own lives to lead and, unlike them, Charlie wasn't eager to pass judgment on Brooklyn's actual or perceived mistakes.

"No, I'll be fine."

Barnett's professional demeanor softened, along with his voice. "You've experienced a substantial trauma. My partner and I can see you home, but you really shouldn't be alone tonight."

Since her own was nonexistent at the moment, Brooklyn relied on Brooke's confidence to help her get through the worst night of her life. "Thank you for your concern, Detective, but as I said, I'll be fine. Don't worry about me. Just find whoever did this."

"My colleagues and I will do our best to bring the perpetrator to justice. Are you sure Ms. Evans didn't have any enemies? Anyone who might have wanted to cause her harm?"

It was a theme he had returned to time and time again during the course of his interview. Brooklyn shook her head, just as she'd done the previous times he'd asked various forms of the question.

"I can honestly say Charlie's the only person I've ever known who is—who *was* universally liked by everyone she met. I've never heard anyone say a cross word about her."

"In this day and age, that's quite an accomplishment. I'm sorry for your loss. We'll be in touch."

"Wait," she said when she saw one of the crime techs slide Charlie's work computer into an evidence bag. "That laptop is company property. Both it and the information on it are proprietary."

"We need to search Ms. Evans's files and emails for possible clues to her killer's identity," Barnett said. "The laptop will be returned to you after the investigation is over."

"How long do you think that will take?"

"Your guess is as good as mine. If we get lucky, we could wrap this up relatively quickly. If not, it could take a while. However it goes, you can rest assured that any info the forensics guys unearth that isn't related to the case will be kept confidential."

"Please do. Charlie backed up all her data in the cloud so I'll still have access to it, but I wouldn't want any of my competitors to get a sneak peek at some of the projects we're working on."

"Understood."

After Barnett and Theroux left, Brooklyn headed to her office. She drafted an email to inform her employees of Charlie's death and to give them the option of working from home, returning to the office, or taking some time off to deal with their emotions. The email was difficult to craft and even harder to send, but having a task to perform helped her focus. Helped her forget. There would be plenty of time for memories later. And when they came, she hoped she wouldn't be swept away by the tide.

She sent the email, then waited for the shocked replies to filter in. She didn't have to wait long. The response was almost immediate. The reactions mirrored her own: initial disbelief, followed by anger and depression. She, like they, would eventually cycle through all five stages of grief, but she didn't expect the process to happen overnight. A loss like this would take months, if not years for her to accept.

She watched the crime scene techs take photographs, bag evidence, and analyze the scene. She heard them discussing entry angles and exit wounds, unable to believe something so surreal was taking place in what had once felt like a place of refuge. She felt like she was watching an episode of a police procedural. She would give anything to be able to change the channel.

A commotion near the door caught her eye. A couple of uniformed officers were wrestling with someone. Brooklyn tensed, fearing it might be the killer. Had whoever shot Charlie come to make sure he had finished the job, or had he selected a new target?

She felt the hair on the back of her neck stand on end as she wondered if she would ever feel safe again. She relaxed a bit when she spotted the face of someone she recognized.

"You can let him in," she said, approaching the officers. "I know him."

Luke Ridley approached her with his arms outstretched. "Are you okay?" he asked, drawing her into a tight embrace. "I came as soon as I heard."

"Bad news travels fast, I see."

She turned her head to keep from getting makeup on his shirt as he pressed her head against his chest. She could feel the pec implants he had always denied having. He claimed the look was natural, but she had never seen him lift a weight heavier than a laptop. The surgical enhancement provided tangible evidence of both his vanity and his propensity to take shortcuts rather than put in the hard work required to accomplish a particularly challenging task.

Setting aside her issues with Luke's personality, Brooklyn allowed herself to take comfort in his strength. They had known each other since they were undergrads at MIT and had been competing against each other ever since. For the highest grades, the hottest girls, and the most lucrative professional contracts. Both had claimed their fair share of victories in their friendly rivalry. She doubted she would be half the businesswoman she was without having him around to push her to greater heights.

"What happened?" he asked, holding her at arm's length.

She stared into his bright blue eyes until the concern she saw emanating from them made her look away. She shook her head and tried not to cry. "I don't know. We were talking about the JapanTech conference and I got up to grab us a couple of beers. When I got back, she was—She was—"

She tried, but she couldn't get the words out.

"That's okay," Luke said, drawing her into his arms again. "You don't have to say it. I can figure out the rest." He glanced at the bullet hole in the window and the darkening stains on Charlie's desk. He swallowed as if he were trying not to vomit, then he hastily looked away. "I'll call someone and have them clean up this mess."

"Don't bother," she said when he started to pull his cell phone out of his pocket. "I already have someone on standby. They're just waiting for the all-clear from the police so they can get started."

"I should have known you had already jumped into crisis mode. What can I do to help?"

Though she and Luke had never been besties, she longed for someone to confide in. For someone to lean on. "Talk to me. Help me try to make sense of this."

He led her to a nearby chair and sat across from her, holding her hands in his. "Do the police have any idea who did it?"

"How could they? No one we know would do something like this. And if we did, what possible motive could they have?"

Luke shrugged. "When something like this happens, you always hear about people having secret lives. Maybe Charlie was into something she shouldn't have been."

Brooklyn almost laughed at the ridiculousness of the suggestion. "Charlie might have pushed boundaries from time to time, but she never went past them. She had a wide variety of interests, none of them illegal. Nothing, in other words, worth losing her life over."

"Perhaps she flirted with the wrong woman."

"That deserves a drink in the face at most, not a bullet in the head, don't you think?"

He shrugged again. "I'm grasping at straws here." His frustration mirrored her own.

"So am I. I can't imagine coming to work and not seeing her holding court."

"She was one of your best programmers. What are you going to do about the projects she was working on?"

"Assign them to someone else or take them on myself, I suppose."

Without Charlie around to distract her, she would have plenty of time to devote herself to work. Finding motivation—and inspiration—however, could prove problematic.

"My team's still struggling with the cell phone program," he said. "How close is yours to coming up with a finished product?"

She welcomed the chance to talk shop rather than continue discussing Charlie's unfortunate demise.

"Are you talking about the app that allows users to access the information on password-protected cell phones?"

"Government agencies would pay dearly for the technology, which would allow them to pull info off of suspects' phones and computers after crimes are committed."

"We shelved that project months ago."

Luke looked shocked. "What? Why? The first company that creates the program will practically have a license to print money. I thought BDV would be the one that hit the jackpot. Charlie told me over drinks one night that you were almost there."

"We were, but I couldn't reconcile the privacy concerns if the technology ended up in the wrong hands or was used in ways other than originally intended."

"You opted to turn down millions—no, *billions*—of dollars in order to stand behind your principles?"

"The choice wasn't as hard as you're making it seem."

"For you maybe. What did the rest of your team say?"

"A few disagreed with my decision, but the vast majority were onboard. As was so clearly reinforced tonight, money isn't everything."

She glanced at the police personnel wandering around the office. Their number had dwindled from over a dozen to little more than a handful. Soon they would all be gone, leaving her alone. Leaving her wondering what the hell she was going to do next. What she was going to do without Charlie.

"Let me take you home," Luke said. "You need to get out of here."

Brooklyn felt the thin threads of her temper begin to fray. "I wish everyone would stop trying to tell me what I need and let me figure it out for myself."

Luke held up his hands to indicate he meant no harm. "I'm just trying to help."

"I appreciate your efforts, but I'm not made of glass. I don't need to be handled with kid gloves."

"I know, and I'm sorry if I overstepped." He gave her hand a squeeze, then slowly rose to his feet. "Give me a call if you need anything. Day or night, I'll be there for you if you need me."

She thanked him for his offer, but after losing her best friend, the only person she planned to depend on from here on out was herself.

## CHAPTER SIX

Santana should have known the Evans job was too easy. She hadn't had to perform any reconnaissance for the hit because all the information she had been told she needed was included in the dossier she had received when she was given the assignment. Evans's list of personal contacts was missing, but her home and work addresses and her favorite hangouts were there, along with a list of her most frequent comings and goings. Santana could have kicked herself for choosing to rely on someone else's intel rather than gathering her own. Yes, Winslow had wanted the job completed as soon as possible, but if she had taken the time to perform even cursory research, she would have known that BDV Enterprises, the company Evans worked for, was owned and operated by the woman she had met on New Year's Eve.

Olaf had a name, and her name was Brooklyn DiVincenzo.

"I've officially made your acquaintance, Brooklyn, but it's not nearly as much of a pleasure as I had hoped it would be."

She pulled up a website on her laptop as she continued her search. Befitting someone of her status, Brooklyn had a prominent social media presence. Santana scrolled through posts both professional and personal in nature. Charlotte Evans appeared in several of them, providing visual evidence of their relationship. Their bond was apparently platonic but obviously extremely close. That explained Brooklyn's dramatic reaction when she had discovered Charlotte's body.

Santana took a sip of whiskey from the cut crystal glass sitting on the coffee table, but the alcohol didn't help her swallow her guilt. Even though she hadn't performed the hit, she still felt responsible for Evans's death. She was determined to find out who had actually pulled the trigger and, more importantly, who had paid them to do it. Winslow had told her to let the matter drop, but she was just getting started.

As she stared at the computer screen, she barely resisted the urge to caress an image of Brooklyn's face. The photograph showed Brooklyn smiling and happy. She looked as she had in Tokyo. Open. Honest. For lack of a better word, carefree. She looked nothing like the terrified woman Santana had seen through her rifle scope a few hours earlier.

"Stick to the objective," she said, admonishing herself.

She ran a hand through her hair, which was still wet from the shower. The clothes she had worn when she witnessed the hit on Charlotte Evans had been washed and were now tumbling in the dryer. Tomorrow, she would get rid of them and discard the fibers that had collected in the lint trap. Some might say she was being overly cautious, but in her mind, there was no such thing. She was too close to finally earning her freedom to spend the rest of her life locked in a cage.

She refilled her glass, then returned to the task at hand.

She started by gathering the information she hadn't been provided, and she had foolishly chosen not to obtain, given Evans's low profile. If she had taken her usual steps, she would have spotted the connection between Brooklyn and Charlotte before the hit was carried out. She might not have been able to prevent Charlotte's murder, but perhaps she could help solve it.

Neither Brooklyn's nor Charlotte's social media profiles raised any obvious red flags. Both seemed relatively straightforward, painting them as smart, independent women who liked to work hard and play harder. Brooklyn's emphasis was more on work, Charlotte's on play. Even though there were plenty of pictures of Brooklyn attending an array of social events in a plethora of exotic locales, her posts appeared to be designed to promote a professional agenda rather than document a good time. Based on the numerous photos of her and her friends playing beer pong or lining up tequila shots while they mugged for an ever-present camera, Charlotte left her professional agenda behind once the work day was done.

Santana closed the website and tapped a finger against her lips. It was becoming increasingly obvious to her that this was a problem she wouldn't be able to solve from afar. She would have to do it from the inside.

She reached for the napkin she had thankfully convinced herself not to throw away. The phone number that had been written on it was slightly smudged but still legible. She grabbed a burner phone she had activated but never used and entered the numbers on the keypad.

The phone rang so long she began to think the call was going to go to voice mail. She didn't want to leave a message, but hanging up and calling back would have felt like an act of desperation. This was no time to panic. She had to play it cool. She nearly sighed with relief when someone finally answered.

"Hello?"

The voice sounded curious, confused, and a bit uncertain. No surprise, given the events that had taken place tonight. Trying to sound reassuring so she wouldn't cause further alarm, Santana made a studied effort to keep her voice calm.

"May I speak to Olaf?"

The sound of her cell phone ringing drew Brooklyn's attention away from the macabre scene taking place outside her office. She was grateful for the distraction.

Mentally preparing herself to act as grief counselor to Charlie's heartbroken parents or one of her stunned employees, she reached for the phone. She didn't recognize the number printed on the display and the caller was listed as unknown. She never answered calls from numbers she didn't recognize because she didn't want to waste either her time or her data dealing with robocalls from random companies trying to sell her products she didn't want.

"My credit record doesn't need repairing, I'm not interested in a timeshare, and I'm not in the mood to hear I've won some stupid contest I didn't even enter."

She started to press the Ignore button, but she thought better of it at the last second. The timing of the call was most likely a coincidence, but perhaps it had something to do with Charlie's murder. Was the killer reaching out to her to make sure he had finished the job? Or, even worse, was he calling to let her know he was just getting started?

She had to admit the idea sounded farfetched, but so was the notion that someone would want Charlie dead. She swallowed to lubricate her suddenly dry throat, then pressed the Accept button and slowly brought the phone to her ear.

"Hello?"

"May I speak to Olaf?"

Brooklyn didn't know whether to feel disappointed or relieved that her fears had proven to be unfounded. She settled on feeling embarrassed for allowing her imagination to run wild.

"I'm sorry," she said, deciding to limit her brainstorming to new technology rather than conspiracy theories. "You have the wrong number."

"Do I?"

"Yes, you—" The caller's voice caused Brooklyn to flash back to New Year's Eve. To the evening she had spent flirting with a mysterious woman who had ridden to her rescue like a knight in an Armani suit. "TDH."

"One and the same."

TDH's voice was even more intoxicating than Brooklyn remembered. Hearing it purring in her ear made her lightheaded. Or perhaps the physical and emotional fatigue she had been ignoring was finally beginning to settle in on her.

"You told me if I ever found myself in New York, I should give you a call. As it happens, I'm in town for a few days so I decided to take you up on your offer. Is this a bad time?"

Brooklyn glanced at the police personnel inspecting what had once been Charlie's workspace but was now a crime scene. "You could say that."

"I'm sorry." TDH sounded taken aback. She probably wasn't used to having one of her overtures turned down. And who could blame her? The woman was flat-out gorgeous. She probably had women throwing themselves at her feet constantly. "I didn't mean to interrupt."

"No," Brooklyn said quickly so TDH wouldn't be tempted to end the call. She could use a touch of normalcy while she tried to deal with a situation that was as far from normal as it could get. "I'm glad you did."

"Are you sure? You sound like you're in the middle of something."

"I am, as a matter of fact," Brooklyn said with a rueful laugh. "A police investigation."

"I beg your pardon?"

Brooklyn laughed again. Luke's visit had made her feel worse instead of better. Talking to TDH, on the other hand, somehow made the situation feel less dire. Funny how a stranger could offer her the comfort her friends had thus far been unable to provide. "You sound as shocked as I feel."

"What happened? Are you allowed to say?"

TDH sounded empathetic. Like she could relate to what Brooklyn was going through. Brooklyn didn't want sympathy. What she needed was understanding.

"A friend—my *best* friend was murdered."

Her voice caught when she finally said the word. Thinking it allowed what had happened tonight to remain an abstract concept. Saying it out loud made it real.

"Her name was Charlie," she said, finally beginning to feel the loss. "Charlotte, actually, but she hasn't answered to that since she was ten. We met at a computer camp half a lifetime ago. She and I were the only girls in attendance that year. The number of women in the tech industry is so small it often feels like the members of my staff and I are still the only girls who've managed to crash the boys' club."

"I'm so sorry to hear you've experienced such a tragedy. You said your friend was murdered. That sounds intentional. Was she targeted, or was she the victim of some random act of violence?"

Brooklyn didn't feel like telling the story for the umpteenth time that night and TDH probably didn't want to hear all the gory details anyway so she decided to be intentionally vague. "No, she was here. In the office. We were alone when it happened."

"You were in the—Wait. You're not you still there, are you?"

"Unfortunately, yes, I am. I'm waiting for the police to wrap things up. Then I can finally head home and try to put this day behind me. Eventually, maybe everything will start to make sense. At the moment, I can't wrap my head around any of it."

"That's understandable. You've been through a lot tonight. Do the police have any suspects?"

"No, it's too soon for that. Right now, they have more questions than answers. As for a motive, that's nonexistent." TDH fell silent so Brooklyn tried to fill the void. "I'll bet this isn't the conversation you were planning to have when you reached out to me, was it?"

"No, it wasn't."

Brooklyn thought she couldn't feel more depressed than she already did, but TDH's response made her heart sink even lower. "I appreciate your honesty. So I'm assuming this is both hello and good-bye?"

"Why would you assume that?"

Brooklyn shrugged, then remembered TDH couldn't see her. "We had fun in Tokyo. When I gave you my number, I was hoping for more of the same. I'm sure you were, too. I wouldn't blame you for bailing. You didn't sign up for all this drama."

"Neither did you."

The statement was so unexpected Brooklyn didn't know how to respond.

"I think it's safe to say you'll have a great deal of unpleasant things coming your way over the next few days," TDH said. "If it gets to be too much or if you simply want to talk, give me a call. You have my number."

"Yes, but I still don't have your name," Brooklyn said before she realized TDH had already ended the call.

She smiled as the disconnect signal beeped in her ear. A few minutes ago, she had felt hopeless. Now she had something to look forward to.

She was tempted to ask if life could get any stranger, but she didn't dare because she was afraid to hear the answer.

## Chapter Seven

Santana felt like an intruder in Brooklyn's life. Like a cat burglar who had broken into her apartment and stolen all of her most valuable possessions while she slept. Their brief conversation had confirmed what she already knew. Charlotte Evans's family and friends had no idea who wanted her dead or what their motive might be. Unfortunately, neither did the police.

Given Evans's lack of name recognition, solving her murder would most likely be deemed low priority. If authorities didn't find the culprit within forty-eight hours, chances were they never would. The matter would be added to their already long list of unsolved cases, and the detectives tasked with solving the crime would perform routine follow-ups every few months or so to see if they could discover something new. By then, the trail would be cold, potential witnesses' memories would have grown fuzzy, and the killer would be long gone. If they weren't already.

By rights, she should already be halfway across the Pacific by now. Instead, she had chosen to remain in New York. Why, exactly?

She was not only curious about the circumstances of Evans's murder. She was curious about Brooklyn, too. About the effect her best friend's death was having on her. She had sounded strong when Santana spoke to her on the phone. Had she remained that way once the initial shock wore off or, more likely, had she fallen apart? When the tears finally came, did Brooklyn have someone to comfort her, or had she chosen to be alone with her grief?

Santana hadn't heard from her since their initial phone call. When she had offered to provide a sympathetic ear if Brooklyn needed one. Tellingly, Brooklyn hadn't reached out to her. She was used to keeping people at arm's length, not the one being held at bay.

Charlotte Evans's obituary had appeared in the local newspapers two days after her death. The write-up managed to provide a comprehensive summary of both her personal and professional accomplishments.

The details of her memorial service were listed in the obituary's final paragraph. The venue was relatively small, which meant the congregation would be as well. In such an intimate locale, Santana couldn't attend the services without drawing unwanted attention, but she needed to be there. Not to mark Evans's passing but to observe those who turned out to mourn her. She needed to keep a close eye on Brooklyn and the people around her to see if any of them struck her as the person who had paid to have Evans killed.

Unlike other hits she had been involved with, this one felt personal. It seemed logical, therefore, that the perpetrator had to be a member of Evans's inner circle. Brooklyn's reaction had ruled her out as a potential suspect. Now Santana had to work her way through the rest of Evans's friends and associates before she could rule them out as well.

She pulled up the obituary online to remind herself when and where the interment was scheduled to take place. Unlike the small church where the memorial service would be held, the cemetery sprawled over several acres.

She opened her favorite search engine. With a few clicks, she managed to find a map of the cemetery's grounds as well as a chart of the hundreds of burial plots located onsite. She downloaded both and forwarded the images to the headset device that looked like a standard pair of eyeglasses but functioned as a computer.

The device was controlled by a series of voice commands and allowed her to access a wide variety of programs hands-free. Today, she planned on using it to surveil Evans's mourners. She wouldn't be able to get close enough to hear their conversations, but she could observe their interactions while she discreetly photographed them. When she returned to her apartment, she would run the photos through an image recognition program to determine who they were and, hopefully, what their relationship to Evans had been.

Some headstones and monuments in the cemetery were several centuries old. Evans's family plot, on the other hand, was relatively new. According to the chart Santana had found, it was located in a tree-lined area near the gated entrance.

She checked her watch. Evans's memorial service was about to begin, leaving her plenty of time to pick up a potted plant from a nearby flower shop and make her way to Jersey City. Once there, she hoped to find a grave that didn't appear to have frequent visitors but afforded her a clear view as Evans's remains were entombed in their final resting place. A simple bouquet might not draw as much attention, but a potted plant would give her a built-in excuse to linger at the gravesite long enough for the interment service to take place.

She dressed in an outfit that was unassuming rather than flashy. Jeans, a gray pullover, and a black overcoat. She opted against gloves because the temperature, though far from balmy, was high enough not to warrant them.

The flower shop she frequented most often was a few blocks from her apartment. Harry Sanders, the owners' son, greeted her as soon as she walked in. "Good afternoon, Ms. Bautista. How may I help you today?"

The high school senior was nearly a head taller than she was. Not so long ago, he had barely come up to her shoulder.

"How many times do I have to tell you, Harry? Call me Vilma, not Ms. Bautista."

Harry's long blond hair flopped back and forth as he forcefully shook his head. "No can do. My dads raised me to respect my…"

Santana arched an eyebrow as his cheeks colored. "Your elders?"

"No," he said hastily, "my customers."

"Nice save."

"Thank you. What are you in the market for?"

Santana looked around the shop, which was packed with so many flowers it looked like a starter kit for a float in the Rose

Parade. "I need a potted plant that's low maintenance and can be kept outside."

"I know just the thing." He set aside the bouquet he was arranging and came around the stem-covered counter. "Stay there. I'll be right back."

He sprinted up the stairs and headed to the shop's second floor. The first floor was filled with dozens of bouquets in a variety of containers. The second floor looked more like a nursery. Potted plants dotted the area. Some were for sale, others meant for eventual use. Harry picked up a ceramic pot containing a fragrant purple plant.

"What's that?" she asked. "I can smell it from here."

"Lavender. If you place it in a sunny spot with at least six hours of sunlight per day, give it the right soil and plenty of drainage, it will practically take care of itself."

"I'll take it."

"Awesome." Harry tucked the container under his arm and headed down the stairs. "Will this be all?"

"Yeah, that'll do it."

"Would you like me to wrap it for you?"

"No, that won't be necessary."

"Cool."

Santana reached for her wallet as Harry began to ring up the purchase. "What?" she asked when he peeked at her through the veil of his shaggy bangs.

"You typically buy bouquets when you come in. The arrangements are beautiful, if I say so myself, but they don't last long. Potted plants imply a sense of permanence."

"And?" she said, trying to prompt him into taking a less circuitous route to get to whatever point he was trying to make.

"Are the flowers for you or someone else?"

"I haven't met the love of my life, if that's what you're asking."

"Oh." His expectant smile faded.

"Why do you look so disappointed?"

He lowered his eyes. "Sometimes you seem lonely. I was hoping you had met someone."

"You're a hopeless romantic just like your fathers."

"Is that such a bad thing?"

She swiped her debit card to pay for the purchase, then picked up the plant she had just bought. "No, I guess it isn't."

"Have a good day, Ms. Bautista."

"You, too, Harry."

His words stuck with her after she left the shop.

"There's a difference between being lonely and being alone," she reminded herself as she headed for the subway.

Lonely wasn't a word she had ever felt the need to apply to herself. It implied she had been forsaken or abandoned. Nothing could be further from the truth. She had been loved. Fiercely and wholeheartedly.

For years, Winslow had used love as a weapon against her. Perhaps the time had finally come for her to return the favor.

## Chapter Eight

B rooklyn had expected today to be difficult, but she hadn't imagined it would turn out to be quite so tough. She had lived the past few days in a fog, stumbling from one self-imposed goal to the next as she tried to keep her emotions under wraps. The numbness that had set in almost immediately after she discovered Charlie's lifeless body had finally worn off at the memorial service when Charlie's inconsolable parents had draped themselves across her flower-covered coffin.

"I would react the same way if that was you or one of your brothers and sisters up there," her mother had whispered as Gail Evans's agonized wails echoed off the church's high ceilings.

Brooklyn had told her mother she didn't need her to accompany her to Charlie's funeral. Knowing how close Brooklyn and Charlie had been, her mother had decided to come anyway.

Brooklyn didn't know whether to feel grateful or annoyed by her mother's presence. She was touched by her mother's concern for her well-being, but she wanted to prove she was a grown woman who could stand on her own two feet, not a little girl who still needed her parents' protection.

A lump had formed in her throat, making it hard for her to breathe. Though the arm her mother had wrapped around her shoulders had provided some much-needed comfort, she had longed to get away. To go somewhere she could pretend the events of four nights ago had never happened, but she had known that place didn't exist. Not even in her fantasies, let alone the real world.

As she stood in the cemetery watching Charlie's pastor read several passages from the Bible over her grave, she prayed for the whole thing to be over. She was still feeling a bit unsteady from the tequila shots she and a group of Charlie's friends had downed during an impromptu wake in Charlie's favorite bar the night before. She had stopped drinking before she had gotten completely wasted, but several other attendees hadn't. No wonder they, Luke included, had been no-shows today.

The evening had been filled with more laughter than tears as everyone took turns telling funny stories about Charlie. Today had been the exact opposite. Brooklyn wished she could cry so she could start to feel better, but her burning eyes remained dry.

She glanced at a solitary figure about fifty yards away. The person's back was to her so she couldn't tell if it was a man or a woman. A fitted baseball cap covered the person's hair, and the upturned collar on their black overcoat hid their face from view.

The person was exchanging the dead flowers at the foot of a grave for a pot filled with what appeared to be fresh lavender. Feeling like she was invading the person's privacy, Brooklyn forced herself to look away. Soon, she would find herself in a similar position. She wouldn't want a stranger ogling her while she visited the grave of someone she loved as much as if not more than a member of her own family.

This whole experience was new for her. Certainly, this wasn't the first time she had lost someone she cared about. Those people were decades older than she was and, in most cases, their deaths had been expected. With Charlie, it was different. She was only twenty-eight. She still had so much to live for. So many goals yet to be accomplished. So many hearts yet to be broken.

Brooklyn knew her broken heart would mend eventually, but she didn't expect the process to take place anytime soon.

"Are you okay?"

The question was asked in a voice barely above a whisper, but Brooklyn flinched as if it had been shouted. She looked around. The interment service was over and most of the mourners had begun to make their way to their cars. Her mother was chatting with

Charlie's parents near the front of the oversized tent that had been erected to shield the mourners from the elements, and employees from the funeral home had already started removing the empty folding chairs.

Brooklyn looked up to see JoAnna Gojowczyk staring down at her. JoAnna had interned for BDV Enterprises during her senior year at Columbia two years ago. After she graduated, Brooklyn had hired her as a programmer. Charlie had been her direct supervisor and biggest supporter.

"The kid has skills," Charlie would say each time one of JoAnna's ideas received a greenlight to go into production. "She must get it from me."

Though she was obviously proud of JoAnna, Charlie had also teased her relentlessly. She had nicknamed her AJ for her tendency to create a finished product in her head and work backward while she strived to turn fantasy into reality. Most people started at the beginning. AJ preferred to start at the end.

"I can leave if you like," she said. "You look like you'd rather be alone."

"No, it's fine." Brooklyn patted the chair next to her. "How are you holding up?" she asked after AJ settled into her seat.

AJ shook her head. Her eyes looked pained as she stared into the distance. "It still doesn't seem real. I keep waiting for the phone to ring so she can ask me what ideas I'm working on or point me in the right direction if she doesn't think what I come up with is up to snuff."

"She could be gruff sometimes."

"I knew she only did it because she was trying to bring out the best in me."

"My favorite teachers were like that. They challenged me rather than coddled me. I've always been self-motivated, but having an extra push from time to time doesn't hurt."

"Are you going to the repast?"

"I haven't had much of an appetite the past few days, so I don't plan on eating anything, but my mom and I will stick around and help clean up after the reception so Charlie's parents don't have to."

"If it's all the same with you, I think I'll skip it. I've never been very good at espousing sympathies with strangers while balancing a paper plate filled with food cooked by well-meaning friends and family members doing their best to mitigate the loss of a loved one. In this situation, I don't think a green bean casserole is going to cut it."

Brooklyn pressed her lips together to keep from laughing. "You sound like Charlie."

AJ flashed a sad smile. "She was my mentor, remember?"

"Do I ever. You two made a great team."

"Yeah, I'm going to miss collaborating with her. Seeing her face light up whenever I managed to solve a problem or brought her an idea she found intriguing. I lived for those moments."

"I'll try to pair you with someone else who can provide the same creative spark."

"Someone like you?"

Brooklyn was usually too busy trying to keep the company afloat to get too involved in the projects that kept it going. She missed being in the trenches. Getting her hands dirty. Perhaps this was a chance to return to her roots.

"I think that could be arranged."

"I'd like that."

AJ rubbed her hands together as if she were trying to gather her courage to ask her something.

"What's on your mind?" Brooklyn asked when no question seemed to be forthcoming.

AJ fixed her with an earnest look. "Frankly, I'm ready to get back to work. I'm ready to return to the office and get back to my old routine. Working from home is a lot less expensive than commuting every day, but I miss seeing everyone. It feels like I'm working by myself instead of with a team, you know?"

Brooklyn hadn't been in the office in days. The cleaners she had hired had been incredibly thorough. Most people walking into the space probably wouldn't be able to tell anything untoward had ever happened there. She, on the other hand, would never be able to forget. She wasn't looking forward to returning to the literal scene of the crime. But she had a company to run and employees to look after. She had to do what was best for both.

"Are you working on something new?" she asked.

"Yes," AJ said with almost palpable excitement. "Last night, I had an idea for a new app. Utilizing a conversational interface powered by artificial intelligence, users would be able to—"

Brooklyn held up a hand before AJ could get too revved up. "Put a presentation together and pitch it to me in a couple of days. If I like it, I'll kick it to the product committee to get their take on it."

"Thanks, boss. I'll see you Monday morning." AJ squeezed her hand before she bounded out of her seat.

As Charlie's parents climbed into the long black funeral car that would drive them home, Brooklyn joined her mother at the front of the tent.

"Was that one of your employees I saw you speaking with?"

"Yes, that was one of my programmers. She was checking up on me and making sure I knew how anxious she is to return to work."

Her mother placed a hand in the crook of her elbow as they slowly walked across the plush grass toward the gas-guzzling SUV parked a few feet away. Brooklyn kept trying to convince her to switch to a vehicle that was more environmentally friendly, but her mother wouldn't hear of it.

"That car's been paid off for years," she would say each time Brooklyn brought up the subject. "A tank of gas costs a whole lot less than a car payment."

"I was skeptical when you said you wanted to start your own company," her mother said as they climbed into the SUV. "I've seen how volatile the tech industry can be. You're on top one year and bankrupt the next. But you're good at what you do. Your employees like you and, more importantly, they respect you. You listen to their concerns, treat them right, and let them know how much they're valued. You've used the qualities it takes to be a good parent in order to be a good boss."

"Did you give Bella and Tessa that same speech?" Brooklyn asked as she fastened her seat belt.

"I tried to talk them out of procreating, but you can see how well that turned out."

Between them, Brooklyn's sisters had seven kids—and the prematurely gray hair to prove it.

"I think your reverse psychology needs a bit of work, Mom."

Brooklyn looked out the window. The figure she had seen kneeling in front of one of the other graves was still there. She took a moment to admire the person's apparent devotion for the friend or relative they had come to visit.

"Someone you know?" her mother asked as she turned the key in the ignition.

"No, just someone who caught my eye."

Something about the figure seemed familiar, but Brooklyn was pretty sure the only thing they had in common was grief.

## Chapter Nine

A s the cars from the Evans funeral procession slowly began to exit the cemetery, Santana gave the verbal command for the camera on her headset to switch to continuous shooting mode.

"Now zoom in."

After the camera regained focus, she captured images of each car's license plate. She might not need the information if the image recognition search came up empty, but she would rather have it and not need it than the other way around.

She waited for the final car to disappear from view before she pushed herself to her feet. She regarded the grave she had tended for the past thirty minutes. The weathered headstone belonged to Melanie Pierce, who had been born in the nineteenth century and had passed away just before the dawn of the twenty-first.

The epitaph below Melanie's name hinted her time on earth had been not only long-lasting but well-lived. Instead of traditional sentiments like *RIP* or *Beloved*, a recipe for fudge brownies had been inscribed in the stone. Seeing a touch of levity in such an incongruous setting brought a smile to Santana's face.

"Thanks for allowing me to spend some time with you today, Melanie." She gave the headstone an affectionate pat. "I hope you enjoy the flowers."

She shoved her hands in her coat pockets to warm them as she turned and walked away. She needed to catch the train back to New York. Downloading and viewing the dozens of photographs she had snapped would take some time. Analyzing them would take even longer. There was no denying she had a long day ahead of her. So why was some part of her hoping she could spend her night with Brooklyn DiVincenzo?

❖

By the time she finished her stint doling out food, making small talk, and placing dirty dishes in the overloaded washer, Brooklyn felt like a waitress in a local diner without the meager tips to show for her efforts. Still, she was happy to have done her part to make life a little bit easier for Pete and Gail Evans. She had long considered them her surrogate parents. She was willing to do whatever she could to ease the tremendous burden they were carrying, even if it meant tying on an apron and standing behind a table laden with enough provisions to stock a soup kitchen for weeks.

"You look thin," Gail said as Brooklyn covered a half-empty casserole dish with aluminum foil. "You should take some of this food home with you. It's way more than Pete and I could possibly eat."

"That's okay. I'm good."

"I doubt that, but thank you for everything you've done for us." Gail held Brooklyn's face in her hands. "I always hoped you and Charlie might—" She shook her head as her eyes filled with tears. "I guess it doesn't matter now. Take care of yourself, okay?"

Brooklyn gripped Gail's hands before she could break contact. "You're acting like we're never going to see each other again. I'll still come to see you as often as I can."

"You've got a company to run and a life to live. Pete and I couldn't possibly ask you to—"

"You're not asking. I'm offering."

Relief washed over Gail's drawn features. "We would certainly love to see more of you. You've always been like a daughter to us. Now you're the only one we have left. You don't mind sharing her, do you, Connie?"

"Of course not." Brooklyn's mother set the cake stand she was holding on the table so she could give Gail a hug. "Sal and I have always had more than enough love to go around."

Seeing her mother and Gail hold on to each other next to a wall filled with Charlie's childhood pictures almost brought Brooklyn to tears. She excused herself so she wouldn't break down in front of them.

She headed outside to get some fresh air. If she were a smoker, she would have pulled out a pack of cigarettes and fired one up. And if the pantry had been stocked with something besides soft drinks, she would have taken a long swallow of her favored libation. Fresh out of vices, she desperately searched for a life preserver to latch on to.

She pulled her cell phone from her pocket and thumbed through her list of contacts. She had seen most of the people listed at the wake last night or the funeral today. The rest she hadn't spoken to in months and, in some cases, years. If she hadn't reached out to them before, she couldn't possibly do so now. Acting on a whim, she selected one of the entries, pressed Dial, and waited for the phone to ring.

"It's Olaf," she said when she heard an increasingly familiar voice in her ear. "Does your offer still stand?"

## Chapter Ten

Santana couldn't believe she had made such a rookie mistake. If someone had eyes on Brooklyn, she had led them practically to her own doorstep. Sure, there were hundreds of residents in the building, but it wouldn't take a skilled assassin long to find a list of tenants. Her name—one of them, anyway—would be on the list. No matter. If someone came for her, she would be ready. Because some risks were worth taking. And Brooklyn was starting to feel like one of them.

She had given Brooklyn her address but still hadn't provided her with a name. She would do that in due time, preferably face-to-face rather than over the phone. She called downstairs to give the staff a heads-up.

"Good afternoon, Ms. Bautista," Samson Diaz said. "How may I be of service?"

The follically challenged concierge bore no resemblance to the biblical character with which he shared a name. Still, Santana hoped there were no women in his life named Delilah. She liked him too much to see him betrayed.

"I'm expecting company tonight," she said. "If a woman approaches you and says her name is Olaf, please direct her to my apartment."

If Samson was taken aback by her unusual request, he was too well trained to let it show. "Of course, Ms. Bautista. Is there anything else?"

"Yes, actually."

"And what might that be?"

"What's your go-to dish when you're trying to impress someone?"

She ran a hand through her hair. Unwilling to admit she needed help from time to time, she rarely if ever asked for advice of any kind. Asking for guidance on an issue this delicate was well outside her comfort zone. Thankfully, Samson treated her request with respect rather than disdain.

"Oh, that's easy," he said cheerfully. "Spaghetti and meatballs. It's a cinch to pull off and if you make too much and wind up with leftovers like I always do, the sauce tastes even better the next day."

"True, but my visitor is Italian-American. I don't want to serve her something she could have any night of the week."

"Plus you don't want to compete with family history."

Santana didn't bother pointing out that she didn't have the world's best track record when it came to dealing with family dynamics.

"I've got another idea," Samson said. "If you don't mind a heavy dish, try steak with wine sauce and truffled mashed potatoes on the side."

"Since I won't be counting carbs tonight, that sounds perfect. Thanks for the tip."

"Happy to help. Would you like me to call the grocery store and arrange a delivery?"

For a split-second, she wondered if he had looked inside her refrigerator and seen how empty it was. She hadn't planned to remain in New York more than a few days. If she extended her stay much longer, she'd have to stock up.

"No," she said, "I think I can manage that part myself."

"Of course. Have a good night."

"You, too."

Santana ended the call, googled the dish Samson had recommended, and called a local grocery store to have the ingredients delivered along with a week's worth of staples. While she waited for the provisions to arrive, she busied herself cleaning her apartment. She grabbed her laptop and all the research materials she had been poring through since she had returned from the cemetery that afternoon and placed them in the wall safe in her bedroom. Before she secured the safe, she looked around her apartment to make sure no traces of her true identity remained.

Vilma Bautista, one of the identities she assumed most often, had money to burn. Accordingly, Winslow had gone to great lengths to fill Vilma's apartment with all the trappings of wealth—high-end furniture, art, and accessories. Not too many, though. She had to live in the place from time to time so she wanted it to feel like a home instead of a museum.

She closed and locked the safe, then covered it with the hinged frame she used to hide it from view. The painting housed within the frame had cost close to six figures. The objects in the safe it obscured were worth considerably less. For her, however, they were priceless. They were not only the tools of her trade. They were the keys to her eventual freedom.

After the groceries arrived, she gave the deliveryman a substantial tip and unpacked the bags. She opened the wine so it could have time to breathe before she incorporated it into the sauce, then she poured herself a glass to help steady her nerves.

Her heart was racing and she couldn't catch her breath. Granted, she didn't entertain guests often. When she did, she didn't react this way before they arrived. What was it about Brooklyn DiVincenzo that had her so on edge? Simple. Brooklyn was dangerous for her in more ways than one. She represented a threat Santana had never faced. Not to her life. She had survived being placed in mortal peril before. This time, the risk was to her heart. Something she had sworn she would never allow herself to lose.

"I guess there truly is a first time for everything."

Brooklyn had lived in New York all her life so she had grown accustomed to seeing the rich and famous come and go. Being among them—seeing where they lived up-close rather than from afar—was new to her.

The salary she paid herself was nice, though not exorbitant. She preferred to invest most of BDV Enterprises' profits in the company or in employee bonuses, meaning her lifestyle wasn't nearly as luxurious as the one she was bearing witness to now. She tried not to seem awed when her Lyft driver dropped her off at the address TDH had given her, but she doubted she did a very good job.

The building looked like something out of a movie. Not the gritty dramas populated by characters who could have doubled for some of the people she had grown up with. More like a glitzy romantic comedy featuring two trust-funded leads who had everything money can buy. Everything except love.

Her family had always been short on money, but they had never lacked for love. It was the one thing they always seemed to have in abundance. Besides bills, of course. She couldn't speak for the current state of her individual family members' finances, but hers were in pretty good shape. Though her personal and business accounts had sizeable balances, neither could compete with those of the people around her.

After the doorman ushered her inside, she stepped into the lobby and inhaled the scent of power, prestige, and privilege. This was the life she had always dreamed about. The one she had always hoped she would eventually lead. As she approached the nattily attired concierge seated behind a marble-topped desk, she was torn between feeling out of place and feeling at home.

"May I help you?" he asked.

"Yes, I'm here to visit a woman who lives here."

"What's her name?" The concierge reached for a phone as he consulted a list of names on his computer screen.

"I have no idea." A fact that made her feel abjectly silly, given their plush surroundings.

"I see." The concierge flicked his eyes away from the computer screen and focused them on her face. Both his voice and demeanor were a touch too calm. As if he were mentally running through the correct steps to take to kick her out without causing a scene. "Let's approach this a different way. What's *your* name?"

"Olaf."

Somehow, she managed to say it with a straight face. Her efforts were rewarded with a smile.

"Ah, yes. I was told to expect you. Follow me, please." He led her across the lobby and punched some buttons on the control panel in the elevator. "That will get you where you need to go."

"Thank you."

"You're welcome," he said as the elevator doors began to close. "Enjoy your evening."

Compared to the day she'd had, even a disastrous night would be an improvement.

As the elevator began to rise, she felt her spirits lift along with it. The elevator in her building was so jerky riding in it was like being trapped inside a cement mixer. In contrast, the elevator in TDH's building rode as smoothly as one of the many luxury cars parked nearby.

"Nice to see someone's rent checks are being put to good use."

Hers must line the building owner's pockets because they certainly didn't go toward repairs. If something in her apartment needed fixing, she knew better than to call the super. If she wanted something done, she had to do it herself. Then again, there wasn't anything unusual about that. The youngest child in large families was often left to their own devices. Fending for herself was nothing new for her. Learning to depend on someone else was.

That was why she had resisted TDH's offer for so long. She hadn't wanted to seem weak or vulnerable. She hadn't wanted to break down. She hadn't wanted to need anyone. But a few hours ago, she was finally forced to admit she did.

The elevator stopped and the doors slid open. TDH was waiting for her when she stepped into the foyer.

TDH wasn't wearing a suit like she had the last—and only—time they'd met, but her outfit was just as luxe. Leather oxfords, sharply creased jeans, and a gray V-neck sweater paired with a crisp white cotton dress shirt.

The sweater was form-fitting and clung to TDH's slender torso. Brooklyn longed to touch it. Not to feel the expected softness of the material but the firmness of TDH's body underneath.

"Welcome to my home," TDH said. "Let me take your coat."

Brooklyn turned and allowed TDH to slide her overcoat off her shoulders. She almost cried out when she felt TDH's strong hands brush against her. The touch was fleeting but electric. Brooklyn felt her body come alive. When TDH asked if she wanted something to drink, she waited until she could trust herself to speak.

"A drink would be wonderful."

"What would you like?" TDH asked as she walked toward a well-stocked bar lined with bottles of alcohol and assorted mixers.

"Anything but tequila. I had a few too many shots of that last night." Brooklyn winced at the memory.

"Were you preparing for today or remembering the past?"

"A bit of both, I guess."

Brooklyn's thoughts were so jumbled she didn't think she was making much sense, but TDH nodded as if she understood her perfectly.

"Two Manhattans coming up."

As TDH busied herself making the drinks, Brooklyn checked out the living room. The space was filled with gorgeous furniture and stunning antiques, but it was the view that impressed her more than anything else.

"We're so high up, I feel like we're in some airline's flight path."

TDH smiled as she stirred bourbon, sweet vermouth, and bitters over ice, then strained the concoction into two chilled glasses. "Sometimes," she said, joining Brooklyn by the window, "I feel that way, too."

TDH held out one of the drinks she had just made. The contrast between her warm fingers and the cool glass gave Brooklyn goose bumps. "What do you do about it?"

"Pinch myself to make sure I'm not dreaming." TDH raised her glass in a toast. "Cheers."

Brooklyn laughed and took a sip of her Manhattan. The drink was smoky yet sweet. It reminded her of the time she and Charlie had drank Scotch and lit celebratory cigars to commemorate what, at the time, had been their most lucrative contract. The combination had made them both so sick they had puked in no time flat.

Would everything always remind her of Charlie, or would she eventually be able to make new memories that didn't involve her?

She turned toward the kitchen, where something was simmering on the stovetop. "What is that incredible smell?"

"Wine sauce. It needs some time to reduce." TDH's expression darkened as if she had been struck by an unpleasant thought.

"What's wrong?"

"I just realized I didn't ask if you were vegetarian or vegan. I planned to make steak and truffled mashed potatoes for dinner, but I can swap the protein for chicken, Portobello mushrooms, or tofu, if you like."

Brooklyn leaned against the reinforced window. "I just realized who you are."

"Who might that be?" TDH asked through narrowed eyes.

"You're one of those women who make the rest of us look bad. The kind who can kick some bad guy's ass, then turn around and whip up a delicious gourmet meal. All without breaking a nail or a sweat."

TDH's response was as self-deprecating as her smile. "I would tell you how far off-base you are, but I won't because I prefer your version of me to the real thing. Your version can make dinner on her own. Mine has to watch how-to videos on her phone."

Brooklyn glanced at the granite countertop, where she saw a smartphone resting next to a bamboo cutting board. The realization that TDH wasn't the superwoman she had thought her to be made her more relatable and, if possible, even sexier.

"Now that I've discovered you were only pretending to be a culinary goddess, does this mean I shouldn't expect you to tell me your real name anytime soon?"

TDH held out her hand. "It's Vilma. Vilma Bautista."

Her name was suitably exotic, yet it didn't seem to fit. No wonder she was reluctant to advertise it.

"Pleased to meet you, Vilma Bautista. I'm Brooklyn DiVincenzo."

Vilma took her hand and led her across the room. "Now that we've gotten the introductions out of the way, sit down, put your feet up, and make yourself comfortable. You've shouldered enough of the load this week. Let someone else do the work for a while."

Grateful tears filled Brooklyn's eyes as she took a seat on the couch. The cushions were so soft she felt like she was sitting on a cloud.

"Dinner should be ready in about thirty minutes," Vilma said. "How do you like your steak, rare or medium?"

"Is well done completely out of the question?"

"Not if it's what you want."

I could get used to being pampered, Brooklyn thought as she watched Vilma putter around the kitchen. Vilma even made an apron look sexy.

"Now that I finally know your name," she said, "am I allowed to ask what you do for a living?"

Vilma put a pot of potatoes on to boil and sprinkled a liberal amount of salt in the water. "I'm a venture capitalist."

Brooklyn knew how much start-up companies relied on venture capitalists to front them the money they needed to get their ideas off the ground, but she had always been too busy making a living at her own profession to research someone else's.

"How does that work exactly?" she asked. "What I'm saying is, how do you make money when, essentially, your job is to give it away?"

"By making sure I invest it wisely." Vilma unwrapped two steaks, placed them on a plate, and set the plate on the counter so the steaks could come up to temperature. "What about you? What do you do to pay the bills?"

"I run a tech company. Our market share isn't large enough for us to enter the lexicon and become a verb like Google has, but I'm proud of the products we've made. Instead of simply keeping up with what's trendy now, we try to predict what will be popular a year or two years from now to make sure we don't get left behind. That's the fun part."

"What's your specialty? Games, apps, social media?"

"We cover all those bases and then some."

"Yes, but what do you do best? Many companies do several things well. The best focus on doing one thing great." Vilma stirred the sauce, then turned to look at her. "If I asked you to name the one thing you're most proud of, what would you say? What's your claim to fame?"

Brooklyn was surprised that the first thing that came to mind wasn't a professional accomplishment but a personal one. "I'm most proud of the relationships I've made. That probably isn't the answer you were expecting."

"No, but it tells me a great deal about you."

"I'm not sure how to take that. Did I just lose you as a potential investor?"

"I invited you here because I'm interested in you, not your company. You can forward me a prospectus if you like. I'll take a look at it and see if your company intrigues me as much as you do."

"I will." Brooklyn channeled some of Brooke Vincent's bravado to emphasize her point. "I think you'll like what you see."

"Believe me. I already do."

Vilma's intense gaze belied her relaxed demeanor. Brooklyn had never met anyone who was such a study in contradictions. Who was this mysterious woman who had entered her life, and what did she have to do to convince her to stay?

"Are you sure you don't need any help with dinner?" she asked.

"I can tell you're used to being in control. You don't form a successful company unless you have the drive to make your dreams come true. Let someone else take the lead for once. Sit back. Relax. I've got this."

"Yes, ma'am."

Vilma's words gave Brooklyn the permission she needed to let go of the uncertainty she had been feeling for the past few days. She made a conscious decision to live in the moment instead of continuing to dwell on the past. And this moment was not about what she had lost but what she might gain.

"Would you like to hear some music?" Vilma asked.

"Yes, please."

A person's music choices often offered telling glimpses into their personalities. She was anxious to get a peek into Vilma's inner psyche because it was obvious Vilma wasn't in a hurry to share the information on her own.

Vilma gave her smart speaker a verbal command. "Will you hold it against me for using a product made by your competition?" she asked as the sultry voice of a woman Brooklyn didn't recognize began to swirl around the apartment.

The singer's voice sounded like honeyed whiskey. The music accompanying her had the same feel. Vilma hummed along to the music as she cooked, her rich alto blending in with the slinky bass guitar. If the song offered a representation of her personality, the woman was sex on legs.

*I can work with that.*

Brooklyn sank lower on the couch. Between the drink and the music, she was finally starting to relax. Her limbs felt lighter as the tension in her shoulders, arms, and legs gradually lessened. "If you promise not to make a habit out of it, I might find it in my heart to forgive you."

"I'll keep that in mind."

Brooklyn loved the back-and-forth. The flirting. The slow process of feeling each other out. She didn't know if it would lead anywhere, but she didn't care. She was too busy enjoying feeling something she hadn't felt in days: safe.

Santana held her hand over the cast iron grill pan to check the temperature. The tutorial she was watching said she was supposed to make sure the pan was screaming hot before she placed the steaks on it, but setting off the smoke detectors might ruin the mood she had gone to such great lengths to set.

She turned the heat down a little just in case. She was about to reach for the first steak when she noticed Brooklyn had grown quiet. An unusual circumstance given how much she clearly loved to talk. Whenever they interacted with each other, Santana didn't have to say much. She just had to ask the appropriate leading questions, then wait for Brooklyn to deliver a minutes-long discourse in response.

If they continued to see each other, Brooklyn would eventually expect her to open up as well. When the time came—*if* the time came—would she be able to do it? More importantly, would she share the details of her own life or Vilma's?

None of the identities she assumed were anything like her real one. Vilma came closest for three reasons. She didn't use wigs or facial prosthetics in order to play her, she had lived with the identity the longest, and she endowed her with the same background. No wonder she often found it easier to be in Vilma's skin than her own. Like now, for instance.

As Vilma, she could admit her shortcomings like she had when she had confessed she wasn't a very good cook. That was the kind of admission she would never be able to make as herself. Santana was tough. She was strong. She didn't have room in her life for failure. On her part or anyone else's. In her line of work, failure was not an option. Because failure could get her captured or killed. Neither was an option she wanted to consider. Not when Brooklyn DiVincenzo was around to provide such a pleasant diversion.

She was wildly attracted to Brooklyn, and she could tell the feeling was mutual. What remained to be determined, however, was if Brooklyn was attracted to her or the woman she was currently pretending to be.

"Are you enjoying the music," she asked, "or are you getting tired of my company?"

She waited for a response but didn't receive one. She placed the first steak on the grill pan, set the timer on the stove for four minutes, and wiped her hands on a dishcloth. Then she tossed the dishcloth on the counter and headed to the living room.

When she reached the couch, she realized why Brooklyn hadn't answered her question. Brooklyn was in the same position she had last seen her in—lying on the couch with her drink in her hand—but she was sound asleep.

Santana didn't know whether she should apologize for being such a boring date or be touched by the fact that Brooklyn felt comfortable enough to so thoroughly let down her guard around her. She gently brushed a stray lock of hair away from Brooklyn's face.

"Let's go with the latter."

Brooklyn stirred but didn't wake. Santana slowly slipped the glass out of her grip, removed her shoes, and covered her with a spare blanket from the linen closet. Then she lowered the lights and turned off the music.

"I guess I'm having dinner alone tonight," she whispered in the sudden quiet.

She returned to the kitchen, adjusted the timer to her liking, and set the spare steak in the refrigerator. After she prepared the mashed potatoes and plated the food, she took a moment to admire her work. Everything smelled incredible and, surprisingly, it bore more than a faint resemblance to the finished product on the tutorial she had been watching. Of all the classes Winslow had subjected her to over the years, none had involved anything practical.

"Why should you learn to cook and clean," he had often asked, "when you're rich enough to pay someone to do it for you?"

Naturally, he had neglected to mention that most of the money she possessed didn't actually belong to her. She had access to it because it was in her aliases' names, but he was the one who truly held the purse strings. Her only real asset was her house, but it was by no means the only thing she had to lose.

She headed to the dining room table and took a few tentative bites of her meal. The food wasn't restaurant-worthy, but the steak didn't taste like shoe leather, the mashed potatoes didn't have the consistency of wallpaper paste, and the wine sauce wasn't broken. All major accomplishments in her book.

"Thanks, Samson," she said, raising her glass in his honor. "I owe you one." Her excitement was blunted by a pang of disappointment as she glanced at Brooklyn's sleeping form. "Too bad I'm the only one who's getting a chance to sample my handiwork."

Brooklyn obviously needed the rest so Santana let her sleep. After she finished her meal, she put her plate and the dirty pots and pans in the dishwasher. She set a bottle of water on the coffee table in case Brooklyn got thirsty during the night and left a light on so she would be able to make her way around the apartment—or out the door if she chose to leave without saying good-bye.

Santana refilled her wine glass and took one last look around. Then she headed to her room, closed the door behind her, and retrieved her laptop. Brooklyn obviously felt safe with her. She wanted to make sure she remained that way.

She booted up her computer so she could continue the research she had started that afternoon. She took a sip of wine as she pored through the images she had downloaded. Faces of dozens of strangers flashed across the screen. She carefully examined each one to see if she could spot a quality she recognized.

"It takes a killer to catch a killer."

## Chapter Eleven

B rooklyn yawned and stretched. She couldn't remember the last time she had woken up feeling refreshed instead of even more exhausted than she had been before she had gone to bed. She blinked to get her bearings, then reality smacked her in the face. She wasn't in her dinky little apartment. She was in Vilma's spacious penthouse. She hadn't gone to bed last night. She had fallen asleep on Vilma's couch.

She covered her face with her hands, wondering if it were possible for someone to literally die from embarrassment. If so, she might be about to accomplish the feat.

She tossed the blanket aside and stepped into her shoes. Now all she had to do was grab her coat, take the elevator downstairs, and make her walk of shame through the lobby.

She checked her watch. It was a little before seven. At this hour, there shouldn't be too many witnesses. She would send her apologies to Vilma later. Right now, she just wanted to—

"Good morning."

She turned at the sound of Vilma's voice. Even dressed casually the way she was now, she still managed to look incredibly put together. Did she wake up at five a.m. each day to start getting ready? Because surely no one rolled out of bed looking that good.

"Good morning." Brooklyn wrapped her arms around her waist to hide some of the wrinkles in her dress.

"How did you sleep?"

Brooklyn felt her cheeks warm. "Quite well, obviously," she said, praying the blush didn't show. "I hope I didn't drool on your throw pillows."

Vilma waved a hand dismissively. "That's what dry cleaners are for. Since you missed dinner, would you like some breakfast?"

Brooklyn's stomach growled before she could say anything.

Vilma grinned. "I'll take that as a yes. I've got a rib eye left over from last night. I'll whip up some steak and eggs."

"Don't." Brooklyn grabbed Vilma's arm before she could head to the kitchen. The muscles felt like corded steel. Her mouth watered as she wondered if the rest of Vilma's body was just as firm. "You've already done enough for me," she said, releasing her grip. "It's time I returned the favor. Let me clean up a little, then I'll make you breakfast. If you've got peppers and onions, I can whip up my famous hangover skillet."

"The master bathroom's that way. If you'd like to take a shower, I've got some clothes you can borrow."

Vilma was a good three inches taller than she was and her shoulders were broader so any of her clothes were bound to be too big for Brooklyn. Given the choice between looking like a clown rather than a down-on-her-luck call girl, she was willing to accept the tradeoff.

The shower was so spacious she could practically run laps in it. The tile looked—and felt—like marble. The showerheads—all five of them—could be adjusted to provide not only the perfect angle but the perfect spray. The one overhead was set to rain shower. The four on the sides had some kind of pulsing action going that was even more relaxing than being stretched out on a massage table. Brooklyn could have stayed in there all day. She eventually forced herself to turn off the water and reach for a towel.

She dried off and slipped into the clothes Vilma had provided for her—a heather gray sweatshirt and black jeans. She pushed the sleeves of the sweatshirt up to her forearms so the cuffs didn't dangle below her hands. Then she folded the hems of the jeans so they wouldn't drag across the floor while she walked.

Even though the clothes had been laundered, they kind of smelled like Vilma. Brooklyn pulled the collar of the sweatshirt up to her nose and took a deep breath, drawing the faint trace of Vilma's cologne into her lungs.

She felt silly, an opinion that was confirmed when she saw her reflection in the bathroom mirror.

"You're the CEO of a rather successful tech company," she told herself. "Stop acting like a teenager with a crush."

When it came to Vilma Bautista, however, that was easier said than done. Vilma was aspirational, offering her a glimpse of who she could eventually become, not who she was. Yet they somehow found themselves in the same orbit. Hopefully, they would continue to move closer without crashing into each other like a couple of meteoroids on a collision course.

"Better?" Vilma asked when she came out of the bathroom.

"Much. Thank you."

Vilma handed her a glass of orange juice. "I took the liberty of sending your dress out to be cleaned. Samson says it should be ready in a couple of hours."

"You didn't have to do that. I could have thrown it in the washer when I got home."

"Yes, you could, but my way gives me a chance to earn more brownie points."

"I think you've already earned more of those than you could possibly redeem."

"Perhaps, but I like to hedge my bets."

"Is that what makes you such a successful investor?"

"That and a high tolerance for risk."

The look in Vilma's eyes made it seem like not all the risks she took were business-related. The idea gave Brooklyn an undeniable thrill. She imagined testing Vilma's limits. And allowing Vilma to help her push past her own.

"So what makes this dish of yours so famous?" Vilma asked. "I would also love to know how it got its name."

Brooklyn set her empty glass down and pulled her hair back into a loose ponytail. "I might have overstated its renown, but

I stand by its recuperative powers. The name is self-explanatory. My hangover skillet is guaranteed to cure what ails after a night of overindulgence. Thankfully, it tastes just as good even when, like last night, only one drink was enough to put me out like a light."

Vilma indicated Brooklyn's empty glass. "More?"

"Yes, please."

Vilma reached into the refrigerator for the container of orange juice, giving Brooklyn a chance to check out what was inside. Potatoes, steak, eggs, onions, and jalapeño peppers.

"Perfect. I'll take these. And those. And this. And this. And this." She gathered the ingredients she needed and carefully set them on the counter. "What are your feelings on cheese? Love, hate, or barely tolerate?"

"I'm flexible."

"Good to know." Brooklyn grabbed a bag of shredded cheddar cheese and closed the refrigerator door.

"I would offer my assistance," Vilma said as Brooklyn began to chop the vegetables, "but you seem to know your way around my kitchen even better than I do."

Brooklyn diced the potatoes first and dropped them into a skillet drizzled with olive oil. They would take longest to cook so she made sure to get them on the heat first.

"I've been cooking since I was ten so I've had lots of practice. I would help my mother and my *nonna* make Sunday dinner. I come from a large family so there was always lots of food to prepare when all of us got together."

"Is that how you learned to make your famous skillet?"

"No, I stumbled upon the recipe for that while I was in college. My friends and I were typical poor college students. We had enough money for pizza and beer but not much else. One morning after we'd spent a late night in a few of Boston's finest bars, we raided each other's mini-fridges and pooled our meager resources." Brooklyn pointed her knife toward the steak resting on the counter. "I think the meat in the first batch was canned ham instead of Wagyu beef, but I didn't hear any complaints."

"You won't hear any from me, either, though the waitress at my favorite diner might make a comment or two about the tip she's missing out on today."

Brooklyn paused before she reached for the jalapeños. "You weren't kidding about being a novice at cooking, were you? Do you go out for every meal?"

"Or have something delivered."

"Then why did you offer to make dinner for me last night?"

Vilma lifted her shoulders in a shrug. "I think I wanted to try something different. The results were better than I expected."

"I'm sorry I wasn't able to share them with you."

"Just because it was better than I expected didn't mean it was fit to be consumed by someone other than myself."

"Even so, would it be presumptuous of me to ask for a rain check?"

"Perhaps, but I like women who go after what they want instead of waiting for it to be handed to them."

"Also good to know."

Brooklyn cracked two eggs in a bowl, dropped a handful of cheese on top, and mixed the concoction with a fork. Then she sliced the steak into bite-sized chunks and seasoned the meat.

"This is turning into quite the production number," Vilma said.

Brooklyn added diced onions to the pan of potatoes. "The whole is greater than the sum of its parts."

She continued to add ingredients to the skillet until each element was properly cooked. Then she grabbed two plates and spooned food onto them.

Vilma reached into the refrigerator and pulled out a bottle of champagne. "A dish that smells that good deserves a mimosa, don't you think?"

Brooklyn watched as Vilma expertly popped the cork on the bottle of champagne and poured some of the contents into a pair of crystal flutes before topping off the champagne with orange juice.

Vilma moaned when she took the first bite. "Now I'm glad you fell asleep last night. This puts my efforts to shame."

"I doubt that, but thank you for the compliment."

Brooklyn was pleased to see that something so simple had appealed to someone with Vilma's refined tastes. As she ate a dish from her past, she felt like she was being offered a glimpse into the future. Was this the only breakfast she and Vilma would share, or the first of many?

"Do you have anything planned for today?"

The question took Brooklyn by surprise because it made it seem as if Vilma couldn't wait to get rid of her. Had she misjudged their rapport? Here she was planning their next encounter while Vilma was anxious for this one to be over.

"Nothing major." Brooklyn moved her food around her plate to hide her disappointment. "What about you?"

Vilma set her fork down, a common precursor for ending a conversation rather than continuing one. "Actually, I was hoping to spend the day with you. Are you up for an adventure?"

"I feel like I've been on one since the night we met."

"Then today sounds like a perfect opportunity to decide where we should go next."

And Brooklyn couldn't wait to get started.

## CHAPTER TWELVE

The facial recognition scans Santana had run the day before hadn't been of much help. Even though she now had a name for each person who had appeared at Charlotte Evans's gravesite, none of the attendees had stood out to her as the person who had arranged the hit. They were just the usual assortment of friends, relatives, coworkers, and current and former lovers. She had been up until four a.m. running thorough background checks on each of them, hoping she would spot something she had missed during her preliminary search. Again, she had come up empty.

The unsatisfying results didn't dent her desire to solve the mystery, though. Instead of giving up, she was determined to try even harder. To dig even deeper into both Brooklyn's—and Charlotte's—personal and professional lives. Now that she had looked into the people who had attended Charlotte's funeral, she needed to research the associates who hadn't. Scheduling conflicts might have kept some of them away, but so could a guilty conscience.

"What would you like to do today?" Brooklyn asked as they cleared the breakfast plates off the table.

"If you don't mind, I'd like to see your office."

The plate Brooklyn was holding slipped in her hands. Santana lunged to catch it, but Brooklyn tightened her grip before it managed to fall from her grasp. "Sorry about that. I'm not usually such a klutz." Brooklyn turned toward the sink, though not fast enough to prevent Santana from seeing the stricken expression on her face. "Why do you want to see my office?"

"Hearing you describe your company has me intrigued. I would love to tour the facility so I can see where the magic happens."

Brooklyn rinsed the plate and handed it to Santana so she could load it in the dishwasher.

"You're shaking." Santana placed her hands on Brooklyn's shoulders to steady her. "What's wrong?"

"I haven't been back to my office since the shooting," Brooklyn said, her voice quavering. "As far as I know, no one has. Tomorrow's our first official day back at work. Everything was cleaned up days ago so the place no longer looks like a crime scene, but I don't know if I'll be able to walk through the doors and pretend nothing has changed."

"No one expects you to do that, but your employees will be counting on you to lead them. They'll be waiting to take their cues from you. If you fall apart, how long do you think it will take for them to follow suit?"

Santana let her hands drop. This situation was new to her. She was used to inflicting pain and occasionally providing pleasure, not offering comfort.

"Returning to a place filled with so many memories, both good and bad, is bound to be difficult," she said, "but you need to face your fears rather than run from them." And she needed to take a look at Brooklyn's office up close rather than through a rifle scope.

"I know."

Brooklyn leaned against the sink as if she thought her legs were about to give way. Santana took a step toward her but didn't reach for her again. Brooklyn had experienced a terrible trauma, as had so many others like her, but she could tell Brooklyn was strong enough to withstand it. A fact she hoped Brooklyn realized as well.

"I've been telling myself that for days," Brooklyn said with a sigh, "but I kept coming up with excuses to prevent myself from doing so. To be honest, that's one of the reasons I called you yesterday."

"To help you face your fears?"

"In a way."

"I don't understand."

"Probably because I'm not making much sense. Let me back up." Brooklyn took a breath and started over. "When I was in high school, I invented an alter ego to help me do all the things I'd convinced myself I couldn't accomplish on my own. Someone who's confident, fearless, and has her shit together instead of being a raging bundle of insecurities who would rather speak in code than emoticons. Whenever I was nervous or anxious—whenever I wanted to ask someone for a date or ace a presentation in class, for example—I pretended to be Brooke Vincent instead of Brooklyn DiVincenzo. I still do that now. It wasn't me who talked the loan officer at my bank into giving me the money I needed to start my company. It was Brooke. It isn't me who gives TED talks. It's Brooke. It wasn't me who shepherded my friends and employees through the hardest week of our lives. It was Brooke. Sometimes, I'm tempted to buy one of those *What Would Jesus Do* T-shirts and customize it so it reads *WWBD* instead."

"What Would Brooke Do? I like it."

"Yesterday, I got tired of being Brooke. I wanted to be Brooklyn again. The way I was with Charlie. The way I was with you."

She placed her hand over Santana's heart. The gesture was so unexpected Santana almost pulled away. The tenderness of Brooklyn's touch, however, kept her rooted in place.

"I know we haven't known each other very long," Brooklyn said, "but I don't feel like I have to pretend with you. I can be myself."

"A lovable snowman whose best friend freezes everything she touches?"

Brooklyn's dazzling smile took Santana's breath away. Seeing it was like watching the sun break through the clouds after a storm.

"I would say you found me out, but I think you've known exactly who I am from the beginning. Not literally, of course. Why would you? I'm nobody. Yet, from the moment you looked at me, you seemed to see the real me instead of the image I often project. And, for some reason, you appeared to like me anyway. Call me selfish, but I wanted more of that. I wanted more of you."

Santana felt herself drifting farther and farther into uncharted territory. The urge to return to safer ground was almost overwhelming. Almost, but not quite. For some reason, the prospect of sex without a meaningful connection except the physical didn't hold the same appeal it had a few days ago. And an idea she had once refused to consider—allowing a woman to touch her soul instead of just her body—was starting to take root.

She preferred to think things through rather than act on impulse. If she had followed her instincts, she would have closed the distance between herself and Brooklyn and taken Brooklyn's face in her hands. After taking a moment to breathe her in, she would have kissed her. Gently at first. Then, as Brooklyn started to respond, with a greater sense of urgency. They would have spent the rest of the day in bed. Exploring each other's bodies with their lips, tongues, and hands. And afterward? What then? Would she send Brooklyn away like she had all the others who had preceded her or, unthinkably, would she beg her to stay? The realization that she had no idea how she would handle that situation prompted her to follow her head instead of her heart.

"I'll make a deal with you," she said. "Despite present circumstances, your office sounds like your happy place. I'll show you mine if you show me yours."

Brooklyn's smile broadened. "What are we waiting for?"

## CHAPTER THIRTEEN

While Vilma tipped the driver of the town car that had brought them from her apartment, Brooklyn tried to keep from falling apart. Her office and the building that housed it had once felt like home to her. A few days ago, that home had been invaded by a nameless, faceless intruder who hadn't even bothered to cross the threshold. Cosmetically, everything looked pretty much the same, but it definitely didn't feel that way.

She looked up at the office windows high overhead. A new pane of glass had been installed in place of the one that had been pierced by a large caliber bullet. It was so clean it gleamed, making it stand out from the weathered panes on either side of it. Brooklyn tore her eyes away from the window as images of Charlie's bloody corpse flashed through her mind.

Tempted to run away, she retreated a step. Then she felt Vilma's hand press against the small of her back. Grounding her. Giving her the courage she needed to face what she had been trying to avoid.

"This is an unusual building," Vilma said. "How did you locate it?"

"I don't own it—I rent the suite of offices on the tenth floor—but I consider it something of a family heirloom. It was originally built as a piano factory. If you look carefully, you can still make out the name painted on the brick." She pointed at the faded lettering on the pocked walls. "My grandfather worked here for almost fifty years. He started when he was a teenager and stayed on until it was time for him to retire."

"What did he do?"

"He was a tuner. It was his job to manipulate the pins on the wires until each key reached the correct pitch. I would have lost my mind after less than a day of being bombarded by all those discordant notes, but he loved it. He and my grandmother would have the funniest arguments sometimes. When he didn't respond after she asked him to do something around the house, she would stand over him in his easy chair and say, 'You can tell the difference between a flat and a sharp, but you can't hear me when I tell you to take out the trash?'"

"They sound adorable."

"They are. They're the ideal couple, too. They've been together so long I can't imagine one without the other. To this day, my grandfather takes my *nonna's* hand every time they cross the street." She smiled to herself as she thought of them making their way through life. A bit slower than they once did but still together. "I had forgotten about that story. Thanks for reminding me of it."

"You're welcome."

Brooklyn felt a sense of peace wash over her as she looked into Vilma's eyes. She couldn't tell if the feeling had transpired because of Vilma's presence or the memory she had prompted her to recall.

"Shall we go inside?" she asked.

"After you."

Brooklyn used her key fob to gain access to the building, then pointed at the list of names printed on a sign in the lobby.

"Several companies are located in the building and there's a coffee shop here on the first floor, so on the rare days I get an actual lunch break, I don't have far to go to find a good place to eat."

"How long have you been in business?" Vilma asked as they boarded the elevator.

"Officially? Five years."

"And unofficially?"

Brooklyn thought back. "I wrote my first program when I was eight. I sold it shortly after that. I only made five dollars for the sale. At the time, it seemed like a fortune. I framed it like most businesses do when they make their first buck, but I ended up spending it when

I had to break into my piggy bank in order to buy a handheld game console I had my eye on but my parents refused to pay for."

"Now you create your own games."

"Among other things, though I'm planning on making some changes to my business model. I have you to thank for that, by the way."

"How so?"

"Last night, you said many companies do several things well, but the best focus on doing one thing great. Tomorrow, I'm going to challenge my staff—and myself—to do something great."

Vilma's smile seemed to hold a hint of pride. "I look forward to hearing about your future projects."

"When the time comes, I'll prepare a formal prospectus for you. Unless you'd prefer a more personal approach."

"Give me a call when you have something concrete and we'll decide how to proceed."

Brooklyn wondered if she needed to write a prospectus for the two of them as well because she was currently at a loss. When they were standing in Vilma's kitchen a few minutes ago, she had been certain Vilma was about to kiss her. Vilma had come close, but not close enough. Had she backed off out of respect for her grief, or was there another reason she had chosen to exercise restraint?

When the elevator reached the tenth floor, Brooklyn unlocked the office doors and turned on the lights.

"This is it. Let me take you on a tour. I like to think of the space as a miniature version of the sprawling campuses favored by companies like Google and YouTube. Same principle but less square footage. The research and development team works here," she said as Vilma trailed her around the room. "The programmers congregate here, the production team works in this area, and the marketing team works pretty much wherever they can find inspiration."

"What about HR and accounting and finance? Do you have teams for those functions as well?"

"I'm in charge of personnel, and an outside firm handles the accounting duties. I have a good head for numbers, but I'd rather leave some things to the experts."

Vilma whistled as she turned in a slow circle. Her gaze seemed to linger on Charlie's desk, but surely that had to be either a coincidence or a trick of Brooklyn's imagination. How could Vilma possibly know which workspace was Charlie's when she had never visited the company before?

"Impressive," Vilma said. "Which work space is yours?"

"I'm in here."

She led Vilma to her office. A whiteboard filled with notes for potential projects covered one wall. The other walls were decorated with framed quotes attributed to some of her favorite tech wizards and business leaders. Most of the shelves on a bookcase to the right of her desk were filled with an array of business manuals. The top shelf, though, contained her collection of shot glasses from some of her favorite dive bars.

"Not what you were expecting?" she asked when she saw the quizzical look on Vilma's face.

"I'm just wondering where Brooke ends and Brooklyn begins."

"Yeah, sometimes I wonder that, too."

"Hey, boss."

Brooklyn turned to find AJ standing in her doorway. She had been so engrossed in her conversation with Vilma she hadn't heard AJ enter the office. "Hey, yourself. I didn't know you were planning on coming in today."

AJ indicated the computer bag slung over her shoulder. "I wanted to put some finishing touches on my presentation before our meeting tomorrow and the internet's a lot faster here than it is in my apartment. I'm also a sucker for dual monitors."

"So am I. I keep meaning to do a similar setup at home, but if I did, I'd probably never leave my apartment."

"You and me both."

AJ glanced at Vilma, which reminded Brooklyn she hadn't bothered to introduce them to each other.

"Pardon my manners. Vilma, this is AJ Gojowczyk, one of my programmers. AJ, this is Vilma Bautista, a venture capitalist I met while I was in Tokyo."

"Pleased to meet you," AJ said as she and Vilma shook hands.

"Likewise."

"Are you looking to invest in BDV?"

"I'm always on the lookout for an attractive arrangement, business or otherwise."

"Aren't we all?" AJ turned back to Brooklyn. "If I had known you were having a business meeting, I never would have poked my head in the door. I didn't mean to interrupt you. I just wanted to let you know I was here. I'll get out of your hair."

"We'll talk in the morning, yeah?" Brooklyn asked.

"I've been practicing my talking points all day. Prepare to be dazzled."

"I consider myself warned." Brooklyn briefly rested her hand on AJ's arm the way she always did when she was trying to be reassuring. Soon, though, AJ wouldn't need such gestures because she definitely seemed to be coming into her own. "Make sure to lock up when you leave."

"Will do."

"She seems…eager," Vilma said after AJ sat at her desk, put her ear buds in, and went to work.

"She was Charlie's protégée. Now I suppose she's mine. Charlie was expecting big things out of her, and I can understand why. She's smart, talented, and driven to succeed. If she wanted to, she could be sitting in this chair in a few years instead of me."

"Does she want to?"

"I think she'd rather be the power behind the throne than the person sitting on it."

"Uneasy lies the head that wears the crown. Isn't that how the saying goes?"

"It sounds vaguely familiar."

"Is there anyone who would like to take your crown?"

"You sound like Detective Barnett. One of the first questions he asked me was if Charlie had any enemies. She didn't, and as far as I know, neither do I. Tech is a competitive industry, but my rivalries are friendly rather than cutthroat. We fight each other for business deals during the day, but we're able to share a few laughs over drinks at night. Luke Ridley is a prime example. He and I constantly butt heads when it comes to the way we do business, but our personal relationship has always been solid."

"Admirable."

"Not admirable. Necessary. Life's too short to spend it at odds with someone."

She turned off the lights in her office and closed the door. She waved at AJ as she and Vilma headed for the exit.

"How did it feel to be back?" Vilma asked.

Brooklyn thought for a moment. After the initial shock had worn off, her comfort level had grown by the minute. Seeing AJ made her long to touch base with the rest of her employees as well. She had seen most of them over the past few days, but she had felt out of place conversing with them at a wake or in a cemetery. Tomorrow, she would be able to see them in their normal environs.

Monday was bound to be hard since it would be their first work day without Charlie in their midst, but with the emotions of the past week behind them, it would be easier to pick up where they had left off.

"Thomas Wolfe was wrong," she said. "You *can* go home again." She squeezed Vilma's hand as they waited for the elevator to arrive. "Thank you for this. Thank you for today."

"Don't thank me yet. The day's not over. We're just getting started."

Santana felt a flicker of jealousy when Brooklyn touched AJ's arm. Brooklyn's gesture hadn't caused the reaction. It was the obvious pleasure AJ had derived from Brooklyn's touch. Brooklyn might not have noticed, but AJ had either a crush, a healthy case of hero worship, or both. If she and AJ crossed paths again, it would take a concerted effort for Santana to view her objectively rather than as competition.

When was the last time she'd had to compete for a woman's attention? Try never. She preferred her relationships to remain uncomplicated so she could walk away from them at any time with no drama and no hurt feelings. Having a rival for Brooklyn's affections might be an interesting new wrinkle, but it was a complication she didn't need. Another in a growing string of them.

The fallout from Charlotte Evans's death was supposed to be someone else's problem, not hers. Yet here she was smack in the middle of a situation that felt like it was starting to spin out of control. She was finally getting a taste of what it felt like to embark on an actual relationship, and she had never been happier—or more frightened. If Winslow found out how much Brooklyn was starting to mean to her, he wouldn't hesitate to use Brooklyn to keep her in check. In his mind, love was something meant to be exploited, not shared. Even though she wanted to spend more time with Brooklyn, she would rather walk away than see her hurt.

"You're awfully quiet," Brooklyn said as a car took them out of town. "Is something troubling you?"

Santana shifted in her seat so she could look Brooklyn in the eye. "I'm wondering if I might have oversold what I have planned for us. I don't want you to be disappointed."

Unlike most of the things she had told Brooklyn since they'd met, this one was true. She cared what Brooklyn thought. Both in general and about her. Talk about interesting new wrinkles.

"If you think I might be bored, think again," Brooklyn said. "I could probably watch paint dry with you and find it fascinating. Based on the address you gave the driver, I assume we won't be doing anything quite that sedate."

They were headed to an upscale shopping center just outside Yonkers. The expansive space featured dozens of high-end retail stores and nearly as many upscale restaurants. It also contained one of the few permanent indoor skydiving facilities in the state. The nearly hundred-foot-tall wind tunnel allowed participants to turn their dreams of flying into reality.

"Have you been to Flyght Zone before?" Santana asked.

"I've considered taking my staff there several times, but I've never followed through."

"Because?"

"Though it could provide the perfect venue for a team-building exercise, the chance of someone getting hurt offsets the potential upside. Nothing ruins a good time faster than a few broken bones."

"Now you tell me."

"Is it one of your favorite hangouts?"

"I try to visit whenever I'm in town. When I'm working, I like to remain as calm as possible. When I'm not, I have to do something to blow off the pent-up energy."

"And indoor skydiving is your method of choice?"

"Of the options that require me to be fully clothed, yes."

Brooklyn's inscrutable expression didn't reveal what she was thinking, but her eyes were a dead giveaway. The look in them was challenging, practically daring Santana to ask the driver to turn the car around and take them back to her apartment.

"I hadn't pictured you as an adrenaline junkie," Brooklyn said before Santana could take the bait.

"What had you pictured me as?"

Brooklyn furrowed her brow as she pondered the question. She probably adopted the same pensive look whenever she was trying to figure out a particularly difficult piece of computer code or resolve a personnel issue. She was such an enticing combination of beauty and intelligence. Santana longed to watch her work, but she doubted any marketing geniuses had created an event called Take a Contract Killer to Work Day. If so, she was ready to sign up.

"I'm not quite sure," Brooklyn finally confessed. "I can't get a handle on you. In Tokyo, you reminded me of James Bond. Elegant, refined, and able to emerge from a full-scale battle royal without so much as a hair out of place. You're not a spy, are you?"

Santana laughed to hide her shock at how close Brooklyn had come to the truth. She had received nearly as much training as Ian Fleming's fictional spy. Weapons training, language lessons, hand-to-hand combat. Winslow had spared no expense as he slowly but surely turned her into someone she almost didn't recognize.

"If I were," she said, "I would sound much, much wittier, and my paramours would all sport sexualized names befitting of a Bond girl. By my reckoning, I fall short of the mark."

"I suppose we'll have to agree to disagree because by my reckoning, you're right on target."

"You flatter me."

"And you intrigue me." Santana tried to break eye contact, but Brooklyn's penetrating gaze held her fast. "I want to know all about you, but I don't want to bombard you with all my questions at once. I suppose I should start with the most important one."

"Which is?"

"Are you single?"

Santana couldn't help but laugh. At herself for expecting the worst. And at Brooklyn for offering such a refreshing change of pace. None of the other women she had been with had bothered to ask if she was involved with someone else or not. All they had cared about was how much pleasure they could derive from each other. Brooklyn was different. And thoroughly intoxicating.

"I had expected a more existential query."

Brooklyn shrugged. "In my mind, the practical approach is often the best approach. It allows me to cut through both red tape and BS with the least amount of effort."

"That's a good strategy. No wonder you're such a successful businesswoman."

"Thank you for the compliment, but you haven't answered my question."

Realizing Brooklyn wouldn't allow herself to be as easily dissuaded today as she had in Tokyo, Santana relented. "Yes, I'm single. I'm almost afraid to ask, but what's your next question?"

"I detect a slight accent, but I can't tell what kind. What is its place of origin? That tiny speck of land in the middle of the Pacific you mentioned before, or somewhere else?"

"I like to say I'm a citizen of the world—my main residence is in 'Ohe Sojukokoro and I have a place here in New York—but if we're being specific, I was born in the Philippines. I left when I was a teenager, but I've never been able to completely shake the accent."

"Is that where your parents were born?"

"My mother's Filipino. My father's American. They met while he was stationed on the air force base in Manila."

"They must be so proud of your accomplishments."

"I wouldn't know. I haven't seen either of them in years. Mixed marriages don't go over well in the Philippines, especially when one of the principals is already married to someone else. My mother and I had a falling out when I was too young to realize I didn't know as much about the world as I thought I did, and I haven't seen my father since he left to return to his 'real' family in the States."

Brooklyn's face fell. "Oh, I'm sorry to hear that. I apologize if I brought up unpleasant memories."

"No need. My family situation is unfortunate, but it is what it is."

Thankfully, Brooklyn didn't try to convince her that she and her parents could eventually work things out. Winslow hadn't included parents or family members in any of her aliases' official biographies in order to keep her true identity a secret. The less information someone snooping around her personal life had to sift through, the better.

Her father had left a wife and two children at home while he was stationed at Clark Air Base. He might have produced more after he returned to the States, but she hadn't bothered to check. Not like she had much to go on. The only thing she knew about his life here in America was he was from West Virginia.

She was curious to know if she and her siblings shared some of the same personality traits or had a family resemblance, though not curious enough to meet them face-to-face. A chapter had ended the day her father walked out on her and her mother. When she left home a few years later, she had closed the book for good.

Some stories weren't worth revisiting while others only grew more satisfying upon multiple readings. She knew which category her backstory fit into. Time would tell how she would be able to categorize her future. And what role Brooklyn DiVincenzo would play in it.

## Chapter Fourteen

After the driver dropped them off at Flyght Zone, Brooklyn followed Vilma inside so they could check in with the receptionist.

"It's good to see you again, Ms. Bautista," the receptionist said perkily. "I see you brought a guest this time." She turned to Brooklyn. "I'm April. Welcome to Flyght Zone. Are you a willing participant, or did she drag you in here kicking and screaming?"

"That remains to be seen."

The lobby walls were made of glass, allowing a clear view of the customers in the wind tunnel and the others anxiously waiting to take their turns. Brooklyn watched as a man wearing a helmet, safety goggles, and a bright red flight suit floated on a cushion of air while an instructor guided him through his paces. The man must have been a first-time visitor because he dropped like a rock as soon as the instructor released her grip on his leg and let him try to navigate on his own. The customers ringing the outside of the wind tunnel cheered after the instructor managed to catch him just before he would have hit the ground. The man looked embarrassed but none the worse for wear.

"Don't be scared," April said. "I'm sure you'll get the hang of it in no time."

"From your mouth to God's ears."

"Let me give you the spiel." April slid several forms across the desk. "This first form is a standard waiver of liability. Feel free to take your time and read it over, but it pretty much says you understand the risk you'll be assuming by participating and agree not to sue us if something goes wrong."

"That's a pleasant way to start a conversation," Brooklyn said as she began to read the two-page document.

"I know. Right? But once you get through the unpleasantness, we can get to the fun stuff."

Vilma quickly signed the form and returned it. Brooklyn followed suit.

"Thank you." April retrieved the forms and filed them away. "Since you haven't been here before, Brooklyn, I'll tell you how things work. After you leave the reception area, you'll head to the locker room to change into your helmets, goggles, and flight suits." She pointed at another form in the stack. "Fill this out to let me know what size you'll need. Our uniforms are unisex, so keep that in mind when you make your selection."

After Brooklyn placed a check mark in the box next to the appropriate size, April handed her a flight suit and a pair of goggles from the stash under the desk. Vilma's information must have already been on file because April handed her a flight suit without asking her to complete a form first.

"Nicole is the instructor on duty today," April said. "After you watch the other students and get a feel for the process, she'll show you how to navigate the currents and move through the air. In other words, she'll teach you how to fly."

"I'll keep the legend of Icarus in mind and try not to get too close to the sun."

"Don't worry," Vilma said. "I'll be there to catch you if you fall."

Brooklyn couldn't think of a better place to land.

"Flight sessions last between one and two hours," April said. "You'll complete the last form after your session is complete. It's a survey that gives you an opportunity to provide feedback on your experience. Ratings are on a scale from one to five. One means you had a truly sucky time and five means you enjoyed yourself so much you can't wait to come back with all your friends in tow."

"What are you thinking?" Vilma asked as they headed to the locker room to change clothes.

Brooklyn was thinking how much Charlie would have loved doing something like this, but she didn't think it was appropriate to bring up another woman while she was on a date. Instead, she held up the baggy flight suit April had given her.

"I was just thinking this isn't my most flattering look."

"If you'd prefer black tie instead, I'll keep that in mind for our next date."

"If I'm still talking to you after today's date, I just might take you up on that."

Vilma opened her assigned locker and began to undress. Though she longed to watch her, Brooklyn turned her back to give Vilma some privacy. She removed her borrowed clothes and slipped into the rented flight suit. When she strapped on her goggles and helmet, she felt like Tom Cruise in *Top Gun*, but the mental illusion was shattered as soon as she looked in the mirror. Her reflection made her seem more like the butt of a joke than the hero of an action film. Thankfully, Vilma didn't appear to hold the same opinion. When Brooklyn turned to face her, the look Vilma gave her was searing.

For the first time, Brooklyn sensed a crack in Vilma's heretofore impenetrable façade. She wanted to slip her fingers into the fissure and spread it wider. To feel Vilma open up to her. To go over the edge with her, then gather herself and make the journey again. If not today, then soon.

*God, please let it be soon.*

Santana watched Brooklyn take her turn in the wind tunnel with her heart in her throat. She wasn't afraid Brooklyn would fall. Nicole was too good at her job to allow anything to happen to anyone in her charge. She was afraid she was starting to fall for Brooklyn.

Brooklyn had that look on her face again. The one that was a mixture of concentration and determination. After Nicole let go and allowed her to fly on her own, the look morphed into one of wonder, then accomplishment.

Santana applauded with the rest of the customers gathered outside the glass wind tunnel as Brooklyn gracefully floated through the air. Emboldened, Brooklyn tucked her arms and legs and turned a tentative somersault. She punched the air when she successfully completed the maneuver without losing altitude in the process.

Santana caught her eye and gave her an enthusiastic thumbs-up.

"Do I need to tell you I had an amazing time in there, or is it self-evident?" Brooklyn asked when she finally came back to earth.

One of a group of teenage boys who had been sitting in the waiting area with Santana during Brooklyn's session gave her a high five. "Dude, you're, like, made for this."

"Yes, she is," Santana said.

And, perhaps, she was also made for her.

## CHAPTER FIFTEEN

When she left her office a few days ago, Brooklyn had felt as low as she could possibly get. She returned to work the following Monday on a high. Even though her session at the indoor skydiving venue had ended several hours ago, she still felt like she was flying. The time she had spent with Vilma was just like that session—filled with the lows of embarrassing gaffes and the highs of unexpected breakthroughs.

Even though she and Vilma had been acquainted for only a few weeks, Brooklyn had said good-bye to her yesterday feeling as close to her as if they had been in each other's lives for years. She couldn't figure out if their bond was due to the unusual circumstances in which they had met, or the more depressing ones in which they had become reacquainted. Whatever the reason, she was looking forward to deepening their connection.

During the ride back to her apartment, Vilma had asked her to go out with her the following weekend. She had kept the details under wraps as Brooklyn had expected she would, but she did offer a tantalizing hint that black tie and tails might be involved. Brooklyn loved the way Vilma treated even a throwaway comment as a challenge meant not only to be met but exceeded. Now it was her turn to do the same.

Most of the staff was already at their desks when she arrived. She felt their eyes on her as soon as she walked through the door. The collective look they gave her was expectant. Like they were wondering what they were supposed to do next and were counting on her to lead them there.

"Good morning, everyone." She faltered for a moment when she noticed several people had placed handwritten notes or mementoes on Charlie's desk, but she forced herself to remain strong. "We've all had a hard week, but now it's time for us to do our best work. Meet me in the conference room in fifteen minutes and bring your best ideas."

The quiet was broken by the sound of people scurrying to locate their notes files or dream boards. She loved that sound. The sound of great minds at work.

She headed to her office so she could check her email before the meeting started. She was thrown off-stride by the large bouquet of flowers sitting on her desk.

*Thank you for a most unusual weekend*, the card read. *Looking forward to the next flight—Vilma*

"We're all wondering who sent those," AJ said. "Whoever she is must have had to pull some major strings to arrange a delivery so early."

Brooklyn dropped the note card in her purse but didn't bother to say who had written it. "I don't kiss and tell," she said as she logged into her computer.

"Are you allowed to say if your meeting with the investor went well, or is that off-limits, too?"

"It was promising."

AJ lowered her voice to a conspiratorial whisper. "So there's a chance we might be going public soon?"

"That depends on the outcome of today's meeting."

"Charlie always said you could be cagey when you wanted to be."

Brooklyn looked up from her email long enough to meet AJ's eye. "You and Charlie talked about me?"

"You were one of her favorite subjects." AJ blushed. "Actually, what she called your 'pathetic excuse for a love life' was."

"Yep," Brooklyn said with a laugh, "that sounds like Charlie."

"Did she know about—" AJ jerked her chin toward the bouquet of flowers.

"No." Brooklyn felt a pang of melancholy when she realized Charlie and Vilma would never meet. Would they have gotten along, or would they have ended up butting heads? It was sad to think she would never know. "Because there's nothing to tell. Not yet, anyway."

"Got it. If you need a sounding board, you know where to find me."

"Thanks, AJ." Brooklyn regarded her for a moment. Aside from company functions, they hadn't spent much time together outside the office. Brooklyn had gleaned a few details about her over the years, but she knew more about the contents of her personnel file than her personal life. The main thing they had in common was Charlie. And now that link was gone. "Are you free for lunch today?"

"Yes."

"Perfect. Let's grab a bite in the café downstairs. Is one o'clock good for you?"

"I'll have to check my schedule, but I think I might be able to fit you in."

"I'm happy to hear that. See you in a few."

"Sure thing, boss."

Brooklyn responded to a few emails and flagged the ones she needed to follow up on later. Then she checked the clock. She had just enough time to send Vilma a quick text.

*The flowers are beautiful,* she wrote. *I'll do my best to deserve them.*

Vilma's response came a few minutes later. *You already have.*

*Looking forward to Saturday night,* Brooklyn wrote back. *Any hints about where we're going?*

Brooklyn waited anxiously for the ellipses on the phone's display to turn into words.

*You'll find out when we get there.*

Brooklyn hated mysteries because she always figured them out way too soon. Vilma Bautista was a mystery she hadn't come close to solving, but, damn, if she didn't enjoy trying.

She strode into the conference room and took her seat at the head of the table. The chair to her right, the one Charlie had always occupied, had been left empty. She was touched by the show of respect.

"You guys are a good team." She watched everyone's faces light up at the compliment before she finished her thought. "But I recently met someone who made me realize that being good isn't good enough. I want us to be great. That's the only thing that's going to separate us from the rest of the pack. If you can do that, BDV won't be known as the fun place to work. It will be *the* place to work. Today, I'm not only challenging you to make that happen, I'm also challenging myself."

She paused to look each team member in the eye.

"Are you ready to meet that challenge? I think you are. Now prove to me that you have as much confidence in yourselves as I have in you. Who wants to go first?"

She leaned back in her seat and waited for someone to take the lead. Everyone looked around, but no one spoke. She had expected them to fight for the chance to kick things off. Instead, no one seemed willing to subject their ideas to external scrutiny.

After a few moments of awkward silence, Trevor Gleason raised his hand

"What's your idea, Trev?"

"It's an app along the lines of—"

Brooklyn held up her hand. "Stop right there. This is for all of you, not just Trev. Don't give me an idea that's like something else on the market but better. Give me something I haven't seen before but can't live without."

"If that's your criteria, it's back to the drawing board for me."

Trevor's comment prompted a chorus of similar ones. More disappointed than frustrated, Brooklyn turned to AJ. "What do you have for me?"

"You want to hear my idea now?"

"There's no time like the present. Do you need time to get set up?"

"No, I'm good."

AJ quickly hooked her laptop into the projection system and opened the file Brooklyn had seen her working on the previous afternoon.

"I'm sure this isn't news to you, but advances in machine learning and AI have sparked a renewed interest in CUI. Most people would rather utilize conversational user interfaces than take the time to type a command. This allows us to use conversation as the primary mode of interaction with technology."

"What's so groundbreaking about that?" Trevor asked. "Google, Amazon, and Microsoft introduced that capability years ago. At this point, Siri and Alexa are household names because everyone and his sister owns one."

Brooklyn prepared to step in to protect AJ from Trevor's verbal assault, but AJ stood her ground.

"But they don't own this."

Brooklyn turned to look at the image on the screen.

"Meet Newton."

"What the hell is that?" someone asked.

"A CUI that interacts with both new and existing technology. With it, anything can be upgraded from manual to verbal control. Once the app is downloaded, you can use it to control anything in your home from your TV to the telephone to the electrical system."

"Like a modern-day version of the Clapper?" Trevor asked. "My grandparents had one of those."

"Mine, too," AJ said, "but this is a hundred times better. In essence, it's a voice-activated universal remote that controls an entire house, not just a TV. What do you think, boss?"

Brooklyn stared at the presentation as she weighed the app's obvious merits against its potential for abuse. "We would have to include a top-notch security system to lessen the chance the system could be compromised."

"Naturally," AJ said. "Does that mean you like it?"

"I do. I'm not crazy about the name, but I love the idea itself."

"Great. I'm also working on something else."

"You've been busy," Brooklyn said as AJ cycled through screens on her computer.

"That's what happens when you don't have a social life."

Brooklyn admired AJ's ability to laugh at herself, a valuable asset in this or any other high-stakes business.

"Technically, what I'm working on might not meet your criteria since it improves on already existing technology, but I've developed a search engine that—"

"Wait," Trevor said. "Are you seriously trying to say you want to take on Google? They're so big they've practically cornered the market on search engines. Every time someone tries to take them on, they either crush them or buy them out."

"Either way, we win," Brooklyn said.

"How so?" Trevor asked.

"Whether the product goes down in flames or is a spectacular success, we'd make a name for ourselves. In this industry, product quality is the key to retaining customers, but name recognition is vital for earning new ones. Why do you think the marketing department gets such a huge chunk of our budget each year? No risk, no reward." Brooklyn waited for the members of her team to connect the dots before she continued the meeting. "Show me what you've got, AJ."

"The working title is Finders Keepers, which I admit is a bit cutesy. I'm still looking for the perfect fit. But here's how it works."

She demoed a product that was lightning fast, visually appealing, and user-friendly.

"I assume advertisers' websites would receive priority positioning on the initial results page," Brooklyn said when AJ was done.

"I know that practice provides valuable ad revenue, but I've always found it disingenuous. And, to put it bluntly, it annoys the crap out of me. Whenever I run a search, I skip the results labeled as ads or sponsored on general principle."

Brooklyn smiled to herself as she noticed several people nodding in agreement. They had finally stopped sniping at each other long enough to find something to agree on,

"We are in the business of making money," she said, playing devil's advocate, "so how do you propose we do that in this instance?"

"I figured I'd leave that part up to you. It's my job to write the software. It's your job to find a way to make it profitable."

"So it is." And AJ had just given her two promising ideas to work with. She reached across the table to give her a fist bump. "Looks like our lunch has turned into a celebration. Does anyone else want to join the party?"

After AJ set the bar, the ideas started flowing fast and furious. Brooklyn dismissed some for lack of originality or because of the prohibitive cost of production, but she thought a few others held potential. By the end of the meeting, her lunch for two had turned into a party of five.

"Good work, everyone," she said as she brought the meeting to a close. "If I had known all I needed to do was ply you with free food to prompt you to give me your very best, I would have done it years ago."

"Free food's good," AJ said after everyone else filed out of the room, "but a big, fat bonus would be even better."

"If your products go over as well as I expect them to, you just earned yours."

"Thanks for the vote of confidence."

"I'm not trying to blow smoke up your ass, AJ. The ideas you pitched today aren't the only things that have potential. You do, too. Pretty soon, you're going to be treating me to lunch instead of the other way around."

"I hope you're right."

"I know I am. Just promise you'll save me a seat at the table."

"Always."

A few days ago, Brooklyn had been wracked with doubts about the future. As she smelled the flowers Vilma had given her and watched her team work on bringing their ideas to fruition, she had never felt more confident about what the future held. For her company or for herself.

Santana listened attentively as Brooklyn told her about her first day back at work since her best friend's death. Even though they weren't in the same room, she could feel the excitement flowing off of Brooklyn in waves. Brooklyn's cadence of speech grew faster and faster as she talked about the staff meeting she had held that morning and the working lunch she had treated several employees to that afternoon. She wouldn't divulge the details of some of the projects she had greenlit, but Santana could sense her obvious enthusiasm for them.

"I knew AJ had promise," Brooklyn said when she finally paused to take a breath. "After today's meeting, I was able to identify several other potential top producers as well. Now I'm looking through the files Charlie stored in the cloud to see if there are any ideas she was kicking around that might bear fruit. It's all your fault, you know."

Santana turned away from her view of the city so she could focus more fully on the conversation. "How so?"

"If you hadn't thrown down the gauntlet this weekend, I wouldn't have convinced myself to get out of the rather comfortable rut I had fallen into."

"Is this the way you usually respond to a challenge? By tackling it head-on?"

"Let's put it this way. When playing Truth or Dare, I'm the one who always opts for the dare."

"Because you have an aversion to the truth, or because you have a fondness for thrill-seeking?"

"Neither. The truth is I'm a terrible liar. I always have been. If you ask me a question, my response will be unfailingly honest every time. But when it comes down to it, anything I have to divulge is guaranteed to be boring. That's why I invented Brooke in the first place. Her adventures are a lot more interesting than mine. An armchair psychologist might say I would rather perform for my audience than reveal myself to them."

Santana was guilty of the same thing. Perhaps that was why she and Brooklyn got along so well. Because they had much more in common than she had initially realized.

"Did you have an epiphany?" she asked after the faint clack of keyboard keys that had underscored their conversation to that point abruptly ended.

"No, but I think I might have found something."

"Another future project?"

"No, the person who killed Charlie."

Santana felt her blood run cold. She had always thought the expression was just a cliché until she experienced it for herself. If Brooklyn had uncovered the information she had been unable to, she might be placing herself in the line of fire. Literally.

"Who do you think it is?" she asked.

"One of Charlie's pet projects was an app that allows law enforcement officials to identify human traffickers as well as victims. We didn't get a chance to bring it to market because a nonprofit spearheaded by a former teen idol perfected it first. Charlie must have continued working on her version of the software in her spare time, though, because it seems she put it through a couple of test runs in a live environment."

"Did she find something?"

"It appears so. I'm looking at a list of suspect names. I recognize the one at the top. Eve Thao was arrested a few months ago after an anonymous tip led police officers to a couple of properties she owned in the Garment District. A sweat shop that employed dozens of undocumented workers, and the squalid apartment building she forced them to live in while they tried to work off the insurmountable debt she claimed they owed her for smuggling them into the country. She hasn't gone to trial yet, but her properties have been seized and her accounts have been frozen."

"And you think Charlie was the person who called in the tip?"

"I can't tell based on the notes in her files. If she was the informant, Eve must have found out about it somehow and sent her henchmen to silence her. Does that sound plausible, or am I grasping at straws here?"

"It *is* a long shot, but it also seems reasonable," Santana said. "With her domestic accounts locked down, Thao could have used an offshore account to arrange the hit. Charlie's death would serve two purposes. It would allow Thao to exact revenge on the person she blamed for her downfall and it would also intimidate potential witnesses so they would be too afraid to testify when she finally has her day in court."

"I guess Detective Barnett wasn't too far off base when he suggested Charlie might have enemies. I should call him so he can direct his forensics team to investigate what I've found. But what if I'm wrong? He'll probably think I'm a crackpot. He might even laugh in my face."

"It's more likely he could end up thanking you for helping him break the case. If the lead doesn't pan out, no harm, no foul. Every bit of information helps."

"I suppose so," Brooklyn said doubtfully. "I'll call him as soon as I can remember where I put his business card. I was in a daze when he gave it to me. I hope it didn't wind up in the trash. I'll talk to you tomorrow."

"Are we still on for this weekend?"

"We'd better be. I bought a dress this afternoon you've got to see to believe."

Santana pictured Brooklyn wearing a sleek and sexy gown that hugged her curves. The image made her mouth water. "I can't wait."

"Neither can I. Have a good night."

"You, too.

After Brooklyn ended the call, Santana felt a sense of relief mixed with trepidation. If Eve Thao had paid to have Charlie killed, it would confirm her suspicions that the hit was personal. It would also mean that, most likely, Brooklyn was safe from harm since she had played no part in Thao's arrest. But what if Brooklyn was wrong?

Eve Thao felt like a logical suspect, but she didn't feel like the right one. She was already facing a potentially long sentence. Why would she risk having additional time tacked onto it? Additionally, the fee Winslow had collected for the hit on Charlotte Evans was much lower than he would normally charge someone with pockets as deep as Thao's. That meant he had either performed a favor for a friend or given a deep discount to a first-time client for whom he hoped to perform more lucrative tasks in the future.

Santana had never gotten involved in the business side of things. Lee Townsend looked after the accounts while she and others like her performed the dirty work. Lee had never been one of her biggest fans—he bristled each time Winslow gave her even a semblance of positive reinforcement—so she knew she couldn't count on him to let her see the details of the transaction.

She hoped Brooklyn's hunch panned out because if it didn't, they would be back to square one.

She picked up the remote and flipped through channels on the television. She stopped on a movie featuring laughable special effects, atrocious acting, and even worse dialogue. The film was supposed to be a horror film instead of a comedy, but she was more amused than frightened. No matter. She didn't plan on watching any of it. She simply wanted noise in the background while she looked into the friends and associates who hadn't attended Charlotte Evans's funeral services.

She checked out Charlotte's social media first. The pages were still active for the time being and were filled with messages from and tributes by her devastated friends. Some of the posts seemed heartfelt. Others seemed designed to garner sympathy for the author rather than express any for the deceased.

Luke Ridley's post was a prime example of the latter model. He had shared a photograph of him and Evans downing flaming shots of something alcoholic in a crowded bar. The post accompanying the photograph was twenty sentences long, and he referenced himself in more than half of them.

"Classic narcissist."

His post said he hadn't attended Evans's funeral because he wanted to remember how she lived, not how she died. Santana was sure Brooklyn felt the same way, but she had found the courage to show up to support her best friend's family in their time of greatest need. If Luke was as close to Evans as his post claimed, he should have been able to do the same.

Santana navigated to Luke's page on the same website so she could take a look at the posts made available for public consumption. Most were business-related. The most recent teased that his company would be making a major announcement in the near future and urged his followers to keep watching his page for further developments. A blog post on the company's website said pretty much the same thing, but neither the social media page nor the official web page divulged any further details. Like everyone else, Santana would have to keep hitting the Refresh button. Unwilling to give Luke the web traffic he so obviously craved, she decided to monitor the coverage on several reputable business magazines' digital outlets instead.

She scrolled through the list of products Luke's company offered. Some seemed just this side of legal, which made her wonder if his organization had ever popped up on Winslow's radar. Not likely. If he had, Winslow would have already added it to the long list of legitimate and shell companies he used to manage his assets.

Her laptop chimed during the horror film's not-so-dramatic showdown between the hero and the titular villain. She turned off the TV when the message she had received proved to be far more interesting than the action on the screen.

"Freedom isn't free," the message read. "Completing this task will allow you to purchase yours."

She read the words twice to make sure she hadn't imagined them. The assignment was a lucrative one. Its exorbitant price tag matched the level of danger involved. The target was a former warlord who was one of the world's most wanted men.

Jusuf Mladić had commanded the Bosnian Serb army during the war that had decimated Eastern Europe in the early- to mid-nineties. He had been found guilty of war crimes, genocide, and crimes against humanity by the International Criminal Tribunal for the former Yugoslavia, but he had managed to escape justice. Now someone was willing to pay one hundred million dollars to ensure justice was finally served.

Santana scanned the file attached to the email. Mladić had been tracked to Iceland, where he was living with a surgically altered face and an assumed name—Josef Magnusson. Like most criminals who used aliases, he had chosen to retain his actual initials. His heavily fortified compound was guarded by a cadre of his former soldiers, whose salaries were paid, no doubt, from the vast amount of cash he had hoarded while he was in power.

The job would be easier to pull off if she had a team surrounding her, but it would take time to find the right people, test their skills, and develop the necessary amount of trust they would need to operate as a cohesive unit. She had always preferred to work alone. It was easier keeping track of all the pieces on the board when she was the only one playing the game, and she didn't like the thought of working with an accomplice who might be willing to turn on her in order to save their own hide.

She drummed her fingers on the sofa as she tried to decide what to do. The job was so dangerous that taking it on could be akin to embarking on a suicide mission. But what choice did she have?

"If you defy me again," Winslow had said after she refused to kill Charlotte Evans, "I won't have someone put a bullet in your mother's head. I will have them put one in yours."

She couldn't turn down the assignment and expect to walk away unscathed. If she chose to ignore it, Winslow would most likely enact the insurance policy he had employed during the Evans hit. Only this time it would be used on her instead of the intended victim.

She pressed the Confirm button and drained the rest of her drink, knowing that, one way or another, her next job would be her last.

## Chapter Sixteen

Brooklyn couldn't believe the nightmare she had been reliving for the past week might be coming to an end. Despite her fears, Detective Barnett had been receptive to the information she had provided him. He had promised to follow through on her hunch to see where it might lead. If her tip panned out, the district attorney's office might be able to charge Eve Thao with conspiracy to commit murder.

"If the charges stick and Thao refuses to talk," he had said, "we might not know who actually pulled the trigger, but at least we'd be able to say who put the gun in his hands."

"If you need me to testify, please let me know. I don't know how much help I can be, but I'm willing to do what I can."

"Thank you, Ms. DiVincenzo. I'll be in touch."

From the beginning, Brooklyn had been more concerned with why Charlie was killed rather than who had committed the crime. Hopeful that Charlie's death was about to be avenged, she took the subway to Jersey City to visit Charlie's grave.

The site looked much different than it had the last time she had seen it. The headstone Charlie's parents ordered had been put in place, and seedlings of grass had started to sprout on the freshly tilled earth.

"I didn't bring flowers because I know they weren't your thing." She placed a bag of candy on the headstone. "Have some Twizzlers instead. I know they were your favorite."

She stood at the foot of Charlie's grave and tried to put her feelings into words.

"I have so much to tell you, I don't know where to start."

A residual shard of grief pierced her heart, bringing tears to her eyes.

"It's almost over," she said, drawing in a shaky breath. "I told the police about the project you were working on. Thanks to you, they think they know who did this to you. She's going to pay for her crimes. The ones she's already charged with as well as the one she committed against you. I am so mad at you for playing amateur detective, but I am so proud of you for having the courage to do the right thing. I would say you're a rock star, but I don't want your ego to get any bigger than it is already."

She laughed despite her tears.

"Do you remember the woman I told you about? The one I met in Tokyo? I ran into her again here in New York. It took some work, but I finally managed to find out who she really is. Her name's Vilma Bautista. She's a venture capitalist from Manila, and she has a place near Central Park that would look right at home splashed across the pages of *Architectural Digest*. I wish you'd had a chance to meet her. I think you'd like her. She seems super serious, but she has a sly sense of humor. Beneath the stern façade, there's a sense of vulnerability about her."

Brooklyn remembered when Vilma had talked about her fractured family. When her carefully chosen words had belied the pain in her eyes.

"In a lot of ways, she reminds me of you. She's not nearly as fond of hearing her own voice as you were, but she doesn't pull any punches and, when she does speak, she's not afraid to say exactly what's on her mind. Like you, she can't cook for shit. Unlike you, she at least managed to give it a try. I only wish I hadn't fallen asleep before she was done. I felt like such an idiot when I woke up on her couch the next day. I thought I'd blown it right then and there. Instead, she acted like it was no big deal. Then she took me to that indoor skydiving place in Yonkers we were always talking about. It was even more fun than I had imagined. You're not the only one who has wings. It's time for me to give mine a try."

She closed her eyes and spread her arms, remembering the dips and dives she had taken while she was in the wind tunnel. Then she opened her eyes and let her arms fall to her sides.

"She's taking me out again this weekend. The dress code's black tie, but she won't tell me where we're going. Yeah, she's kinda big on mystery. If this goes anywhere, I suppose I'll have to start getting used to that. And if it doesn't, well, it's already been a hell of a ride."

A strong breeze kicked up. Brooklyn shoved her hands in her coat pockets to ward off the chill.

"You're the first person I've told about her. I haven't said anything to my family yet. I tell myself it's because I'm enjoying keeping her to myself for a while, but in the back of my mind, I keep thinking I'm going to wake up tomorrow and realize this was all a dream. That she's not really here, and you're not really gone. I'm old enough to know that plot twists like that don't happen in real life, but I'm still young enough to hope they might."

She adjusted her purse strap to keep it from sliding off her shoulder.

"I almost forgot my other bit of news. AJ kicked ass during the team meeting today. Congratulations on turning her into a miniature version of you. Watching her take point today was almost like watching you. The next time I come, I'll tell you all about it. You did a great job molding her. I promise I won't let her talent go to waste." She pressed her fingers to her lips, then placed her hand on Charlie's headstone. "I love you, buddy. Rest easy."

She walked away. Curiosity led her toward one of the other headstones rather than toward the exit.

She approached the grave that had caught her attention during Charlie's internment service. The one that was being so lovingly tended by the mysterious figure in a black overcoat.

According to the headstone, the grave belonged to Melanie Pierce. The cheeky epitaph engraved on the stone brought a smile to her face. So did the flowers resting at the foot of the grave. The potted lavender looked so fresh it could have been placed there that morning rather than several days before.

Brooklyn dropped to one knee, cupped a blossom in her hands, and inhaled the heady scent. She wondered which florist had been responsible for providing such a beautiful specimen, but there was nothing to identify the vendor because the plant had been removed from its original container and placed directly in the ground so it could continue to prosper rather than wither and die like the cut flowers that dotted other graves.

She didn't know why she felt such an affinity for a complete stranger's final resting place. Was it because Melanie and Charlie appeared to have shared the same off-kilter sense of humor? Though their paths hadn't crossed in life, fate had managed to bring them together in death.

She had never been a big believer in fate, but she was starting to become a convert. Fate had drawn her and Vilma together. Perhaps their meeting hadn't been a happy accident. Perhaps it was something that was meant to be.

She pushed herself to her feet. As she rode the subway home, she wondered what else fate had in store.

## Chapter Seventeen

Santana had been given access to the finer things in life for so long she had forgotten how much joy they could bring. She remembered how excited she had been the first time she had flown in an airplane, slipped into a designer suit, or eaten a decadent meal. Such things were so commonplace for her now she had started taking them for granted. The look on Brooklyn's face when she picked her up on Saturday night made her feel like she was experiencing those luxuries for the first time. In a way, she was. Because she was experiencing them with Brooklyn.

"You look amazing," she said as their driver ferried them through traffic.

"So you've said."

"I thought it bore repeating."

Brooklyn was wearing an off-the-shoulder black evening gown that hugged her body in all the right places. Her hair was worn up and away from her face, drawing Santana's attention to the exposed expanse of skin from her neck to her cleavage. The taffeta material was cool to the touch, providing a stark contrast to the heat Santana could feel building inside her.

"You still haven't told me where we're going," Brooklyn said. "I checked the social calendar. There are no gala events, charitable or otherwise, scheduled for tonight, and if you were planning to take me to the opera or the ballet, we're headed in the wrong direction."

Santana reached across the leather seat and gave Brooklyn's hand a squeeze. "You don't give up, do you?"

Brooklyn returned the pressure. "I'm told persistence is one of my strong suits."

"Stubbornness is one of mine, so I think you might have met your match."

"So do I."

Santana had meant her comment in jest, but Brooklyn's reply was decidedly serious. The earnest tone of her voice made Santana's stomach do a funny little flip. She had never experienced anything like it. She felt butterflies every time a woman she was interested in made it clear the feeling was mutual, but that sensation was nothing like this. She wasn't prepared for the intensity, the unexpected depth of emotion.

Even in the darkened confines of the limousine's back seat, Brooklyn's face glowed with excitement. Her eyes darted back and forth, looking for clues each time the driver tapped the car's brakes or made a turn.

"Here we are," Santana said when the driver finally came to a stop at the NYC Manhattan Downtown Heliport.

Brooklyn peered out the tinted windows. "Do you bring all your dates to the East River?"

"Only the special ones. It's not the most romantic choice of venue, but it has its merits." She tried not to smile when Brooklyn's face fell. "Follow me and let me know if you agree."

She took Brooklyn's hand and led her toward the helipad a few feet away. A uniformed woman strode toward them.

"I'm Captain Sandra Wyatt," the woman said. "I'll be your pilot this evening. Our trip should last around thirty minutes. Our flight path will allow us to have perfect aerial views of the Manhattan skyline, the Empire State Building, and the Brooklyn Bridge. After we circle the Statue of Liberty, I'll bring you back here so you can enjoy the rest of your evening."

"Thank you, Captain," Santana said.

"Thank you for choosing Big Apple Helicopter Tours. Welcome aboard. Your headsets will protect your ears and allow us to communicate while we're in the air. Please fasten your seat belts. After my copilot and I complete our instrument check, we can take off."

After they settled into their seats, Brooklyn turned to Santana, her eyes wide. "You did all this for me?"

Santana repositioned the microphone on Brooklyn's headset so she could get a clearer view of Brooklyn's luscious lips. "Few people take the time to act as tourists in their hometown. Even though you grew up in New York, I doubt you've ever seen it like this."

The helicopter rose into the air and banked over the water. Below them, the lights of New York City twinkled. The landmarks Captain Wyatt had mentioned seemed to pass right outside their windows. Brooklyn gasped when the Statue of Liberty came into view.

Captain Wyatt flew so close to the colossal statue Santana could practically count the hairs on the great lady's head. She had never seen anything so beautiful. Not the landmark that had stood sentinel in New York Harbor for almost two hundred years. The look on Brooklyn's face as she was treated to a bird's-eye view of it.

"When I was in middle school," Brooklyn said in a voice filled with awe, "my classmates and I took a field trip to Liberty Island. I remember boarding the ferry, sailing across the Hudson River, and waiting in line to climb up to the crown. There are three hundred fifty-four steps inside, the equivalent of twenty stories. When I finally got to the top, I felt like I couldn't get any higher. Now I know better."

Santana felt the same way. Each day she spent with Brooklyn felt like it couldn't be improved upon. Then the next one came along and proved her wrong.

She turned to look out the window as Captain Wyatt began the return trip to the heliport. The trip had seemed to end in the blink of an eye. She wanted more time with Brooklyn, not less.

After they landed at the heliport, she thanked Captain Wyatt and her copilot for the problem-free flight.

"Do you plan to keep one-upping yourself?" Brooklyn asked. "Are each of our dates going to be more extravagant than the last?"

Santana didn't respond as she helped Brooklyn into the car.

"Where to next?" the chauffeur asked.

"Change of plans."

Santana gave him an address that was a world away from the Michelin-starred restaurant at which she had made reservations for the evening.

She was enjoying showing Brooklyn some of the things money could buy, but perhaps it was time for her to share something priceless: herself.

## CHAPTER EIGHTEEN

The chauffeur drove Brooklyn and Vilma to Woodside, Queens, an area of the city Brooklyn had never visited before. The vibe—bustling narrow streets lined with dozens of small restaurants and mom-and-pop shops—reminded her of Chinatown but with a fraction of the tourists.

"Where are we?" she asked after Vilma told the driver he was free to go.

"Little Manila. More than half of New York City's Filipino population lives here. I like to visit whenever I start feeling homesick. I brought you here because I wanted to show you where I grew up. Even though this isn't the exact location, it's a close approximation."

Brooklyn placed her hand in the crook of Vilma's elbow as she took a look at her surroundings. The small working-class neighborhood Vilma had brought her to bore faint resemblance to the ritzy Central Park enclave she called home.

Brooklyn took in the bustling markets, small storefronts, and even smaller restaurants. Some places featured seating on the sidewalk rather than inside.

Vilma led her to a restaurant on Roosevelt Avenue. "Brgy?" she said, reading the name on the marquee.

"It's short for *barangay*, the native term for a village, suburb, or neighborhood. A way of letting everyone know where you're from. Your *barangay* is Queens, for example, and mine is Payatas."

The name sounded vaguely familiar. Then Brooklyn remembered where she had seen it: in a news article describing the tragic deaths that had occurred at a landfill there after a wall of garbage suddenly collapsed and entombed two hundred people who were scavenging for something they could eat, wear, or sell.

"Were you there when the landslide happened?"

"No, but I know several people who died. If things had been different, I could have been one of them."

Vilma requested a table for two, and they were escorted to the crowded restaurant's second floor. Brooklyn had barely settled into her seat before a waiter came to take their drink orders and ask if they would like to see the dinner menu.

Vilma conversed with him in a language Brooklyn couldn't understand. The cadence was lilting. Almost poetic. She was entranced by its beauty.

"Was that Tagalog?" she asked after the waiter headed downstairs.

"No, it was Waray. There are over one hundred seventy languages spoken in the Philippines. Along with Tagalog, Waray is one of the most common."

Despite the brisk temperatures outside, the interior of the restaurant was warm. Almost uncomfortably so. Vilma unbuttoned her tuxedo jacket and draped it across the back of her chair. Even in her shirtsleeves, she still managed to look debonair rather than dressed down.

"I hope you don't mind," she said, "but I took the liberty of ordering for the both of us."

Brooklyn usually preferred to make her own choices rather than have them dictated to her. Vilma's actions didn't seem to be a matter of overstepping her boundaries. Instead, they seemed designed to bridge a gap. "I willingly place myself in your hands."

"I'll be gentle, I promise."

Vilma's smile hinted she didn't always have such a delicate touch. The thought made Brooklyn's pulse race.

The waiter brought out a bottle of wine and poured some in Vilma's glass. She swirled the clear contents, took a quick sniff, then drained her drink. After she signaled her approval, the waiter filled both their glasses.

"This is *arrack*," Vilma said before Brooklyn could ask the question. "It's wine made from coconuts. The taste is subtle, but it has a potent kick."

"You're not trying to take advantage of me, are you?"

"Hardly. When we're together, I want you to be fully cognizant of everything we're doing."

The intensity of Vilma's gaze almost made Brooklyn drop her glass. She took a sip of her wine while she tried to regain her composure. The potent kick Vilma had warned her about was offset by a finish that was slightly sweet. It reminded her of an umbrella drink. Seemingly innocuous but possessing the ability to knock her on her ass. She told herself to go slow so she wouldn't end up falling asleep again. She could get away with doing that one time. More than once would send the wrong signals. She didn't want Vilma to think she wasn't interested in her. In truth, she had never met anyone more fascinating. Or mysterious.

"I'm sensing there's a reason you brought me here," she said as she pushed her glass away from her.

"There is. As I said, this neighborhood reminds me of home. My mother and I didn't have much money when I was growing up."

"Purse strings were tight in my family, too. Hand-me-downs were pretty much worthless by the time they finally got handed down to me. Did you put yourself through school?"

"Yes," Vilma said with a laugh, "the school of hard knocks."

"If you don't mind my asking, how did you go from such humble beginnings to living on Central Park?"

"How did I get so rich, you mean?"

Brooklyn blushed. "I must sound like a gold digger."

"No, you sound understandably curious. To answer your question, I wrote my success story with these." Vilma held out her hands, which were well-manicured but undeniably strong. "And with this." She pointed to her head, which contained a brain with which Brooklyn was increasingly enamored. "In my life, I've always found it's better to be street smart than book smart. Being lucky helps, too. The rest is all about timing. Otherwise, you and I might not have met."

"It is funny to think we've lived in the same city for years but didn't meet until we both walked into the same bar almost seven thousand miles away from home."

Brooklyn took another sip of her wine. She thought she couldn't be more impressed by Vilma than she was already, but Vilma's confession proved her wrong. She liked the fact that Vilma had earned her money rather than inheriting it. Perhaps the adage about hard work paying off had merit after all. If so, there was still hope for her.

"I didn't mean to interrupt you," she said. "You were telling me about your life in the Philippines."

"I grew up on a diet of street food. It was cheap, it was easy, and even though it shared similar price points with the fare in fast food restaurants, most of it had actual nutritional value." Vilma leaned back in her chair when the waiter brought out a platter laden with several small dishes. "These were some of my favorites." She pointed to each of the dishes one by one. "Fish balls, banana cue, *sisig*, *isaw*, and *tokneneng*. Make sure to save room for dessert because we still have dirty ice cream to come."

"Everything looks so interesting I don't know where to start."

Vilma placed a deep-fried orange ball on her plate. "Try the *tokneneng*. It's like a Scotch egg without the layer of sausage."

Brooklyn had expected the dish to be heavy, but the tempura batter and sweet-and-sour dipping sauce combined to make it surprisingly light. "God, that's good. What's next?"

Vilma indicated the *sisig*. "Do yourself a favor and taste it before you ask what's in it."

"I'm not sure I like the sound of that, but okay." Brooklyn took a cautious bite. The meat in the dish seemed to taste like pork, but the intense spices made it hard to tell which cut. "I give. What's in this?"

"Pork jowls, ears, and liver seasoned with calamansi and chili peppers."

"I'm glad I asked you after I tried it rather than before. Are any of the other dishes quite that exotic?"

Vilma glanced toward the plate of *isaw*, which featured a grilled protein of some kind on wooden skewers.

Brooklyn picked up one of the skewers. The meat on it was chewy but incredibly flavorful. "I won't bother asking what that's made of. I don't want you to shatter the illusion."

Fortunately, the fish balls didn't require explanation. The spicy curry sauce they were served with made Brooklyn's taste buds sing.

"The banana cue is the perfect item to lead us into dessert," Vilma said.

The deep-fried banana covered in caramelized sugar seemed to be a stripped-down version of Bananas Foster. It tasted so good Brooklyn didn't miss the ingredients that had been left out.

"There's more to come after this?" she asked after she barely managed to convince herself not to lick the spoon.

"Yes, dirty ice cream, which is also known as *sorbetes*. It's a Filipino version of ice cream made from local fruit, usually mango, avocado, melon, coconut, jackfruit, or strawberry. Which flavor would you like?"

"Strawberry, I guess."

"Why the uncertainty?"

"Too many flavors to choose from. I'd love to sample each of them, but I have to limit myself if I want to keep fitting into this dress."

Vilma looked at her over the top of her wine glass as she took a sip of the *arrack*. "You do wear that dress spectacularly well."

Brooklyn's skin prickled as Vilma's eyes slowly tracked over her body. Forget a bowl of ice cream. She would need to swim in a whole vat of the stuff in order to combat the heat from Vilma's gaze.

"I have a suggestion," Vilma said.

Brooklyn leaned forward, hoping Vilma was about to recommend they order dessert to go so they could enjoy it in Vilma's apartment, preferably the luxurious confines of her bedroom after several rounds of vigorous sex.

"I'll order the avocado and you can have some of mine," Vilma said. "Next time, we can try two more flavors. Would you like that?"

"Sounds like a plan to me." Brooklyn was looking forward to the additional ice cream, but she was even more excited by the fact that the glimpse Vilma had offered into her life wouldn't be a one-time thing. "Thank you for this," she said as the waiter set two bowls on the table.

"For offering to share my ice cream?" Vilma asked with a teasing smile.

"No, thank you for tonight. For taking me on the best date I've ever had and for letting me get to know the true you. I feel like tonight is the actual night we first met."

Vilma dipped her spoon in the generous scoop of green-tinted ice cream in her bowl and held it out for Brooklyn to taste. Brooklyn nearly moaned when the ice cream hit her tongue. It was the perfect combination of sweet and savory. Like candied bacon or chocolate-dipped pretzels but ten times better. "I'm definitely ordering that next time."

"Using your scenario, does that mean our next date will be our second instead of our fifth?"

"Certainly not."

"Why?"

"Because that would mean tonight is our first date." Brooklyn paused to make sure she had Vilma's undivided attention. "And I never sleep with someone on the first date."

Vilma's eyes darkened with desire. "What about the fourth?"

Brooklyn offered a teasing shrug. "It's been known to happen."

Vilma reached into her wallet and tossed two large bills on the table when one probably would have been sufficient to cover the tab and provide a substantial tip. "Then let's make it happen."

After Vilma stood and put on her coat, Brooklyn reached for her proffered hand. "I thought you'd never ask."

## CHAPTER NINETEEN

When Santana had picked Brooklyn up earlier that night, Brooklyn had met her in the lobby of her apartment building but hadn't invited her upstairs. Santana hadn't been offended by the omission. She had chalked it up to Brooklyn being anxious to get the evening started. She had felt the same way. She was anxious now, too. Not in anticipation of how the evening might go but how it would end.

After Brooklyn unlocked her apartment door and turned on the lights, Santana took a careful look at her new surroundings. Like her office, Brooklyn's apartment seemed to be an extension of her personality. The small loft in upper Manhattan was functional yet quirky. The open concept space was filled with furniture that looked comfortable without being over-the-top. The exposed brick walls were decorated with posters from an assortment of science fiction movies whose titles were as eye-catching as the accompanying artwork. Magazines, a sheaf of scribbled notes, and several spreadsheets littered the coffee table, a vintage crab trap that had been repurposed and topped with a thick pane of glass to provide a stable display area/work surface.

"Excuse the mess." Brooklyn gathered the magazines and printouts and stacked them into neat piles. "If I'd known we would end up here tonight, I would have cleaned up first."

"No worries." Santana's apartment felt more like a showroom than a residence. Brooklyn's, in contrast, felt lived-in. It felt like her.

Santana could picture her making herself comfortable on the well-worn couch while she worked on a project. She could practically see her whipping up a quick but hearty meal in the compact kitchen. And she didn't have to imagine Brooklyn reclining on the throw pillow-covered bed because she was about to witness it for herself.

Brooklyn hung her coat in the closet next to the front door. "Would you like something to drink? I don't have any *arrack*, but I have plenty of beer and I think there's a bottle of red wine floating around here somewhere."

"We could go on the hunt for it, but I'd prefer if we dispensed with the niceties."

"So would I." Brooklyn's shoulders drooped as she visibly relaxed. "I've never been any good at playing happy hostess."

"Then I shouldn't expect breakfast in bed in the morning?"

"I can't think about breakfast yet. My mind's still on dessert." Brooklyn came over to her and tugged at her bow tie until the intricate knot came free. "What about you?"

When Brooklyn unbuttoned her tuxedo shirt and slid her hands against her skin, food was the last thing on Santana's mind. She put her hands on Brooklyn's waist and pulled her closer. Brooklyn tilted her head up and parted her lips, inviting her to kiss her. Santana eagerly accepted the invitation.

She covered Brooklyn's mouth with her own. Though she ached to claim Brooklyn right away, she forced herself to go slow. The kiss was languid. Unhurried. Brooklyn sighed as she slipped her arms around her neck. The move usually made Santana feel trapped. Tonight, she felt like she was exactly where she was meant to be.

She traced the tip of her tongue across Brooklyn's mouth, then slipped it inside. Brooklyn's fingers snaked into her hair, holding her in place. She ran her hands along the length of Brooklyn's spine. The task was made easier because the open back of Brooklyn's dress dipped close to the rise of her hips. She cupped Brooklyn's ass and broke the kiss long enough to nuzzle the side of her neck. "I adore you in this dress, but I think I'll like you even more out of it."

Brooklyn smiled and turned her back to her. "In that case," she said, sweeping her long hair aside, "I'll let you do the honors."

Santana unzipped Brooklyn's dress and let it fall to the floor. Brooklyn stepped out of the puddled material and kicked off her heels. When Brooklyn turned to face her, the sight of her took Santana's breath away.

Brooklyn was wearing a black lace thong and matching bra. The sexy undergarments accentuated her hourglass figure. "You are the most beautiful woman I have ever seen," Santana said as she traced her fingers along the dangerous curves.

"And you are wearing far too many clothes." Brooklyn pushed Santana's jacket off her shoulders and tossed it on the couch. Her tuxedo shirt quickly followed. After Santana slipped off her shoes, Brooklyn unbuckled her belt and unzipped her pants. When the cool air hit her overheated skin, Santana almost forgot her vow not to rush.

Brooklyn ran her fingers over the ripples in Santana's stomach. "I've never slept with an Amazon before."

Santana picked her up, carried her to the bed, and gently laid her down. "There's a first time for everything," she said as she slowly peeled off Brooklyn's underwear.

Brooklyn unhooked her bra and slipped her arms out of it. Then she pulled Santana's sports bra over her head and tossed it aside. Santana's boxer briefs came next. "I have a feeling I'm going to remember this first time for a while," she said as she pulled Santana in for another kiss.

Santana had a feeling she would never forget it. She trembled when Brooklyn wrapped her legs around her waist and began to move against her.

"God, you feel good," Brooklyn said. She arched her back when Santana slipped first one, then two fingers inside her. "And that feels even better."

Santana teased one of Brooklyn's pebbled nipples with her tongue, then drew it into her mouth. Brooklyn cried out and began to grind harder against her fingers. She reached for Santana's free hand and placed it on her other breast.

"I've got two of those, you know."

Santana couldn't help but smile. She loved women who knew what they wanted in bed and weren't afraid to tell her how to give it to them. She twirled one of Brooklyn's nipples between her fingers while she kissed and sucked the other. Brooklyn's cries grew louder and louder as she drifted closer to the edge. "Your neighbors are going to hate you."

"They've subjected me to far worse over the years," Brooklyn said breathlessly. "They deserve a little payback."

Santana made sure to make it worth their while. If the sound she made when she came was any indication, Brooklyn seemed to enjoy it, too. She kissed Brooklyn until her breathing returned to normal, then rolled onto her back and drew Brooklyn into her arms.

Brooklyn combed her tousled hair with her fingers. "What would you like?" she asked as she rested her head on Santana's chest.

Santana pressed a kiss to her forehead. "Giving you pleasure was enough for me." Though her clit throbbed insistently, she didn't feel an all-encompassing need for release. She felt as satisfied as if Brooklyn's orgasm had been her own.

Brooklyn lifted her head to get a better look at her. "Are you sure?"

"I have rules, too."

"Such as?"

"I never sleep with a woman on the fourth date."

Brooklyn smiled to show she was in on the joke. "What about the fifth?"

Santana used Brooklyn's own words against her. "It's been known to happen." She kissed the tip of Brooklyn's nose. "I have to head to Switzerland tomorrow for a business trip. Zurich, to be precise. We'll get together when I get back."

"How long will you be gone?"

"Just a few days. I need to meet with some people and get the lay of the land before I decide if I want to invest in their company. If I like what I see, I'll request a formal sit-down in a few months so we can talk numbers."

Lying came so easily Santana could do it without breaking a sweat. For the first time, though, it also came with a healthy dose of guilt. She wished she could be honest with Brooklyn about who she was and what she really did for a living, but she knew Brooklyn could never understand, let alone accept the truth.

"Is that how you make all your business decisions?" Brooklyn asked. "By following your instincts?"

"Paired with a generous amount of research, yes. Instinct only goes so far. That's why I never make a move until I've studied all the angles and taken everything into account."

Except in this case. Her instincts had told her to put as much distance between herself and Brooklyn as possible. She had chosen to ignore her own advice rather than heed it. Time would tell if she had made the right decision or one she—and Brooklyn—would come to regret.

"I'll miss you," Brooklyn said, "but I know the perfect way to welcome you back."

Santana had been looking forward to performing reconnaissance on her final assignment. Now she had something entirely different to look forward to. The Mladić job could earn her her freedom, but it could also get her killed. Which did she want more, she wondered, to risk her life or to share it with Brooklyn?

## CHAPTER TWENTY

B rooklyn went to work on Monday exhausted but satiated. She tried to be productive so her team wouldn't think she was slacking off, but she couldn't stay on task because her mind kept wandering to the events of the weekend. She couldn't stop thinking about the jaw-dropping helicopter tour she and Vilma had taken on Saturday, the amazing dinner they had eaten in Brgy afterward, or the incredible sex they'd had in her apartment at the end of the night. Yesterday, she had woken up in Vilma's arms. She had tried to head to the kitchen in order to make them breakfast, but Vilma had pulled her back into bed and given her something to remember her by before she left to pack for her business trip.

As she had on Saturday, Vilma hadn't allowed her to reciprocate. Though somewhat disappointing, that might have ended up being a blessing in disguise. By the time Vilma was done with her on Sunday morning, she hadn't been able to feel her fingers, let alone use them to pleasure someone. She was eager to make Vilma feel all the wonderful sensations she had treated her to, but she would have to wait at least a week to get her chance since Vilma wouldn't return from her trip to Zurich until then.

Venture capitalism was a globe-trotting profession. On some level, Brooklyn had known Vilma would eventually have to leave her behind in order to take a meeting in some exotic locale. Still, she had quickly gotten used to having her around. To having her be only a few minutes away rather than several hours.

"I'm experiencing separation anxiety and today's only the first day."

She had newfound empathy for addicts going through withdrawal. Because she was hooked on Vilma Bautista. Going cold turkey wouldn't be easy. She needed a distraction. And today, work wasn't cutting it.

She locked her computer, pushed her chair away from her desk, and walked over to AJ's work station. AJ was toiling on a project that wasn't due for a few more months. Based on the work product displayed on her computer screen, she was several weeks ahead of schedule. The perfect time to take a break.

"Do you have plans tonight?" Brooklyn asked after AJ paused the music she was listening to on her phone.

"Nothing that can't be changed," AJ said as she set her ear buds on her keyboard. "Why? What do you have in mind?"

"Come to Game Bar with me. My treat. It'll give us a chance to talk about something other than work while I kick your ass at Donkey Kong."

AJ leaned back in her chair and laced her fingers behind her head. The move was so reminiscent of Charlie it make Brooklyn's heart hurt. "Isn't that the place where people drink craft beer and cocktails while they play a shit ton of vintage video games?"

"The one and the same." She and Charlie had hung out there at least once a week. It felt almost blasphemous to even consider going there with someone else, but she didn't want to abandon all of her old haunts because Charlie was no longer around to enjoy them with her.

"I've always been partial to Tetris," AJ said, "but I'm willing to try something different. Don't expect me to take it easy on you just because you're the boss, though."

"I wouldn't have it any other way. See you tonight at eight?"

"I'll be there." Brooklyn turned to head back to her office, but AJ's question stopped her in her tracks. "Should I bring a plus one?"

"If you like." Surprised by the unexpected conversational turn, Brooklyn folded her arms across her chest. "I didn't know you were seeing anyone."

"I'm single and ready to mingle, but I get the feeling you might be off the market. I don't want to run the risk of making anyone jealous since tonight's not a *date* date. Is it?"

Brooklyn heard what sounded like hopefulness in AJ's voice. She had always taken AJ's eagerness to please her as a sign she wanted to impress the boss. Perhaps it was interest AJ had been displaying all that time rather than ambition. If so, she would have to tread carefully. Office romances had never been her thing, especially ones that involved superiors and subordinates. They ruined workplace morale and, more often than not, ended up in litigation. "What makes you think I'm seeing someone?"

"If you want my honest opinion," AJ said, lowering her voice, "you look like you spent the weekend in bed. And not alone, if you know what I mean. Is it someone I know?"

Brooklyn started to deny everything AJ was saying, but she was in such a good mood she wanted to share the news about Vilma with someone. Preferably someone who didn't share her last name so she wouldn't have to deal with the subsequent teasing from her siblings about how far she thought the relationship might lead or the requisite questions from her parents about the possibility that there might be more grandkids in the offing. As if there weren't enough little DiVincenzos running around already. "You don't know her, but you have met her."

"When?"

"Remember the woman I introduced you to last weekend?"

AJ thought for a minute, then her eyebrows shot up. "The venture capitalist? She was hot."

"I know."

"I thought you two seemed pretty cozy that morning," AJ said. "I had a feeling I'd walked in on something more than a business meeting." She looked away, confirming Brooklyn's suspicions she might be harboring feelings for her. "Does this mean you two are a thing?"

"If by 'a thing,' you mean a couple, I have no idea. It's much too soon for labels. If something changes, I'll be sure to let you know."

AJ turned back to her. "Does this make me your new confidante?"

"Not yet. You have to pass the audition first."

"Challenge accepted."

Brooklyn felt like she had a challenge of her own: finding a way to lead AJ without leading her on.

That night, AJ made things a bit easier for her by showing up at Game Bar with a couple of people from the office in tow. Their presence turned what could have been an awkward encounter into an unexpected team-building opportunity.

"I didn't know you and Trevor were friends," Brooklyn said as he and Dominic Rhodes from R&D headed to the bar to order a round of drinks.

"He loves to try to get under my skin, and he can be a bit of an asshole sometimes, but I seem to have an affinity for assholes."

"That sounds like the same kind of relationship I have with Luke," Brooklyn said. "I respect him, but I trust him about as far as I can throw him."

"It might sound crazy, but when I first heard what happened to Charlie, I thought he might have had something to do with it. He was so gung-ho on beating us to the market on the code-breaking technology he seemed willing to do anything to impede our progress."

"Luke can be ruthless when it comes to business, but he's not entirely heartless. When he came to see me that night, he seemed as broken up about what had happened as I was."

"I just hope the police are able to determine who was truly responsible. I hope they can find out who pulled the trigger, too. In the end, I guess it won't matter as long as they know who ordered the hit in the first place."

"It's interesting that the first conclusion you came to was professional hit. Even now, I have a hard time coming to terms with the idea."

"There's no way an amateur would have been able to pull off a shot like that and get away without being seen." AJ jerked her thumb at one of the dozens of arcade games surrounding them. "Or maybe I spent way too much time playing these as a kid while the rest of my friends were shopping for jeans at Forever 21 or trying to impress some guy they met in the food court."

"That sounds like me. My sisters could hang out at the mall all day, but I'd be bored senseless after five minutes."

"What did you do for fun when you were younger?"

"When I was younger? You make me sound like I'm old enough to be your grandmother."

Brooklyn was only pretending to take offense, but AJ's cheeks colored nevertheless. "Sorry, I was just—I mean—"

Brooklyn smiled to take AJ out of her misery. "It's okay. Some days, I *feel* old enough to be someone's grandmother."

"Rest assured you don't look a day over forty-five."

"Hey." Brooklyn tried to give AJ a not-so-playful punch in the arm, but AJ stepped out of range before she could make contact. "So much for that substantial pay raise I was planning on giving you."

Trevor and Dominic returned carrying a tray of drinks and a platter of nachos.

"Is it too late to amend my answer?" AJ asked as she handed Brooklyn the Manhattan she had ordered.

"You bet it is." Brooklyn took a sip of her drink. It wasn't bad, but the one Vilma had made for her was better. She longed for another taste. Of the drink and of Vilma.

*God, this is going to be a long week.*

"Who's up for a little competition?" she asked. "I know AJ's in. How about you guys?"

"I'm down," Trevor said.

Dominic raised his hand. "So am I."

"Awesome," Brooklyn said. "Let's split into teams so we don't hog the console too long. Otherwise, we might have to fight our way out of here."

Even though it was a weekend, the place was growing more crowded by the minute. The line in front of Pac-Man was six people deep, and the one in front of Frogger wasn't far behind.

"You can pick the teams as long as I can pick the game," Trevor said.

"Okay, AJ and I will be one team, you and Dom the other."

"Cool." Trevor looked around the room, then pointed to a console a couple of rows away from where they were standing. "Let's play Galaga. In case you don't know how it works, the object of the game is to destroy the flying insects that swoop down and drop bombs on your spaceship."

Brooklyn rolled her eyes as he continued to mansplain a game she had played thousands of times. Winning hadn't been her original goal tonight. Now losing wasn't an option. "Is that it?" she asked when he finally stopped talking.

"Yeah, I think that covers it."

"Since we're playing in teams," Dominic said, "how are we going to do this? Are we going to switch players after each round and add each team member's scores together, or what?"

"I have a better idea," Brooklyn said. "Let's have both team members play at the same time. One can be the navigator, the other can be the shooter."

Trevor rubbed his hands together as if he had lured them into a trap. "Oh, you two are going down. You navigate, Dom. I'll handle the weapons." He flexed his fingers. "Ask any of the girls I've dated. Each one will tell you I've got the fastest draw this side of the Mississippi."

AJ grimaced. "Thanks for the imagery, Quick Draw. Though I guess that explains why you don't have a girlfriend."

Brooklyn took a sip of her drink so she wouldn't burst out laughing. She didn't want to dent Trevor's confidence when he seemed to need a bit of bravado to push himself to succeed at his job. "Since you're the self-proclaimed subject matter expert," she said after she regained her composure, "why don't you and Dom go first?"

"I'd be happy to. Watch and learn, ladies. Watch and learn."

Dominic and Trevor positioned themselves in front of the game console. Brooklyn and AJ stood off to the side so they could get a clear look at the screen. The bickering began right after the game did.

"I thought you guys were supposed to be battling a common enemy rather than each other," AJ said when the game ended.

"Don't blame me," Trevor said. "My shots would have been on target if my navigator had done his job."

"I did my part," Dominic said. "It's not my fault if you didn't get your shots off in time. I would have been better off playing by myself."

Brooklyn stepped in before the burgeoning argument could get too heated. "No, the two of you would have been better off working as a team." She felt more than a bit like her mother as she waited for her words to sink in. "Ready, AJ?"

AJ set her empty glass down and flexed her fingers. "Watch and learn, fellas. Watch and learn."

"I navigate, you shoot?" Brooklyn asked.

"Works for me."

When the game started, Brooklyn made sure to do what Trevor and Dominic hadn't. She communicated with her teammate rather than shutting her out.

"Coming up on your right," she said when a bomb-laden insect began to attack their position.

"I see it," AJ said just before she shot the bug out of the sky. "Quick! Two bogies on your left!"

"On it." Brooklyn jerked the joystick in the opposite direction just in time for AJ to repel the attack.

Working as a team, they continued to pile up points. Their luck eventually ran out, but not before they had quadrupled Dominic and Trevor's score.

"Sweet," AJ said after she and Brooklyn shared a high five. "Do you guys want to go again?"

Dominic shook his head. "One round of embarrassment is enough for me. I'll take another drink, though. Anyone else want one?"

"Sure," Brooklyn said. "Put it on my tab."

Trevor held up a hand. "No, this round's on me. Consider it a small price to pay for a valuable lesson learned."

Despite his contrite expression, AJ couldn't resist needling him. "Thanks, Quick Draw. Beer's always better when it's free."

"Don't push him too far," Brooklyn said, "or he might be tempted to spit in yours."

"You might be right."

AJ looked as if she wanted to say something else, but she remained quiet.

"What's eating you?" Brooklyn asked.

"Nothing, really. Just a hunch I have. It's probably better if I keep it to myself, though. I don't want to wind up getting on your bad side now that we're getting along so well."

"With an opening like that, you can't possibly leave me hanging. What's on your mind?"

AJ shifted her weight from one foot to the other. "I checked out the woman you're seeing."

Brooklyn didn't know whether to be touched or offended. She was glad AJ was concerned about her well-being, but she was a little miffed that she didn't seem to trust her judgment. "Why did you do that?"

"I've never seen you with anyone so I was curious to know what kind of woman you're attracted to."

"And?"

"That's just it. I wasn't able to unearth much of anything because her internet profile is practically nonexistent. I saw a couple of photos of her at various business meetings, but I couldn't locate any social media accounts in her name and I didn't see any real biographical information. All I could find was her name, where she was born, and her current place of residence. Nice place, by the way. Some apartments in that neighborhood can cost up to eight figures, occasionally nine."

"Perhaps that's why she keeps such a low profile. So she doesn't make herself a target for con artists and opportunists." AJ didn't look convinced so Brooklyn continued to press her case. "Not everyone lives her life virtually, you know. People in our industry just wish they did so we can chalk up a few more sales."

"Even so, it's incredibly difficult to do anything these days without leaving a digital trail behind—or paying a mint to have it erased. I'm not saying she's up to something hinky and you shouldn't get involved with her, but how well you know her?"

"How well does anyone really know someone else's heart? I know plenty of people who ended up being taken by surprise by someone they thought they knew inside and out. I might not know all of Vilma's innermost secrets, but I know enough. More importantly, I trust her."

"Are you trying to convince me or yourself?"

Dominic and Trevor returned before Brooklyn could respond to AJ's question, but she knew she couldn't avoid it forever—or ignore the ones that were starting to form in her own heart.

## Chapter Twenty-one

Santana reached under the seat in front of her to retrieve her carry-on bag after her flight landed at Keflavik International Airport in Reykjavik, Iceland. When the flight attendant gave the all-clear to use electronic devices, she was tempted to send Brooklyn a text to let her know her flight had landed safely. Then she remembered she had intentionally left all traces of her Vilma Bautista identity behind.

Stay in character, she mentally chided herself. Brooklyn had never met the person she was currently pretending to be. If she forgot that even for a second, she wouldn't make it home to her.

She regarded her reflection in the battered plexiglass window. The platinum blond wig, colored contacts, and facial prosthetics she was wearing made her look like a surfer on the hunt for the next big wave. Her wardrobe—a cable knit beanie, a black leather jacket, low-slung jeans, a long-sleeved T-shirt, and worn skateboard shoes—made the image complete.

She waited her turn to make her way down the narrow aisle. The flight from Montreal was supposed to land at six a.m., but the pilot had touched down a few minutes earlier than expected. By the time she made her way off the plane, cleared Customs, and secured ground transportation, the sun, which was just starting to peek over the horizon, should have risen in earnest. She wanted to get settled in the house she had rented before the man she had come to observe began his day.

Though the trip wasn't as above-board as she had made it seem when she described it to Brooklyn, her mission was the same. She was here to observe. To get a sense of Jusuf Mladić's daily routine and check out his security detail to see if she could detect any weaknesses. She didn't need many. One would do as long as the hole was big enough for her to slip through.

The two-bedroom bungalow she had rented was located in Vesturbær, an eight-neighborhood district west of the heart of Iceland's capital city. The area was mostly residential, though there was an increasing commercial presence in Grandi, which was close to the harbor. Knattspyrnufélag Reykjavíkur, commonly referred to as KR or KR Reykjavik, was also headquartered there. The oldest and most successful team in the Icelandic soccer league, KR had won dozens of titles over the years and was the first team to represent Iceland in the lucrative European Cup. Santana wasn't much of a soccer fan, but she knew someone who was: Jusuf Mladić.

Mladić's life in exile wasn't as isolated as she had expected. According to the intel she had been provided when she accepted the assignment, he never missed one of KR's home games. He was too smart to sit in the same seat each time, but an eagle-eyed observer was bound to spot him somewhere in the stands.

Did she dare try to take him out in front of thousands of potential witnesses, or would she be better off attempting to breach a compound that, from the looks of it, seemed impenetrable?

"That's what you flew five hours to find out."

Instead of making her way to Iceland via a nonstop flight from LaGuardia, she had traveled to Canada by train so she could switch identities first. Delphine Durand, her current alter ego, was a perennial slacker who worked odd jobs from time to time, but didn't have a steady income or permanent address.

When she traveled as Delphine, she always booked a room in a hostel because, for anyone who might be watching, that was all Delphine's limited resources could handle. She had deviated from her usual pattern this time because hostels were notorious for their lack of privacy as well as their practically nonexistent security. She had enough things to concern herself with on this job without having to worry about sharing a room with one or more complete strangers, waiting in line to use the communal bathroom and shower, or having her belongings stolen if she was foolish enough to leave them unguarded.

The most convenient part of the Delphine persona was the need to travel light. Without luggage to claim, she was able to cut down on expenses as well as travel time. When she finally made her way through the long line in Customs, she was able to avoid the ones in the baggage claim area because she didn't have a checked bag. All of Delphine's belongings had been shoved into her carry-on because she couldn't afford the checked bag fee.

She couldn't afford cabs, either. Train tickets, thankfully, were relatively inexpensive. Santana pulled out a few crumpled Icelandic krónas to pay the fare for the two-mile trip to the city center. Once she reached the heart of Reykjavik, she walked the short distance from the train station to her rented house.

The rental was long-term. Though she didn't plan to remain in the country for the entire duration of her six-month lease, she planned to put in enough face time in her temporary digs so that her new neighbors would come to accept her as one of them rather than seeing her as a stranger. She wanted to be someone they trusted rather than someone they feared. At the same time, she wanted to be someone they quickly forgot rather than someone they remembered. Though maintaining the balance would be tricky, it was one she had been striking for years. If she could pull off the feat one more time, she would never have to do it again. Then she could return to 'Ohe Sojukokoro, put her feet up…and do what exactly?

She had no idea how she wanted to spend the rest of her life. She simply wanted the option to figure it out for herself rather than having her fate dictated by Winslow Townsend's whims. In a few months, she would be able to do just that. For better or worse, her life would finally be her own.

Unlike their country's subarctic climate and occasionally barren landscape, Icelanders were a warm and welcoming people. There were less than three hundred fifty thousand citizens in Iceland, making it the most sparsely populated country in Europe. No wonder the people were so friendly. They were probably just happy to have someone to talk to besides themselves.

The owners of the house Santana had rented weren't onsite when she arrived, though she hadn't expected them to be. According to one of the many emails they had sent her after she contacted them to express interest in renting the property, they were currently touring Europe in their RV and had no plans to return home for the foreseeable future. The money they earned from rental income helped finance what they hoped would be a year-long trip around the world. Santana had made sure to pay them a bit more than the price they had agreed on so they wouldn't have any excuses to bring their trip to a premature end due to lack of funds.

Vesturbær was one of the most expensive districts in Reykjavik in terms of real estate pricing, but the house Santana had rented was relatively modest. So was the surrounding neighborhood. The age range was all over the place. College kids in town for only a few years mingled with long-time residents. Each took the time to look her in the eye and say hello when she passed them on the street. Her grasp of Icelandic was nonexistent, but good manners didn't require translation. A nod and a smile, she quickly found, went a long way.

Still, she felt a sense of relief when she located the hidden key to the house, let herself in, and closed the door behind her. She desperately wanted to take a few moments to stop pretending and just be herself, but she didn't dare. She had to act as if someone had eyes on her at all times just in case they did. Was she being overly-cautious? Perhaps, but a healthy dose of paranoia had gotten her this far. It was too late in the game to change her ways now. She left her disguise in place but reverted to her natural stance and gait as she treated herself to a tour of the house.

She was pleased to see that the pictures that had been posted on the internet were accurate. The rooms were a nice size, the furniture was comfortable, and the small kitchen was stocked with the only two appliances she intended to make use of: a refrigerator and a microwave. As she had noticed during her walk from the train station, a grocery store, a coffee shop, and several restaurants were located a few blocks away.

"Perfect."

Now that her creature comforts were taken care of, she addressed her other dilemma: transportation. Reykjavik was small, especially in comparison to sprawling New York City, but she wouldn't be able to go everywhere she needed on foot. Public transportation was an option. Unless she was in a hurry to get away. Then she wouldn't have time to sit and wait for a train's or bus's next scheduled arrival.

Fortunately, her landlords' hospitality was apparently limitless. They had left her the keys to a pair of motorcycles parked in the small, attached garage. She flipped on the overhead light as she examined the well-maintained vehicles.

One was a bright red crotch rocket with an aerodynamic body shape that encouraged the driver to lean forward. The bike would be good for a casual tour of town or a high-speed trek through the countryside. If she needed to defend herself from armed pursuers, though, she might have a hard time steering and returning fire at the same time.

The other motorcycle was a better fit for her purposes. Basic black so it wouldn't draw undue attention, relatively lightweight so it could be easily handled, and blessed with speed to burn.

She patted the soft leather seat, then settled onto it. She turned the key in the ignition, then smiled as the engine rumbled to life.

"Hey, girl," she said, reaching for a helmet. "How would you like to go for a ride?"

She cinched the helmet into place, opened the garage door, and gunned the engine a few times before she shifted the bike into gear.

Mladić's compound was located near the waterfront. The Grandi area was the main hub of Reykjavik's fishing industry and was also home to some of the city's best restaurants. Santana doubted either the mouthwatering food or the breathtaking views were the reason Mladić had chosen to live in what was humorously referred to as the Fishpacking district. Access was. If one of his many enemies managed to track him down, he could escape by water or on land. Or he could simply stand his ground and let his security team do all the work.

Santana slowed as she approached a building with a view of the harbor. Before the property had been rezoned from commercial to residential, it had once been an office complex. Now Jusuf Mladić was the principal occupant.

She wondered if one of Mladić's former employees had let his enemies know where to find him. Not likely, considering the fact that when Mladić chose to terminate someone, it was more than just a figure of speech. That meant the informant was most likely part of his inner circle. Someone who had grown tired of playing second fiddle and wanted to be first chair.

Santana parked the motorcycle and walked into a nearby café. She selected a table near the window so she could keep tabs on the exterior of Mladić's compound without being too obvious about it.

When the waitress approached her table, she paused her surveillance long enough to take a look at the menu. She ordered pancakes, fruit, a bowl of skyr, and a cup of coffee, then returned her attention to the view across the street.

A fleet of cars surrounded the building. Each car was probably armored. The telltale bulges under the ill-fitting suits of the eight men patrolling the perimeter left no doubt that they were packing heat.

"Eight men outside. Probably at least a dozen more inside. All armed to the teeth."

Unless she conserved her ammo, she could run out of bullets just trying to get into the building. Once there, she would have to resort to hand-to-hand combat, a tedious process she wouldn't have time for if she wanted to get away before the police showed up. It wouldn't take them long to respond to a firefight. Especially in a country where gun violence was practically unheard of rather than a common occurrence.

"Would you like something else?" the waitress asked after she brought out Santana's food and set a bottle of birch syrup on the table. Her English was much better than Santana's Icelandic.

"A different profession might be nice."

"Are you new to town?"

"I'll be visiting off and on for the next few months," Santana said noncommittally.

"Once you get used to the cold, you'll love it here. There are plenty of jobs to be found in the tourism industry, and the labor market is a lot more relaxed than it is in the rest of Europe. Probably because there isn't a whole lot of competition. In case you haven't noticed, there aren't too many of us around here. It's always nice to see a new face." She flashed a flirtatious smile. "Especially one as striking as yours. Can I expect to see you in here again?"

The waitress was attractive, she seemed to have a nice personality, and she filled out her uniform in all the right ways, but Santana was too focused on the job at hand to even consider falling into bed with someone. Especially someone who wasn't Brooklyn. Having a contact on the ground, however, could prove invaluable.

"What's your name?" she asked.

"Hekla Gudmondsdottir. My mother owns this café and does most of the cooking, too." She pointed behind her to a slightly plumper, gray-haired version of herself searing reindeer sausage on a flat top. "I'm not as adept in the kitchen as she is so I got stuck serving the food rather than preparing it."

"Lucky for me. If these pancakes taste as good as they look, you and your mother can expect to see me every day."

Hekla's bright blue eyes glittered as she smiled. "If that is the case, I will see you tomorrow, yes?" She leaned over to refill Santana's coffee cup—and offer her a view of her cleavage at the same time.

A movement in the corner of her eye drew Santana's attention out the window. She turned to see the man she had been assigned to kill exit the building and climb into the back of one of the armored SUVs parked out front. She was tempted to skip breakfast and follow him, but she didn't want to make her move too soon. Or alert his security team to the fact that he had someone on his tail. To pull this off, she needed to be patient rather than impulsive.

She turned back to her newfound friend as the car carrying one of the most notorious warlords in modern history sped away. "I'm already looking forward to it."

## Chapter Twenty-two

B rooklyn felt like she had been ghosted. Vilma had been gone for three days, and she hadn't heard a word from her during that time. Not one phone call. Not a single text. Nothing except radio silence.

She hoped Vilma hadn't only been out to get her in bed and was now done with her after she had gotten what she wanted. She preferred to think Vilma was simply too busy meeting with her potential business partners to pay any attention to her personal life. She could be single-minded when it came to business, too, but she always made time for the people she cared about.

"Maybe that's the problem," she said as she headed to her kitchen to open a pint of her favorite frozen pick-me-up. "I might have been a meaningless hookup rather than someone she thought she could have a relationship with."

The explanation might have made sense if Vilma hadn't gone to such great lengths to open up to her during their visit to Little Manila. Vilma had invited her into her life that night. Offered a glimpse of her gritty true self, not the smooth, polished image she normally projected. After letting Brooklyn get so close to her, why was she being so standoffish now?

Brooklyn sighed in frustration. She wouldn't be flipping out like this if AJ hadn't put doubts in her head.

AJ's questions about Vilma had sown a seed. And, damn, if that seed hadn't grown roots. Now Brooklyn had to face the unwanted realization that, even though she felt close to Vilma, she didn't know very much about her. Vilma was obviously a private person, but did she, as AJ seemed to intimate, also have something to hide?

"I might not be the world's best judge of character, but I can usually tell when someone's playing me."

All the moments she had spent with Vilma—even the embarrassing ones—felt real.

As out of sorts as she was, she would probably make quick work of the ice cream she had pulled out of the freezer so she leaned against the counter rather than returning to the living room. Surprisingly, she had her fill after only a couple of bites. The sweet treat, like everything else these days, reminded her of Vilma. Of sharing a platter of food with her while Vilma told her about her childhood.

She tossed the dirty spoon in the dishwasher and placed the container of mint chocolate chip ice cream back in the freezer. Then she returned to the living room, where she sat on the couch, grabbed one of the oversized throw pillows, and hugged it against her chest.

There were many things she missed about being in a relationship. The closeness, the chemistry, the inside jokes. She hadn't missed this. The endless processing. The overthinking. The uncertainty of not knowing when to obsess over a potential problem and when to just chill and allow things to play out.

If for no other reason than to preserve her sanity, she decided to take Vilma at face value. Before she boarded a flight to Zurich, Vilma had said she would get in touch with her when she returned. Would she stick to her word, or would she continue to be as elusive as she was now? Brooklyn could only wait and see.

She reached for her ringing cell phone. Her heart sank when she saw Detective Barnett's number rather than Vilma's printed on the display.

"I've got an update for you," Barnett said.

"Based on the tone of your voice, I almost don't want to know what you have to say, but tell me anyway."

"I ran your theory about Eve Thao up the flagpole, but no one saluted. There's no evidence to tie her to Ms. Evans's murder. The forensic accountants examined her bank statements with a fine-toothed comb, but there were no transactions that might indicate she hired a professional to perform the hit. We scanned her email communications as well, and those didn't raise any red flags either."

"Are you sure?" Brooklyn had been so certain the whole ordeal was about to be over when it was apparently just beginning.

"Unfortunately, yes. I'm sorry your potential lead didn't pan out, but please don't hesitate to pass along any additional information you think might be of use. My guys and I have heavy caseloads, but we'll continue to give this one the attention it deserves."

Brooklyn was fully aware that the longer the case remained open, the less likely it would ever be closed.

"Great," she said to herself after she ended the call. "Just when I thought my night couldn't get any worse."

Santana wasn't used to being faithful to someone. Probably because she had never had anyone she needed—or wanted—to be faithful to. Now she found herself trying to do just that.

During the week she had spent in Reykjavik, Hekla had done everything except take out a full-page ad in the local newspaper to let her know she was interested in her. Santana had initially chosen to ignore Hekla's advances, but she couldn't do that forever. Especially since Hekla's questions during her daily forays to the Arctic Fox Café were beginning to turn from casual to personal.

"I love your accent," Hekla said as she poured her a cup of coffee.

Santana had become such a familiar presence that Hekla no longer bothered taking her order. When she walked in each morning, Hekla would pour her a cup of coffee and let her know that her usual breakfast would be ready in a few minutes. Santana appreciated the shorthand, but she wondered if her plan to fit in had worked a bit too well.

"Have you always lived in Montreal?"

"Yes."

The French-Canadian accent Santana affected when she pretended to be Delphine had taken years for her to perfect. Lessons from her tutors had given her a solid foundation, but immersing herself in the culture had proven to be the best learning tool. She had lived in Montreal for a year to develop the Delphine character, and occasionally returned just for fun when she was looking for a change of pace or had a craving for authentic poutine.

"When are you going back?" Hekla asked.

"Actually, I'm flying home tomorrow."

Hekla's face fell. "Seriously? Do you plan on returning to Reykjavik someday soon?"

"In a few months, yes."

Hekla's dour expression brightened. "If you are here in April, we can attend the *Deildabikar* together."

"What's that?"

"It's one of the most important football competitions in the country. KR usually does really well each year. If you would prefer to see one of the women's teams play, we could do that instead." Hekla paused to enjoy a laugh at her own expense. "I am being presumptuous. Do you even like football? And, more importantly, do you have a girlfriend?"

Santana knew how to answer the first question, but she had no idea how to respond to the other. Delphine was single, but she wasn't so sure she could say the same about herself. She and Brooklyn had been on a few dates and had slept together more than once, but was that enough to make them an item? They hadn't agreed to be exclusive and they certainly hadn't declared their undying love for each other. Yet Brooklyn was the only woman she desired at the moment and the only one she wanted to share things with. Each time she witnessed something memorable, she wished she could experience it with Brooklyn by her side. And even when she was supposed to be concentrating on Jusuf Mladić, her mind often wandered from the man in her sights to a woman who was two thousand miles away.

When she responded to Hekla's question, she decided to be true to her cover even though it felt like she wasn't being true to herself.

"Yes, I like football," she said flirtatiously, "and, no, I don't have a girlfriend."

"Good. On both counts. I will be back in a moment with your breakfast."

Hekla headed to the kitchen, and Santana sipped her coffee as she stared out the window. She had been watching Mladić for five days and had a relatively good handle on his patterns.

The lights went on in his bedroom every morning at six thirty, but he never made an appearance until at least ninety minutes after that.

Most days, he would head to a local facility to play soccer against a series of handpicked opponents. He scored goal after goal past one hapless goalie after another while a coterie of hangers-on dotted the stands and his bodyguards ringed the field. Getting a shot off from ground level would leave her vulnerable to return fire, but the colorful banners and flags attached to the top of the stadium obstructed the view from above, removing a long-range shot from her list of options.

The Blue Lagoon in Grindavik was one of Mladić's favorite haunts, too. Located in a lava field twelve miles from Reykjavik, the man-made geothermal spa was one of the most visited attractions in Iceland. The warm waters, which averaged between ninety-nine and one hundred two degrees Fahrenheit, were rich in minerals such as sulfur and silica. Bathing in them was thought to be beneficial for people suffering from skin diseases such as psoriasis. Mladić, who sported patches of reddened, scaly skin on his back and arms, visited the Blue Lagoon every afternoon.

Bathers were required to shower before entering the lagoon. The showers were communal but divided by gender. Unless she disguised herself as a man, Santana wouldn't be able to take advantage of Mladić while he was in a vulnerable position. There were too many potential witnesses in the lagoon itself and the nearby geothermal power plant that supplied both the water and the heat used to warm it.

The only other location Mladić had visited while she tailed him was to KR-völlur, the stadium where Knattspyrnufélag Reykjavíkur played its home games. The small venue held less than three thousand people. The roofed-in area where Mladić preferred to sit provided cover from the elements as well as protection from a potential long-range shooter.

Santana preferred to carry out her kills from a distance so she could allow herself to remain somewhat detached, but the more time she spent observing her latest target, the more she realized she would have to perform this job up close. She needed to devise a more subtle approach. Something as equally effective as an armed assault but not nearly as dramatic.

The day before, she had followed one of Mladić's security guards to a local drug store. While she pretended to browse for sunscreen, the guard had conferred with the pharmacist, who grabbed several prescription drugs from the shelves behind him. Each medication seemed designed to cater to Mladić's vanity rather than treat a serious malady. There were pills to prevent hair loss and creams to tighten skin, as well as the instantly recognizable blue diamond-shaped pills often used to deal with erectile dysfunction or simply to enhance a sexual experience. If she was able to replace one or all of the medications with a lethal counterpart, all she would have to do was bide her time and wait for the inevitable to happen.

"Pancakes, fresh fruit, birch syrup, and a bowl of skyr."

The order was familiar, but the person delivering it to Santana's table wasn't. Santana was surprised to see Hekla's mother had abandoned her post in the kitchen in order to try her hand at waitressing.

"May I join you?" The question was moot because Hekla's mother claimed the seat she had indicated before Santana could formulate a reply. "My name is Sigrun. You, I gather, are the woman my daughter has been raving about for the past few days. She tells me you are leaving tomorrow but plan to return soon. Is this true?"

"Yes, I like it here. The people are nice, and the food is even better."

Sigrun rested her arms on the table and leaned forward. Her visit, though unexpected, didn't exactly come as a surprise. Santana had shown Hekla just enough attention to keep her on the hook. Now

Sigrun had taken it upon herself to see what her intentions were. She could imagine having a similar conversation with Brooklyn's parents. Hopefully, she would be able to delay that tête-à-tête until she had something more substantial to offer Brooklyn than a few interesting dates and a series of well-rehearsed lies.

"I appreciate your business," Sigrun said, "but I would like to know what brings you into my café each day. Is it my daughter, the food, or the view across the street?"

Santana carefully examined Sigrun's face. Her stern countenance showed no traces of mirth so Santana chose not to toss out a flippant reply.

"Everyone in this area knows who lives in our midst," Sigrun said matter-of-factly. "We don't like it, but we have come to terms with it. You are not the first person who has sat in that chair plotting something that is bound to get you or someone else hurt or killed."

Santana started to deny Sigrun's characterization of her, but she could tell they were already past that point. "Who do you think I am?" she asked, trying to determine if Sigrun had evidence to back up her suspicions.

"I don't know and I don't care. All I care about is keeping my daughter safe."

The reply should have reassured her, but Santana couldn't seem to find her footing as she fought to maintain her equilibrium on what was proving to be increasingly shaky ground. Once more, she thought of Brooklyn. She had inserted herself in Brooklyn's life in an attempt to protect her from harm, but perhaps she might end up exposing her to it. If not now, then at some point in the future. Provided, of course, they were still together by then. She was living proof that no one was guaranteed tomorrow.

"If I help you get close to Mladić or whatever name he has chosen to go by," Sigrun said, "will you promise me you will do everything in your power to make sure my daughter is kept out of danger?"

Santana wished someone would stand up for her the way Sigrun was standing up for Hekla. What she wouldn't give for someone to love her that much. Her mother had once. When her life was her own again, perhaps she and her mother would be able to make up for all the years they had lost.

As she pondered what Sigrun had said, she tried not to overreact. This could be the opening she had been looking for. On the other hand, it could be a trap. Sigrun might be offering to help her out of love for her daughter. If she was on Mladić's payroll, however, she could be setting her up to take a very hard fall. Sigrun's concern for Hekla was clear, her intentions decidedly less so.

"How do I know I can trust you?" Santana asked.

"You don't, but I can certainly say the same about you." Sigrun extended a hand across the table. "Do we have a deal or not?"

"Yes," Santana said after a moment's pause, "we have a deal."

"Good." Sigrun placed her palms on the table and pushed herself to her feet. "Enjoy your breakfast. When you return to Reykjavik, we will have a great deal to talk about."

And Santana would have a great deal to think about. Beginning with finding a way to let Hekla down easy and ending with potentially doing the same to Brooklyn. Somewhere in between, she would have to find a way to defeat an army single-handed.

Winslow had once told her that the first kill was always the hardest. He was wrong. For her, the hardest kill wouldn't be the first but the last.

## CHAPTER TWENTY-THREE

*I'm back. I missed you like crazy. Can't wait to see you. Dinner tonight? I know a place that serves great ice cream.*

Brooklyn smiled as she read the message displayed on her phone. She couldn't remember the last time she had been so happy to receive a text. She wanted to be mad at Vilma for leaving her in the dark for over a week, but she couldn't manage the feat. Vilma's message was short but sweet. And oh-so-welcomed.

*It's my turn to plan an outing for us*, she texted back. *Meet me at eight and I promise to make it worth your while.*

*Intrigued*, Vilma replied a few seconds later. *Send me the address and I'll see you there. Just don't count on me giving you half of my dessert.*

*Party pooper.*

Brooklyn texted her the address of the venue she had in mind, then tried not to count the minutes until they could begin their date. It couldn't have been a little more than a week since they had seen each other because it seemed like a hell of a lot longer than that. She planned to spend a significant amount of time getting horizontal with Vilma before the night was over. Seeing her in a public setting without being able to touch her the way she craved was going to be torture. The most exquisite kind of torture, but torture nevertheless.

The place she had chosen for their date was located in midtown Manhattan. When she arrived, Vilma was waiting for her out front. In her blazer, button-down shirt, and slim-fitting corduroy pants, she looked like she had stepped out of the pages of *GQ*.

Brooklyn's stomach turned a flip worthy of an Olympic gymnast when Vilma spotted her and smiled. The expression on Vilma's face almost stopped her in her tracks. Vilma looked at her with such tenderness, such kindness, such…devotion that it made Brooklyn's heart swell.

*I don't give a shit about her backstory as long as I get to be part of her continuing narrative.*

"It's good to see you," she said after Vilma greeted her with a quick kiss and a lingering hug. "How was your trip?"

"I can't divulge any of the details because there's a nondisclosure agreement in place."

Brooklyn wasn't surprised. Business negotiations were kept secret for a reason: because far too many of them ended up falling apart rather than falling into place. She could understand Vilma's reluctance to talk about something that might never come to pass.

"But I don't think I would be talking out of turn if I admitted I saw some things I liked and some I didn't," Vilma said.

"Did the pros outweigh the cons?"

"By a narrow margin, yes. I'll reconvene with the company's leaders in a few months to see if some of the wrinkles I noticed have been ironed out. If so, we'll talk numbers. If not, I'll walk away and wait for the next opportunity to come along. But enough about business." She took Brooklyn's hand and spun her in a slow circle. "Is it possible you became even more beautiful while I was away?"

Brooklyn's face warmed at the compliment, but she decided not to let Vilma off the hook quite that easily. "Well, it has been a while since we've seen—or heard—from each other."

Vilma looked like the proverbial kid who had been caught with her hand in the cookie jar. "I deserve that."

"Is there a reason you didn't call? Or return any of mine?"

Vilma frowned, but she seemed more bemused than angry. "I could blame a host of factors and put most of the onus on the six-hour time difference, but the truth is I'm not used to checking in with someone. To having someone worry about me. It's new. It's different. It requires an adjustment on my part—and plenty of patience on yours."

Brooklyn was touched by Vilma's unexpected confession. Vilma always seemed to be in complete control of herself and her surroundings. It came as a bit of a surprise to hear her admit to being just as flummoxed about what was going on between them as she was. "This is new for me, too." She held out her hand. "But I'm willing to give it a try if you are."

Vilma laced their fingers together. "Does this mean you accept my apology?"

Brooklyn squeezed Vilma's hand. "Yes, but I might be making you one in a few hours. You're not claustrophobic, are you?"

Vilma took a hard look at the building's signage. "The Great Escape? What have you gotten me into?"

"I know you're probably used to calling all the shots. Both in your professional life and your personal one. Tonight, I thought it would be fun to have you follow someone else's lead for a change."

Brooklyn pulled the door open and ushered her inside. Ten oversized posters were displayed on the walls of the lobby. Each depicted a different scenario patrons could place themselves in and, hopefully, find their way out of before time expired.

"Do you need some help choosing your adventure?" one of the employees asked. He was wearing khaki shorts and a matching camp shirt, making him look like the leader of a jungle safari. "My name's Kevin, and I'm here to answer any questions you might have. The Haunted Room is one of our most popular escapes. It's a bit advanced so I wouldn't recommend it if this is your first time playing an escape game. If you're a seasoned player, be aware that the Haunted Room requires a minimum of ten people and has a two-hour time limit so be sure to choose your partners wisely because you might be stuck with them for a while."

"We'll keep that in mind for next time, thanks," Brooklyn said. "Which ones are your two-player games?"

"If you're looking for a more intimate experience, these two are right up your alley. The maximum number of players is four, and the minimum is two."

"Perfect," Brooklyn said.

Vilma turned to her after they read the short descriptions printed on each poster. Lights Out challenged players to solve an art heist in a museum before a crowd arrived to witness the unveiling of a new painting. In Jail Break, players had to find a way to escape their cell before their jailers could thwart their plans. "Which would you rather do, catch a criminal or become one?"

"In my opinion, the villain is usually more interesting than the hero."

"Jail Break it is then."

Kevin glanced at a display panel that contained a series of clocks, each one counting down the remaining time in a different game. "The room should be available in fifteen minutes at the most. I can take your payment whenever you're ready."

Brooklyn followed him to a workstation on the other side of the lobby, where she paid for the adventure she and Vilma had chosen.

"What's the fastest time someone has posted in Jail Break?" Vilma asked while Brooklyn signed the receipt.

"A couple completed the challenge in eighteen minutes," Kevin said, "but the guy had played the game before and knew where to locate all the clues. He was trying to impress his date by showing her how smart he was. It worked until they ran into one of his exes in the lobby. She was playing another game the same night and spilled the beans."

"Do you have any tips for us before we start?" Brooklyn asked. "Besides remaining on the lookout for vindictive ex-girlfriends out to ruin our good time."

"No matter which game you choose, the object in each is the same. Players need to find clues or objects and use them to solve puzzles and progress to the next stage of the game. Each room has multiple stages that need to be completed in order to advance the plot. As I said before, some adventures can take up to two hours to complete. We have one that can be accomplished in as little as fifteen minutes. Remember to work as a team. Share the clues with each other and communicate often. If one of you struggles with a puzzle, switch off and let the other give it a try. Work quickly, but don't rush. If you do, you might miss something important.

And make sure to look everywhere. Every item in the room could potentially be a clue. If you need help, my fellow escapologists and I are available to help you. And last but not least, don't forget to have fun. If you have to spend time locked in a room with someone, you might as well enjoy yourself in the process."

"Good advice," Vilma said. She turned to Brooklyn after Kevin returned to his post at the register. "If you wanted to confine me in close quarters for an hour, you could have locked me in my bedroom. I have a pair of handcuffs you could borrow if you'd like to experiment with a different kind of adventure sometime."

"Yes, please." Brooklyn felt her temperature spike a good twenty degrees, giving her a sneak preview of what menopause would be like. "But we need to find our way out of this one first."

Santana knew it was just a game, a mindless amusement people paid good money to play, but she felt a definite sense of panic when Kevin showed her and Brooklyn to the room they had chosen and locked them inside. The room didn't just look like a jail cell. It felt like one, too.

"I've spent most of my adult life trying not to wind up in prison," she said. "Why did I agree to spend time in one 'for fun'?"

"Because I batted my big brown eyes and did my best to appeal to your more sympathetic nature."

"That might have had something to do with it, but I think the greater incentive was the idea of spending some quality time with you."

She cupped Brooklyn's face in her hands and kissed her. The kiss they had shared on the street a few minutes earlier had been just a peck. This one was anything but.

She pulled Brooklyn's lower lip into her mouth and applied gentle pressure. Then she slowly traced her lip with her tongue, memorizing every contour.

"You taste like honey," she said when they finally parted.

"If you like the taste so much, I'll let you borrow my lip gloss." Brooklyn used both hands to gently push her away. "Because if you keep kissing me like that, I won't be able to concentrate on any of the clues. You want to get out of here before the time limit's up, don't you?"

Santana checked her watch, then began quickly but methodically examining each object within arm's reach. "We have less than fifteen minutes if we want to break the record."

Brooklyn chuckled. "How did I know you would be this competitive?"

Santana picked up a box containing an unfinished jigsaw puzzle. A note on the bottom of the box said the puzzle needed to be completed in order for players to advance to the next stage of the game. She opened the box and removed the twelve pieces inside. "Because you know me so well."

"Do I?" Brooklyn asked as she joined two of the pieces together.

Santana looked away from the puzzle they were working on so she could examine Brooklyn's face. "Yes, you do. Better than anyone I've ever met. I feel like I can be myself with you."

"I bet you say that to all the girls."

She looked Brooklyn in the eye so Brooklyn could see that, even though they were in an escape room, she wasn't playing games. "No, I don't."

Brooklyn's smile faded as her expression turned serious. "Why now?" she asked, the puzzle seemingly forgotten. "Why me?"

Santana didn't have to look at her watch again to know they were running out of time, but she no longer cared about beating a random stranger's record. She only wanted to let Brooklyn know how much she had come to care for her.

"Sometimes I feel like you came to my rescue on New Year's Eve instead of the other way around. Before I met you, relationships were something meant for other people, not me. I didn't have the time or the interest to give one a try. But you make me want to find the time because you definitely have my interest." She moved closer. How could she not? She was already well past the point where instinct usually told her to run away. "Before you, I had no idea what I was missing. Now that I do, I don't want to let go."

"Don't worry. I don't plan on going anywhere." Brooklyn tilted her head back and smiled up at her. "I think this is the part where you're supposed to kiss me."

Santana tapped her index finger against Brooklyn's chin. "I would, but you said you needed your powers of concentration in order to bust us out of here, remember?"

"I did say that, didn't I?" Brooklyn pressed the final puzzle piece into place and examined the overall image the individual pieces had created. She snapped her fingers when the image directed her to the location of a hidden key. "Get your lips ready, handsome, because I just found the way out." She slipped the key into the lock on the door and turned it. Or tried to. The triumphant look on her face changed to dismay when the door didn't open. She dropped the key into the basket that had been provided to collect objects that had been used and discarded during the course of the game. "Maybe this won't be as easy as I thought."

"Falling in love never is. Or, at least, that's what I've heard."

"So have I." Brooklyn walked toward her. She didn't stop until their bodies were touching up and down. "But would you like to put the theory to the test?"

"Yes, I would," Santana said against her better judgment. "And I'd like to do it with you."

"Are you saying you want us to be exclusive?"

"I'm saying I want to see this through to the end, no matter where it leads."

She just hoped the ending would be one both of them could live with.

Brooklyn had never felt so flustered in her life. She and Vilma had managed to find their way out of the escape room before the deadline, but the task had taken much longer than she had expected. Probably because she was too distracted by the conversation she and Vilma had shared about the status of their relationship to concentrate on the clues. She didn't know what the future would hold for her and

Vilma, but at least they were giving themselves the opportunity to find out.

"If that was an intermediate challenge," she had said when they finally located the key that unlocked the door, "I'm not too sure I want to try an advanced one."

Vilma had draped an arm across her shoulders. "We'll do better next time."

"You're determined to break that record, aren't you?"

"Not tonight. Tonight, I'd prefer to take my time."

Vilma's kiss had felt like a tease, offering an enticing hint of what was to come.

"My sentiments exactly."

"Your place or mine?"

Vilma's place was closer, and it also offered more privacy. Unlike the last time she and Vilma were together, Brooklyn didn't want to worry about disturbing the neighbors.

"Yours," she had said as she used an app on her phone to arrange for a car to pick them up. "Then I plan to spend the rest of the night making you mine."

"I like the sound of that."

And Brooklyn loved the feel of Vilma's bare skin against hers. She imagined the sensation as they waited for the car to arrive, then suffered through what felt like an interminable elevator ride to Vilma's apartment. When they finally made it upstairs, she reminded herself to show a modicum of restraint rather than giving in to an urge to rip Vilma's clothes off. There was a twenty-four-hour dry cleaners around the corner that also performed repairs and alterations, but she didn't want to waste precious time running errands when she could be spending that time with Vilma.

They slowly undressed each other, then spent several minutes simply taking each other in. Though they had slept together before, tonight felt different somehow. Tonight wasn't a casual hookup. Tonight was so much more. Rather than the culmination of a brief but dogged pursuit, it seemed to mark the beginning of an epic journey. One they had vowed to take together.

Vilma lay on the bed and beckoned to her. "Make me yours," she said in a voice thick with desire.

Vilma's words were the first either had spoken since they had arrived at her apartment building. They had been chatty all night but had fallen silent the moment the elevator doors slid shut. In that instant, Brooklyn had felt the weight of the moment settle on her shoulders. Vilma's words, however, set her free.

"Your wish is my command." She sighed contentedly after she covered Vilma's body with her own. "I missed this."

Vilma arched her back, rising to meet her. "I missed you."

That did it.

Brooklyn took her in every way imaginable. First with her hands, then her mouth. A few toys might have come into play at some point, but Brooklyn wasn't thinking too straight by then. She was too entranced by the wondrous sensation of making Vilma come again and again and again.

"I could get addicted to this," she said as Vilma tended to the insistent throbbing between her legs.

"Good. Because I'm already addicted to you."

Brooklyn closed her eyes as she exploded against Vilma's hand. She reminded herself to thank Vilma for the fireworks display. Once she regained the power of speech, that was.

"Thank you for a night to remember," Vilma said, drawing Brooklyn into her arms.

"It's definitely one I'll never forget." Brooklyn rested her head on Vilma's chest. She could hear Vilma's heart beating double time. "Thank you for the workout."

Vilma rolled out of bed and pulled Brooklyn with her.

"Where are we going?" Brooklyn asked as Vilma dragged her across the room.

"What are you supposed to do after a workout except hit the showers?"

Brooklyn smiled as she remembered the multitude of strategically placed shower heads in Vilma's bathroom. Never had getting clean sounded so dirty. She couldn't wait to get started.

❖

In the bathroom, Santana turned on the water and waited for it to get warm. She thrust her hand into the spray to make sure it wasn't too hot before she gave Brooklyn the okay to follow her inside.

Brooklyn piled her hair into a loose bun, then stepped into the shower. Santana closed the door behind her. When Brooklyn rubbed her slippery body against hers, Santana felt herself grow wet in places the five jets of water hadn't yet reached.

"When my brothers and sisters and I were younger," Brooklyn said, "our mother was always yelling at us to save water. If I'd known conservation was this much fun, I would have done it a long time ago."

Santana directed Brooklyn to turn around. Then she squeezed body wash onto a shower sponge and rubbed the sponge across the nape of Brooklyn's neck. Brooklyn quivered when a line of soap suds trickled down her back.

"If this is the treatment I receive when you come home," Brooklyn said with a sigh, "I might have to ask you to go away more often."

Santana soaped Brooklyn's shoulders and arms. "What did you do while I was away?"

"I played arcade games with a group of people from work." Brooklyn ducked her head. "It sounds juvenile when I say it out loud."

"No." Santana turned Brooklyn to face her. "It sounds like you. Did you have fun?"

"Yes, but I discovered AJ isn't as enamored with you as I am."

Brooklyn seemed to find the comment amusing, but it caused Santana more than a bit of concern. She had known from the moment they met that AJ would be trouble. The only question was if she would turn out to be a minor annoyance or a major one.

"Because?" she asked cautiously.

Brooklyn slipped her arms around Santana's neck. "Apparently, you keep too much of a low profile for her liking. She googled you and became alarmed when she couldn't come up with anything concrete."

"That's a good thing, isn't it?" Winslow's tech wizards had taken great pains to keep her internet profile as generic as possible. Apparently, their efforts had worked.

"I thought so, but she warned me I shouldn't get involved with you. She thinks you're too much of a mystery."

"What do you think?"

"I think it's a bit late to avoid getting involved, don't you?"

"Not yet. There's still time for you to walk away."

"If I didn't know better, I'd say you were trying to get rid of me."

"Hardly. You're the best thing that's ever happened to me. I just don't want to come between you and your friends."

Brooklyn stood on her tiptoes and kissed her. "Let me worry about my friends."

"And what would you like me to do?"

Brooklyn glanced at the bath sponge in her hand. "I could be wrong, but I think there are a few spots you might have missed."

Santana slowly slid the sponge down Brooklyn's body. "We can't have that, can we?"

She set all her other thoughts aside so she could concentrate on Brooklyn. She had always prided herself on being good at multitasking. From now on, though, she would have to take one thing at a time. For her sake and Brooklyn's.

## CHAPTER TWENTY-FOUR

B rooklyn hummed to herself as she walked down the street. She drew a couple of strange looks from a few passersby, but she didn't care. She felt like Gene Kelly without the raindrops and the lamppost doubling as a dance partner. She couldn't remember a coffee run ever being so much fun. Or maybe it wasn't the coffee itself but the thought of who she would be sharing it with.

"Does she like savory breakfast pastries or sweet ones?" she wondered aloud as she stared at the selection of baked deliciousness in the coffee shop a few blocks from Vilma's apartment.

"When in doubt, get one of each."

Brooklyn glanced at the gangly teenage boy who had joined her at the counter. His friendly face was framed by a mop of curly blond hair. "Good advice." She ordered two bear claws and a pair of breakfast sandwiches.

"Do you live around here?" the boy asked after he ordered two macchiatos and an espresso.

"No, I'm just visiting. How about you?"

"My dads and I live a few blocks over. They own the flower shop across the street. I help them out from time to time."

Brooklyn looked in the direction he had indicated. "Hey, I know that place. My girlfriend bought flowers for me there." Girlfriend. That was the first time she had used the word to describe Vilma. It gave her a thrill hearing it out loud.

"Awesome. Tell her she has great taste. And I don't just mean in flowers."

"You're a born salesman, aren't you?"

"I was hoping it didn't show. What's your girlfriend's name? Maybe she's one of our regulars."

"Vilma Bautista. Do you know her?"

The boy grinned. "So you're the one."

"The one what?"

He lowered his voice to a conspiratorial whisper. "She'll probably kill me for talking out of turn, but I inherited my dads' love of gossip. Ms. Bautista often pops into the shop to buy bouquets for her lady friends, but you're the first one she ever bought a potted plant for."

"A potted plant? No, she sent a bouquet to my office."

"Bouquet? So the lavender I sold her a couple of weeks ago wasn't—Shit." The boy covered his mouth with his hands. The gesture highlighted rather than hid the expression of abject panic on his face. "My dads are right. I do talk too much. Forget I said anything."

"No worries. We all have a past, don't we?" And today, she was more interested in the future.

"Thanks," he said, looking relieved. "And tell her Harry said hello."

"Will do."

After the barista called her name, she picked up her order and headed back to Vilma's apartment. Something struck her before she made it halfway there. Harry had said the potted plant he had sold Vilma was lavender. The flowers she had seen the mysterious figure tending to during Charlie's interment service were lavender, too. Was it a coincidence, or was Vilma the person she had seen that day? Vilma was the same height and size as the person she had spotted, but what reason would she have to trek all the way out to Jersey City? She had said her mother still lived in the Philippines and she and her father weren't close. That meant she couldn't have been visiting family. And her friends probably wouldn't be caught dead outside of Manhattan unless they were taking the scenic route to one of their summer homes.

Perhaps she was the reason.

Perhaps Vilma was taking her role as protector more seriously than Brooklyn had initially thought. The idea was sweet but probably far-fetched. And a bit creepy, too. New York was a large city and lavender was a fairly common flower. What were the chances Vilma had bought the ones that had been placed at the grave of a woman who just happened to share the same piece of real estate as Charlie?

"Try slim and none."

Yet life was often made up of coincidences. If it hadn't, she and Vilma never would have met in the first place.

"You were gone a while," Vilma said when Brooklyn returned to her apartment.

"I ran into a friend of yours."

"Who?"

"Harry from the flower shop. He says hello, by the way."

"Judging by the frown lines on your forehead, that isn't the only thing he said." Vilma lowered the newspaper she was reading and patted the spot next to her on the couch. "What's up?"

Brooklyn handed Vilma the Americano she had requested. "I'm being silly."

"Tell me anyway."

Brooklyn tucked her feet underneath her as she wrapped her hands around the warm cup of vanilla latte in her hands. "Do you know a woman named Melanie Pierce?"

"No, should I?" Vilma took a sip of her coffee. "Who is she?"

"*Was.*"

"Okay, who *was* she?"

Brooklyn shrugged. "I don't know her either."

"Was she one of Harry's customers?"

"I doubt it. She died before he was born."

"Now I'm curious." Vilma set her cup of coffee down. "Why is a woman you don't even know a topic of conversation?"

"Someone planted a pot of lavender at her grave during Charlie's interment service. When Harry told me he'd sold you the same plant during that timeframe, I thought the person I saw that day might have been you."

"Sorry. I can honestly say Melanie Pierce and I have never met. But I'm glad to know you think about me so much you're imagining my face on other people's bodies. As long as you don't do the opposite when we're in bed, we won't have a problem."

Brooklyn laughed. At Vilma's joke, but mostly at herself. "Like I said, I'm being silly. It's early and I haven't had nearly enough caffeine." She reached for the box of pastries. "I bought breakfast."

"So I see."

Vilma snagged one of the breakfast sandwiches. Brooklyn grabbed a bear claw. As they ate, her high spirits began to dim. She couldn't deny the relief she had felt at hearing—and seeing—Vilma's nonchalant response to her question. The realization made her wonder if she trusted Vilma as much as she had initially thought.

Santana chewed mechanically. The sandwich was delicious, but she could barely taste it. Beside her, Brooklyn appeared to be lost in thought. Harry's slip of the tongue could turn out to be costly.

He was a good kid. He was probably being his usual chatty self. She couldn't blame him for this snafu. No, this was on her. She should have been more careful when she visited the cemetery. More than that, she should have walked away after she had refused to perform the job she had been assigned to do rather than sticking around and getting involved with the victim's best friend.

She could still extricate herself from the situation if she chose to, but the time to do it painlessly had passed. Leaving now would hurt.

Her answers to Brooklyn's questions about the flowers at Melanie Pierce's grave seemed to have appeased her, but Brooklyn looked far from satisfied. Santana could tell Brooklyn wouldn't let this go. Like she had in the escape room, Brooklyn would keep searching for clues until she solved the mystery.

How was she supposed to fix this? She had only two choices. She could either keep feigning ignorance or find the strength to come clean. The truth was supposed to set you free. In her case, it could cost her Brooklyn.

"Thanks for breakfast," she said, tossing the crumpled sandwich wrapper on the coffee table.

"I had to do something to earn my keep." Brooklyn flashed a wan smile, letting Santana know she would have her work cut out for her doing damage control.

"You did a fine job." Santana licked the sugar stuck to Brooklyn's fingers, then laid her down on the couch. "Now let me earn mine."

## Chapter Twenty-Five

Being with Vilma felt like a fantasy. A dream come true. On Sunday afternoon, Brooklyn found herself craving a serious dose of reality. She begged off of Vilma's invitation to dinner at one of the best—and most expensive—restaurants in town so she could spend some quality time with her family and have some home cooking.

When she was growing up, Sundays had always been reserved for two things: morning mass and family dinners. Both were steeped in tradition and each possessed nearly as much pageantry.

Brooklyn didn't make it to church in time to take part in the services, but she did arrive at her parents' house in time for dinner.

"Look what the cat dragged in," one of her brothers said when she walked into the crowded living room. "Are you sure you didn't get lost on your way to some swanky event?"

"Thanks, Gianni. I can always count on you to break my balls."

"That's what big brothers are for, little sis. If I hadn't been so hard on you, you wouldn't be the kickass businesswoman you are today." He handed the youngest of his three sons to his wife so he could give Brooklyn a hug. "Have you made your first million yet?"

"You know we don't brag about how much money someone makes," Brooklyn's father said.

"Probably because we've never had anything to brag about," Gianni said. Like their father, he had been a blue-collar worker all his life. And like their father, he had more calluses than cash.

"Gianni."

"Sorry, Pop." Gianni held up his hands to show he meant no harm. "It's good to see you, sis. It's been too long."

"Yes, it has."

"I was sorry to hear about Charlie. Ang and I planned to go to the service, but we couldn't find anyone to watch the kids."

That wasn't a surprise. Gianni and Angie's boys were so rowdy their babysitters often felt entitled to combat pay.

"Way to make the family look bad," Brooklyn's brother Stefano said.

Even though Brooklyn was the youngest member of her family, her brother Stefano, who was two years older, seemed to be the most immature. He couldn't maintain a job or a relationship for longer than a few months at a time and seemed destined to end up living in their parents' basement for the rest of his life. If Vilma represented everything she had always aspired to be, Stefano embodied everything she didn't. But he was her brother and she would love him no matter what. It remained to be seen whether she could extend that kind of unconditional love to someone to whom she wasn't related.

"What are you talking about?" she asked.

"I shouldn't have to remind you, but I will." Stefano tossed his stringy hair out of his eyes. He had the long, unkempt mane of a rock star, but he didn't have the musical talent to match. "When we were kids, people used to think we were mobbed up because we're Italian-American and Pop worked construction. Those things always go hand-in-hand, right?"

"Not this again."

"I'm just saying it looks kind of sketchy for your BFF to get popped like that."

"Really, Stef?" Brooklyn usually tried to exercise patience when Stefano went off on one of his infamous tangents. Today, though, her patience was in short supply. "I haven't seen you in weeks, and this is the homecoming you give me?"

"Ignore him," Angie said as she tried to soothe Enzo, her restless eight-month-old. "After dinner, we'll send him back to the basement so he can smoke more weed and cook up another batch of conspiracy theories."

Stefano shook his head to deny he participated in either of those activities, but they had all seen evidence to the contrary. His room was littered with empty dime bags and books written by some of his favorite wingnuts. "Besides, it's not a theory if it's true."

"Anyway," Angie said before he could begin another rant. "How are you holding up, Brooklyn?"

"It gets a little bit better every day. Thanks for asking."

"Are the cops any closer to finding the scumbag who did it?"

"They're doing everything they can, but they haven't found anything yet."

"I pray Charlie's parents will eventually have someone to blame," Brooklyn's sister Bella said. "Someone they can point to and say, 'He's the one who's responsible for taking our baby from us.' That's more than a lot of people can say when they lose a loved one."

"One day," Brooklyn said, "I want to be able to look that person in the eye and tell them exactly what I think of them. I want to ask them if the money they received was worth taking someone's life."

"All or nothing. That's always been the case with you. But I guess that's better than settling for whatever you can get."

"I'm right here, hon," Bella's husband, Paulie, said. "You know I can hear you, don't you?"

"And you know I'm not going anywhere. It's been twelve years, babe. You're like my favorite teddy bear."

"Yeah," Gianni said, giving Paulie's balding head an affectionate rub. "Thin on top and soft in the middle."

Paulie poked Gianni's rounded stomach. "You're a couple of cans short of a six-pack yourself, pal."

"Blame it on Ma's good cooking. Right, Ma?"

"Keep buttering me up all you want, son, but you're still not getting the house. You and your brothers and sisters will be entitled to equal shares of it when your father and I pass on. Maybe, when the time comes, the lot of you will finally be able to agree on something."

"Good one, Mom," Brooklyn said. "Do you need any help in the kitchen?"

"No, but I could use the company. Something tells me you could, too."

"I've given up on trying to figure out how you always know what's on everyone's mind."

"It comes with the job once you become a mother. I would say you'll find out when it happens to you, but you don't seem to be in that much of a hurry to join the ranks."

"Call me in a few years. I still have too much growing up to do before I can even think of showing someone else how to do it." Brooklyn followed her mother to the kitchen, which was filled with the mouth-watering aromas of oregano, garlic, and tomato sauce. "Please tell me that's lasagna I see in the oven."

"It might be. You'll have to act fast if you want to beat Tommy to one of the crispy end pieces."

Brooklyn rubbed the scar on the back of her right hand, a four-pronged reminder of one of the dinner table battles she and Tommy had waged over the years. When she was six and he was ten, he had stuck his fork in her hand when she reached for the last piece of garlic bread. She had ended up with the prize and he had wound up being grounded for two weeks. A win-win in her book. "I'll take my chances."

Her mother smiled as she chopped fresh vegetables for a mixed green salad. "You're in a much better mood than you were the last time I saw you. What's her name?"

Brooklyn grabbed a handful of black olives from a jar on the table. "How did you know I had met someone?" Though she had been tempted to tell her parents about Vilma, the only people she had confided in were Charlie and AJ. Charlie was gone and AJ didn't approve.

"Wasn't it less than five minutes ago that we established I have the ability to read my family members' minds?" She pointed her knife in Brooklyn's direction. "And if you keep snacking like that, you're going to ruin your appetite for dinner. Now stop stalling and tell me all about her."

"I wish I could."

"What's the matter? Did she force you to sign one of those PDA things?"

"I think you mean NDA. And, no, she didn't."

"Then why can't you tell me about her?"

"Because she's a bit of a mystery. I adore the things I know about her, but I'm starting to wonder how much I don't."

"That sounds like the plot of a romance novel I read once."

"Did it end well?"

"I can't remember, but I do recall Fabio looking absolutely dreamy on the cover. That is one handsome man. Just don't tell your father I said so."

"Don't worry. My lips are sealed."

Brooklyn's mother wiped her hands on a towel and poured two glasses of red wine. She was a teetotaler most of the time, but she could be a bit of a lush when she was cooking a big meal. No wonder Sunday was her favorite day of the week. "So tell me what you do know. First of all, how did you meet her?"

Brooklyn told her about her trip to Tokyo, her unwelcome visit from the tipsy businessman who had tried to pick her up, and the gorgeous knight in Armani armor who had ridden to her rescue.

"I take that back," her mother said. "This is even better than a romance novel. Did you hook up that night?"

"Mom!"

"Isn't that the expression your generation uses? We used to call it putting out. Would you rather I asked if you knocked boots instead?"

"I'd prefer if you didn't ask about my sex life at all, please and thanks."

"I've got to get my thrills somehow. Heaven knows your father doesn't—"

"Mom!" Brooklyn covered her ears with her hands so she wouldn't be able to hear how her mother finished her sentence. She knew her parents had always had an active sex life since they had so many kids to show for it, but she didn't want to hear a play-by-play.

"Fine. Be that way. How did the two of you find each other again? Or is that off-limits, too?"

"She called me the night Charlie was killed."

"What?"

"I know, right? Talk about bad timing. I couldn't talk to her then because I had what seemed like half the NYPD roaming around my office, but I reached out to her a few days later when I needed to talk to someone who could speak objectively about what I was going through. She was in town for a few days and invited me to her place for dinner."

"She lives here in New York?"

"Not full-time, no. She's originally from Manila and she has an apartment near Central Park, but her permanent home is on some remote island in the Pacific."

"Have you been there yet?"

"To her apartment, yes. To her home, no. I did some research on it after she told me the name of the country."

"And?"

"It's so far out it's a pain in the ass to get to."

"She sounds like a woman who enjoys her privacy. Can't fault her for that."

"I suppose not." Brooklyn swirled the contents of her wine glass. "She doesn't like talking about herself. When she does, I'm intrigued by the stories she relates, and I want to hear more. I can tell she's been hurt before so I don't want to push her into doing something she's not ready for."

"But?"

"I don't want to waste my time developing feelings for someone who can't be trusted."

"What makes you think you can't trust her? The actions you've described have been nothing less than honorable, and I personally want to thank her for taking such good care of you in your time of need. Has she betrayed you in some way?"

"Not exactly." Brooklyn thought about how abandoned she had felt while Vilma was away on a business trip. Vilma's behavior had been regrettable, though not reprehensible. "It's just—People I know have expressed their misgivings about her."

"Do those people have your interests at heart or theirs?"

The question gave Brooklyn pause. She knew AJ was harboring a crush on her, but she didn't know if AJ's feelings for her had helped or hindered when AJ formed an opinion about Vilma. "I have no idea. All I know is this is Vilma's first real relationship and she doesn't have a handle on the rules."

"Do you?"

Brooklyn laughed. "You've seen all the messy relationships I've had over the years. Does it look like I know what I'm doing?"

"Hell, I've been married for over forty years and I'm still trying to figure things out."

"You and Pop are good together. You always have been."

"Because we work at it. Believe me, none of it comes easy."

"It doesn't look that way."

"Then that means we've been doing our jobs." Brooklyn's mother set her knife down and refilled their glasses. "I don't do this often, but I'm going to take a minute to toot my own horn. Your father and I have never had much money, which means we've never had much to give you and the rest of our kids, materially speaking. You never had the must-have toys or the latest fashions unless you got jobs and paid for them yourselves. That's the thing I'm proudest of. That Sal and I molded you into strong, independent people who are able to stand on your own two feet and make your own decisions. Most of you, anyway. Stefano still needs help wiping his own butt from time to time, but you didn't hear me say that."

"So what are you trying to say, Mom?"

"You only get one shot at life, Brooklyn. Don't let someone else try to tell you how to live it. The person you've described sounds like someone who deserves the benefit of the doubt. I could change my mind when I finally get a chance to meet her—hint, hint—but if you love her, I'm sure Sal and I will, too."

"Wait. I never said I was in love with her."

"I know." Brooklyn's mother patted her hand. "You didn't have to."

## CHAPTER TWENTY-SIX

Santana was trying to plan the most important job of her career and she couldn't concentrate. Every time she tried to buckle down and focus on the task at hand, her mind inevitably drifted to something else. Not something. Someone. Instead of devising a strategy to infiltrate Jusuf Mladić's compound, she couldn't stop thinking about Brooklyn and what she needed to do in order to make things right between them.

Brooklyn had kept her distance for three days now. Each time Santana reached out to her, Brooklyn said she was swamped at work and didn't have the time to get together. Her excuses sounded plausible, but part of Santana wondered if Brooklyn was still obsessing over the conversation she'd had with Harry and the subsequent questions it had raised.

Instead of pressing her, Santana decided to give her some space. Brooklyn needed the downtime and so did she. She needed to get her act together. Because if she failed to complete the job she had been tasked with, she wouldn't have a future to worry about.

She powered up the burner phone tied to her Delphine Durand identity and checked her messages. She had a few missed texts from Hekla, most requesting a detailed explanation for why she had dumped her so unceremoniously.

Before she left Reykjavik, she had followed through on Sigrun's edict by telling Hekla they couldn't see each other anymore. Hekla had been confused by the abrupt end to their burgeoning courtship, and she hadn't wanted to hear any of the tried-and-true "it's not you, it's me" excuses Santana had trotted out to explain her decision.

*Which lie am I supposed to believe?* Hekla's last text read. *The one where you said you weren't seeing anyone or the one where you said my mother didn't have anything to do with your change of heart about me?*

Santana was tempted to respond to Hekla's missives, but she knew anything she wrote, no matter how carefully crafted, would only make the situation worse instead of better. Some of the assignments she was given occasionally resulted in collateral damage. If the fallout from this one turned out to be nothing more serious than a broken heart, that was a result she could live with. Hekla, too.

She closed her text messages and opened her email, not expecting to find anything of note. The message indicator said she had four emails. The first three were spam that had managed to slip through the filter somehow. She deleted them without giving them a second thought. She started to dismiss the fourth email as well until she realized who it was from: Sigrun.

The subject line read *Help Wanted*. The body of the email contained a description for a cater waiter job advertised by one of Sigrun's competitors. The restaurant, the email went on to explain, had been hired to provide the food for a private party hosted by Jusuf Mladić and needed to supplement its wait staff for the event.

*The owner of the Midnight Sun is a friend of mine*, Sigrun had written. *I gave him your name and recommended you for the position. The job can be yours if you complete the attached form. I have held up my end of our bargain. The rest is up to you. Good luck in your endeavors, and thank you in advance for being a woman of your word.*

Santana checked the date listed in the email. The party was scheduled to take place in a little over a month. That gave her plenty of time to gather the items she needed, book a return flight to Reykjavik, and do what needed to be done. But first, there was someone she needed to see.

❖

Brooklyn's trip home had given her a lot to think about. Her brain had been overloaded ever since. She had known for a while now that she was developing feelings for Vilma, but she hadn't realized those feelings ran so deep. Her mother's statement about her being in love with Vilma had hit home. More often than not, her parents had been accepting of the women she had dated, but they hadn't always approved of some of them. In those instances, her parents' instincts had turned out to be more accurate than hers. Having her mother give Vilma her blessing meant the world to her, but it also rattled her.

Family, she had realized as she took a seat at the crowded dinner table, could turn out to be a sticking point. Vilma didn't have a relationship with her own family and Brooklyn's was dysfunctional with a capital D.

No wonder she found it so easy to pretend to be someone else because she had spent so much of her life wishing she was someone else. Especially after one of her brothers or sisters did or said something embarrassing, which was practically a daily occurrence,

Stefano's asinine comments when she arrived had brought all those feelings back. Did she want to subject Vilma to that? Would Vilma think less of her if she exposed her to her family and all its flaws? If she and Vilma continued to see each other, she would have to introduce her to them at some point. She shuddered to think what might come out of Stefano's mouth when that moment finally arrived.

It wasn't like her to run scared, but that was certainly what she was doing now. She wished she and Vilma could remain in their hermetically sealed bubble forever. She had tried to delay their entry into the real world, but she had a sneaking suspicion she had only been delaying the inevitable. She had been avoiding Vilma for days, coming up with one reason after another for why she couldn't spend time with her. She knew the day would eventually come when Vilma would tire of her excuses and refuse to take no for an answer. Today appeared to be that day.

An incoming text message drew her attention away from the PowerPoint presentation she was working on. The text was from Vilma.

*You have to eat sometime. Meet me downstairs in ten minutes so I can buy you lunch.*

Vilma's message felt more like an ambush than an invitation. Brooklyn had used the same tactic before—meeting someone in public so they would be less likely to cause a scene when she broke up with them. Now it was apparently Vilma's turn to flip the script.

"I've made a royal mess of things. If I were her, I wouldn't want to date me either."

She locked her computer and reached for her purse.

*Be right there*, she texted back

Her breezy response belied the sense of dread she felt as she rode the elevator downstairs. She had never felt this insecure about a relationship. Probably because none of her previous relationships had meant this much. No wonder she was freaking out.

When she reached the café on the ground floor, she spotted Vilma waiting for her at a table by the window. Vilma rose to greet her as she approached the table.

"Long time, no see," Vilma said, giving her a kiss on each cheek.

"I'm sorry I've been so busy this week."

Vilma resumed her seat and draped a napkin across her lap. "You don't have to explain yourself to me. You have a company to run. I understand that."

"So you didn't invite me here to break up with me?"

A smile tugged at the corner of Vilma's lips. "Is that what you thought I had in mind?"

"I wouldn't blame you if you did. I've been MIA the past few days."

"If I remember correctly, so was I not too long ago. Turnabout is fair play, after all."

"I'm not trying to enter a game of one-upmanship with you."

"That's good to hear, especially considering I need to go on another business trip."

"So soon?"

Vilma held up a hand to let the waitress know they needed more time before they put in their orders.

"That's the reason I asked you to meet me for lunch. I wanted to prepare you for what's to come. The management team for the company I recently met with has addressed the issues I noted during our initial meeting and is on track to get them resolved in a few weeks. I'm scheduled to meet with them again next month. This time, hopefully both sides will end up satisfied."

"How long will you be gone?"

"A few days. A week at the most. But I'll be out of touch most of that time and I don't want you to feel as uncertain as you did the last time I was away."

"Yeah, that wasn't one of my best moments. You must think I'm the neediest person in the world."

"I think you're adorable, but that goes without saying. I'm also willing to admit I need to step up my game in terms of communication. If I want to share my life with you, I need to learn to share myself with you."

"Ditto."

"I'm glad to hear we're on the same page. When I get back, do you think we can find the time to have a conversation that lasts longer than the length of a text message string or the duration of a business lunch?"

Brooklyn finally felt herself begin to relax. "I'd like that."

"So would I." Vilma beckoned for the waitress. "Now what would you like for lunch?"

Brooklyn paraphrased a line from one of her favorite movies as she took Vilma's hand in hers. "More time with you."

"This was fun," Brooklyn said after she finished her Caesar salad. "Not as much fun as a quickie, but close enough."

"I'll keep that in mind for next time," Santana said. "Or are you suggesting there's no time like the present?"

"What makes you think I would suggest such a thing?"

Brooklyn's smile straddled the line between wicked and whimsical. Like everything else about her, Santana found it utterly charming. If she weren't careful, this woman could prove to be her undoing. Then again, she had left careful behind a long time ago. Now she was flying by the seat of her pants. And what a ride it was turning out to be. The question was what lurked around the corner, a clear path or an obstacle she wouldn't be able to avoid?

"I have no idea." Santana placed two bills on the table and told the waitress to keep the change. "I'll walk you back to your office."

"No need. I think I can manage to get from point A to point B without having to leave a trail of bread crumbs behind."

"I'm sure you can, but perhaps, as you so eloquently put it a few minutes ago, I'd like to spend a bit more time with you."

"When you put it that way, how can I possibly say no?"

Santana offered her arm. "I've been told I can be rather convincing when I set my mind to it."

Brooklyn headed to the elevator. "Does that approach make you a success in the boardroom, the bedroom, or both?"

It was Santana's turn to smile. "I've always been my worst critic so I'll let you be the judge of that."

"I haven't gotten a look at your skills in the boardroom yet," Brooklyn said as she punched the number for the appropriate floor. "As for your skills in the bedroom, I'd have to give you a nine out of ten."

Santana waited for the elevator doors to close before she drew Brooklyn to her. "Only a nine?"

Brooklyn rested her palms on Santana's chest. "I'm just trying to provide you with the proper incentive. We don't want you to get stale, do we?"

"No, we definitely don't want that."

Brooklyn groaned when Santana kissed the side of her neck. "If you keep that up, I'll be tempted to hit the emergency stop button and give the guards a show." She pointed to the recessed security camera overhead. "I've gone this long without having a sex tape leaked to the internet and I don't want to break my streak now."

"Point taken." Santana held up her hands as she took a step back. "Sometimes I forget you're an influential CEO with both a company and a rep to protect. Did I say something wrong?" she asked when she noticed Brooklyn's smile falter a bit.

"Part of that conversation we're supposed to have at a later date."

"The agenda for our sit-down is growing by the minute. I'm going to have to block off a significant part of my calendar when we finally find time to talk."

"So will I."

Brooklyn's tone was a bit too somber for Santana's liking. She ran a finger across Brooklyn's furrowed brow as she wondered what was weighing on her mind. "There's nothing you can't say to me. I'll be here for you, no matter what."

"I hope you mean that."

"We've all got baggage. Some more than most. Fortunately, I have plenty of space to stash them in."

The elevator doors opened, but Brooklyn moved toward her instead of heading for the exit. "Do you think you might have room for mine?"

Santana tried to keep the moment light as she offered Brooklyn the reassurance she so obviously needed. "Have you seen my closets?"

"Seen them? I was planning on asking if I could sublet one of them since they all have more square footage than my apartment does."

Santana held her hand in the opening to keep the elevator doors from closing. "I'm glad I could put a smile on your face because you've definitely put one in my heart."

Brooklyn cocked her head. "I can't decide if that's the most romantic thing I've ever heard or the cheesiest. I'll get back to you when I have an answer."

"I'll be waiting."

Brooklyn gave her a quick kiss and turned to leave. Santana waited a beat before she said, "I hate seeing you go, but I love watching you walk away."

"No wait time on that one. Definitely cheesy."

"Just making sure. See you tonight?"

"Count on it. You're still on the hook to make me dinner."

"I'll try to do it without instructions this time as long as you promise not to judge me too harshly on the results."

"I promise."

"Good. Because I can do a mean PB and J. Would you like yours with crusts or without?"

"Surprise me."

Santana hoped the other surprise she had yet to reveal wouldn't end up being a deal-breaker. She pulled her hand away and pressed the button for the ground floor. Just before the doors closed, a hand appeared in the small opening.

"Going down?" AJ asked.

"So it seems."

AJ's shoulders stiffened as she took her eyes off her phone's display and looked at Santana for the first time. "Never mind. I can wait for the next one." She pressed the Door Open button like she was working the controls on a pinball machine.

"Are we really going to play that game?"

"What game?"

"Brooklyn told me you have doubts about me."

"Are you going to hold that against me?"

"Why should I? You're entitled to your opinion. As am I. With that being said, you can't avoid me forever, you know."

"I don't have to avoid you forever," AJ said defiantly. "Just until Brooklyn wakes up from the sex coma she's in and realizes how much of a phony you are. That shouldn't take much longer."

"Ride with me, JoAnna."

AJ seemed taken aback, either by hearing the sound of her real name or by seeing the stern look on Santana's face. She meekly stepped back inside the elevator car. "Do you have something you want to say to me?" she asked as the car finally began to descend.

"No, but there is something I would like you to do."

"What might that be?"

"Take care of Brooklyn for me."

"How very patriarchal of you. In case you haven't noticed, Brooklyn's a strong, independent woman. She doesn't need anyone to 'take care' of her."

"If I wanted a lecture on gender norms and societal expectations, I would have asked you for one."

"Then what are you asking me for? Are you going somewhere?" AJ's expression was a mixture of hope and confusion. Santana might have laughed if the circumstances had been different.

"Not by choice, no, but it never hurts to have a contingency plan. Even though you and I don't see eye to eye, I can honestly say you're a good and loyal friend to Brooklyn. If something ever happens to me, I'm not asking you to take her by the hand. I'm asking you to lend her an ear if she needs one. I'm asking you to be there for her. Can I count on you to do that?"

AJ looked at her for a long, wordless moment. "I initially thought you were jerking my chain, but you're being serious right now," she said at length. "Are you in some kind of trouble?"

"If I were experiencing legal difficulties, chances are I wouldn't be here enjoying a leisurely lunch, followed by a fun-filled elevator ride with you."

"Fine. You don't have to tell me anything if you don't want to, but is there something Brooklyn should know?"

"You're Brooklyn's friend, not mine. I don't need you to worry about me. I don't even need you to like me. I just need you to do what I asked. Can I count on you? Yes or no?"

"Yes," AJ said, "you can count on me."

"Thank you."

When the elevator reached the ground floor, AJ followed her out.

"Before we join hands and start singing 'Kumbaya,' let's get one thing straight. I'll do what you asked me to do because I care about Brooklyn, but I want you to know that doesn't change anything between me and you."

"I didn't expect it to."

The hope went out of AJ's expression, leaving confusion behind. "You really don't give a shit whether people like you or not, do you?"

"As long as they respect me, their personal opinion of me is irrelevant."

"I finally see it."

"See what?"

"What Brooklyn sees in you. You're your own woman, I'll give you that. I just wish you were an honest one."

"Is everything okay here?"

Santana looked past AJ to see Luke Ridley striding across the lobby. His company's headquarters were on the other side of town. What the hell was he doing here?

"We're fine," AJ said. "This is Vilma Bautista, the woman Brooklyn's been seeing. We were having a...discussion."

"If you say so." Luke stuck out his hand. "I didn't know Brooklyn was seeing anyone. It's good to meet you, Vilma. Will you be joining AJ and me for lunch?"

"No," AJ said before Santana could respond. "She has someplace she needs to be. Give me a second to wrap up our conversation, and I'll meet you at the restaurant we agreed on, okay?"

"I'll go grab us a table," Luke said. "I'm looking forward to our chat."

"Are you planning on leaving BDV?" Santana asked after Luke headed outside with his cell phone plastered to his ear. "I thought you were happy here."

"I am," AJ said with a shrug, "but if someone is willing to make me an offer, the least I can do is listen."

Santana wondered if AJ's potential defection was the major announcement Luke had been teasing for the past few weeks. His money had obviously managed to get AJ's attention. When she returned from Reykjavik, she would have to take a hard look at what else he might have used his money to buy.

## Chapter Twenty-seven

Brooklyn loved spooning. It wasn't quite as much fun as sex but close. Thankfully, Vilma was great at it. Incredible, in fact. But that didn't come as a surprise. Vilma's only apparent fault was her decided lack of skills in the kitchen, but the flaw was not only endearing but humanizing. Brooklyn liked knowing someone who was so accomplished in the business world could suck so badly at something that came naturally to her.

She didn't get a chance to try the peanut butter and jelly sandwich Vilma had bragged about earlier because their hello kiss at the door when she'd arrived at Vilma's apartment that night had gotten so heated they had bypassed the kitchen and headed straight to the bedroom. Several hours later, Vilma put in a call for dinner. They would have to get dressed and answer the door when the delivery arrived, but Brooklyn wasn't in a rush to do so. She liked it just fine where she was.

"I have a confession to make," she said as she snuggled closer. Vilma's skin was warm and her body molded around Brooklyn's like they were made for each other.

"That's an ominous conversation starter. Perhaps you should have said something before I made you come four times."

"Three, but who's counting?"

Vilma brushed Brooklyn's hair aside and kissed the back of her neck. "We can go for four if you like. We have a little bit of time before the food arrives. I'll be quick, I promise."

Vilma began to burrow under the covers, but Brooklyn stopped her. "Later," she said, turning to face her. "There's something I want to say first."

"Of course." Vilma lay next to her. "What did you want to talk about?"

"I wanted to tell you the reason I've been so distant lately. The *real* reason."

"This afternoon, you said you've been busy at work."

"I was, but no more than usual."

"I don't understand."

"I know you don't now, but I'm hoping you will." Brooklyn could tell she wasn't the only one feeling vulnerable in that moment. She combed Vilma's tousled hair with her fingers. "A few weeks ago, you and I talked about taking our relationship to the next level. That sounded great at the time, then I started to realize exactly what that entailed."

"And?"

"And I freaked out a little bit. You're not close to your family and mine is…difficult, to say the least. I didn't want you to meet them and realize you'd made a huge mistake by getting involved with me."

"You thought I would walk away from this—from us—because I didn't like your family? It's customary for people to hate their in-laws, isn't it?"

"But it doesn't have to be. Knowing your past, I don't want to willingly put you through something like that in the future. I want you to love my family as much as I love them, and I want them to care about you as much as I do."

"And if neither of those things happens?"

"That's the possibility I've spent the last week trying not to consider. I want to be with you, but I don't want to force you into a situation you might not be comfortable with."

Vilma moved closer. "We promised to take things slowly, didn't we?" she asked once their heads were on the same pillow. "So let's take this the same way. Instead of meeting all of your family at once, which sounds like it could be a bit overwhelming for both of us, why don't I start with your parents?"

"Like have dinner or something?"

"No, that's too formal. It would feel more like an audition than a meal. What do they like to do for fun?"

"They have six kids. What do you think?"

"Besides that." Despite the serious conversation they were having, Vilma still managed to laugh. Surely that had to be a good sign.

"When my siblings and I were younger, my dad would take us fishing. We'd grab our poles and a bucket of bait and head to Prospect Park Lake in Brooklyn or, if we were feeling really adventurous, trek over to Central Park. My dad would grill whatever we caught for dinner and whoever snagged the biggest fish got to sit at the head of the table. My mother loved those trips because she had the house to herself all day and didn't have to cook that night."

"What happened? Why did you stop?"

"The usual. My siblings and I grew up. My sisters discovered boys, my brothers and I discovered girls, and none of us had time for anything other than the pursuit of same."

"Then that's what we'll do."

"Chase girls?"

"No, go fishing. I'll rent a cabin in the Catskills, arrange transportation for your parents, and make sure the refrigerator's stocked in case the fish aren't biting. We can drive up Friday afternoon and make a weekend out of it while we get to know each other better. How does that sound?"

"It sounds amazing."

"Great." Vilma grabbed her phone off the nightstand. "I'll text my travel agent and ask her to set it up."

"Later." Brooklyn pulled the phone out of Vilma's hands and tossed it aside. "First, I want to make you come for the third time."

Vilma's eyes slid shut as Brooklyn's mouth closed around her warm, wet center. "Fourth," she said with a contented sigh, "but who's counting?"

❖

Santana was nervous. The thought of taking on Jusuf Mladić and his personal army no longer kept her up at night, but the idea of spending time under the same roof as Brooklyn and her parents had her stomach tied up in knots. What had she been thinking when she suggested the idea? That's right. She hadn't been thinking at all. She had been acting on impulse. Something she had been trained not to do.

The rules she lived by, she had come to realize, didn't apply when it came to Brooklyn DiVincenzo. If they did, she would be going for a run in 'Ohe Sojukokoro right now instead of shopping for groceries in a tiny town with breathtaking views but spotty cell phone service.

The Catskill Mountains were less than a three-hour drive from New York City, but in most respects the two locales felt like they were a world apart. Gone was the hustle and bustle of crowded Manhattan. Towering mountains replaced the statuesque skyscrapers, and rustic cabins dotted the landscape instead of chic high-rises.

Santana loved the energy of New York City. The Catskills were known for picturesque hiking trails and ski resorts as well as the rich selection of wildlife located in the nearby forest preserve, which meant that for the next two days, she would have to settle for crickets as background noise instead of car horns.

"We won't be here very long," Brooklyn said as she navigated the grocery store's narrow aisles. "Two bottles of wine should be enough, don't you think?"

"You'd better toss in one more just in case." Because if the weekend went sideways, she might end up downing one bottle herself. "Do you think there's a liquor store around here?"

"Probably, but we don't need to drive around town looking for it. I have a bottle of Japanese whiskey in my suitcase."

"I think I love you."

"I bet you say that to all the girls."

"Just the ones who pack premium spirits in their overnight bags."

"I had to hedge my bets somehow. As much as I'm looking forward to this weekend, I don't expect it to be easy." Brooklyn carefully placed the additional bottle of wine in their shopping cart, then gave her a quick kiss. "Thank you for doing this."

"Hold that thought until the weekend's over. If it goes well, then you can thank me all you want."

"And if it doesn't?"

"One of us will have to come up with an appropriate punishment."

"When you put it that way, part of me hopes this weekend sucks."

"Have you already selected your preferred form of discipline?"

Brooklyn bit her lower lip. A move that was as beguiling as it was sexy. "I guess we'll find out in a couple of days, won't we?"

Santana followed Brooklyn to the produce section. She didn't know if this would turn out to be the best weekend of her life or the worst. There was no question, however, that it would definitely feel like the longest.

Brooklyn stood in front of a pile of lemons and began methodically squeezing each one as she tried to find the perfect specimen.

"Is it wrong of me to say you are seriously turning me on right now?" Santana asked.

Brooklyn held a lemon in each hand, subtly but intentionally drawing Santana's gaze to her breasts. "I was planning on squeezing these over the fish tonight, but perhaps I should save one for later."

"Or we could buy some of these instead." Santana reached past her and grabbed a couple of oranges. "Then we can have fresh-squeezed orange juice for breakfast. Or did you have something else in mind?"

Brooklyn did that sexy lip-biting thing again. "I'll never tell."

"Do we have everything we need?"

Brooklyn took a quick look at the contents of their cart. "I think so. Why?"

"The driver should be here in about an hour. That gives us just enough time to unpack the groceries, call dibs on the best room, and christen the bed before your parents arrive."

Brooklyn tossed the lemons in the cart without seeming to care where they landed. "Like I said, I like the way you think."

## CHAPTER TWENTY-EIGHT

The cabin Vilma had rented was located near the base of Slide Mountain, the highest point in the Catskills. A two-mile hiking trail meandered through the woods outside and a huge lake was located less than fifty feet away. Brooklyn could already picture herself sitting by the water with a cup of coffee in her hands as she watched the sun rise the following morning.

The front part of the cabin was open concept, allowing inhabitants to easily carry on a conversation while they watched TV in the living room or prepared a meal on the gas stove in the kitchen. The stainless steel grill on the back deck was also gas-powered, adding to the cabin's rustic feel. There was nothing rustic about the two bedrooms, however. Each featured king-sized beds, ample storage space, private bathrooms, and unobstructed views of the lake. Plus they were located far enough apart that privacy shouldn't be an issue.

"You've got to give me your travel agent's contact information," Brooklyn said. "If she can set up something like this on the spur of the moment, I'd love to see what she's capable of when she has more time to prepare."

She pulled her damp hair into a ponytail. She and Vilma had taken a shower together after they finished making love, but their leisurely pace hadn't left her enough time to dry her hair before her parents' expected arrival.

Her heart skipped a beat when she heard a car's tires crunch on the gravel in the driveway outside. She peered through the blinds on the front window and spotted her parents climbing out of a black luxury sedan.

"Are you ready for this?" she asked as Vilma joined her by the window.

"No, but let's do it anyway."

"Are you always this fearless?"

"No, I just bluff really well."

"Remind me never to play poker with you."

She took Vilma's hand in hers so they could present a united front when they opened the door. Outside, her parents were arguing over whether they should tip the driver.

"Didn't you hear him?" her father asked. "You were standing right next to me when he told us the fare and incidentals are already paid for."

"I don't care what he said." Her mother gave her father a not-so-gentle nudge with her elbow. "Give him a little something anyway."

As her father reluctantly reached for his wallet, Brooklyn tried to hide her mortification. The weekend could only get better from here, she told herself, because it certainly couldn't get much worse.

The driver took her parents' bags from the trunk and, using Vilma's directions, carried them into the house.

"How was your drive?" Brooklyn asked after she gave each of her parents a hug.

"Fantastic," her mother said. "He was really good to us. That's why I told Sal to slip him a little something to show how much we appreciated his efforts." She perked up when the driver emerged from the cabin. "Good-bye, Tim. Have a nice drive back to the city."

"Thank you, ma'am. Enjoy your weekend."

"Oh, I'm sure we will."

"I think your mother has a bit of a crush," Vilma whispered.

"You think?" Brooklyn whispered back. "My dad used to be the jealous type when he was younger, but he's gotten much more laid-back over the years. At this point, my mom's constant flirting with cab drivers, airport security guards, or practically any man in uniform is more of a source of amusement than a point of contention."

"What's her pet peeve about him?"

Brooklyn thought for a moment. Her parents bickered over many things, but only one subject truly got her mother riled up. "Even though he knows it's against every rule of style, both written and understood, he insists on wearing black socks with his sandals whenever he goes to the beach."

"That's an image I won't be able to shake any time soon."

"Try therapy. It's worked wonders for me."

Tim tipped his cap. "Ladies. Sir. I'll be back Sunday afternoon at four."

"Sounds good, Tim." Brooklyn's father motioned toward the pocket where Tim had stashed the ten-dollar tip he had given him a few minutes earlier. "Don't spend all that in one place now."

"I'll try not to, sir."

Tim climbed into the car. When he turned the key in the ignition, Vilma looked like she was tempted to hitch a ride with him. Brooklyn couldn't blame her. She had told her parents to be themselves this weekend, but she hadn't expected them to take her quite so literally.

As the four of them watched Tim drive off, Brooklyn's mother glanced from Brooklyn to Vilma and back again. "Are you going to introduce us to your friend, or are you going to make us do it ourselves?"

"Mom, Pop, I'd like you to meet Vilma Bautista. Vilma, Salvatore and Concetta DiVincenzo."

"Call me Connie."

"And I'm Sal."

Vilma stepped forward and shook both their hands. "It's a pleasure to meet you both. Brooklyn and I are so glad you could join us. Would you like us to show you around?"

"All you have to do is tell me where to find the bathroom and the kitchen," Brooklyn's father said before he turned and pointed to the lake. "Because I can tell you now I'll be spending the rest of my time right over there."

"He's been as excited as a kid in a candy store ever since you suggested this trip, Brooklyn."

"I wish I could take the credit, but this weekend was Vilma's idea."

"Was it now? That was sweet of you, Vilma." Brooklyn's mother seemed suitably impressed as she gave Brooklyn's father another shot to the ribs. "Why can't you be spontaneous sometime, Sal?"

"I gave up on trying to surprise you a long time ago."

"That's true. He can't keep a secret to save his life. I always told him if he ever decided to have an affair, I would know about it before he did."

"It doesn't pay to stray. That's always been my motto. Actually, the people who stray usually end up paying through the nose, but that's neither here nor there." Brooklyn's father grabbed one of the fishing rods leaning against the side of the cabin and gave it a quick once-over. "Fluorocarbon lines rather than monofilament. Nice. Fluorocarbon lines are harder and thinner than monofilament ones, yet they have the same breaking strength."

"You sound like the host of a wildlife show," Brooklyn's mother said.

"I just know quality when I see it. Do you have any cold beers running around here, Vilma?"

"Yes, sir. Brooklyn made sure to stock the refrigerator with your favorite brand."

"Then what are you waiting for, kid? Pack a cooler, grab a pole, and let's go fishing."

"Now?" Brooklyn's mother asked. "I was hoping the four of us could sit down and have a nice chat."

"You and I have been sitting for almost three hours and the four of us have all weekend to talk. Besides, if you want to have fresh fish for dinner tonight instead of the store-bought kind, Vilma and I need to catch it first."

"You two have fun getting your hooks wet. Brooklyn and I will have just as good a time wetting our whistles instead. You did remember to buy wine, didn't you, honey?"

"Of course. I figured you'd disown me if I didn't."

"I knew I raised you right. Now how about that tour you promised me? I need to visit the powder room. I'm sure your dad does, too, since he can't make it for more than a few hours without having to pee. I'm surprised he didn't ask Tim to stop at every gas station we passed during our drive up here. I swear he's worse than the grandkids sometimes."

Brooklyn jumped in before her mother could steer the conversation into even more of a scatological direction. "Follow me."

She led her mother inside and showed her around the cabin. While her parents took a quick bathroom break before they began their respective adventures, she joined Vilma in the kitchen.

"Do you think they're separating us on purpose?" Vilma asked as she packed six cans of beer and half a bag of ice into a Styrofoam cooler they had picked up at the grocery store.

"The phrase 'divide and conquer' does come to mind." After several minutes of searching, Brooklyn finally located a corkscrew and opened a bottle of red wine. "Good luck," she said as she poured two glasses. "Because I have a feeling the fish you and my dad are hoping to catch won't be the only things that get grilled tonight."

Santana watched the bright yellow fishing line drift across the crystal clear water. She kept her thumb on the reel so she could feel the vibration if a fish decided to take the bait. She was starting to wonder if the worms the guy at the bait shop had sold her were defective. She and Mr. DiVincenzo had been fishing for almost half an hour and had yet to get so much as a nibble. At least the beer was cold and the conversation sparse. She was finally discovering what the phrase "comfortable silence" was all about.

"Careful," he said as he set his beer in the cup holder built into his collapsible fishing chair. He had brought it, his lucky fishing hat, and a pair of rubber waders with him. "If the current takes your line too close to that downed tree over there, your hook might get caught up in the roots. You weren't planning on going swimming today, were you? Even in the middle of summer, lake water's cold enough to make your ass pucker."

"Good to know. Thank you, sir." Santana dutifully reeled in her line and cast it out again. She liked the whir the reel made as it spun on its axis.

Mr. DiVincenzo looked exactly as she had imagined him. Tall and handsome with thick, dark hair liberally streaked with gray. His beefy arms were corded with muscle, and his round belly and hearty laugh indicated his appetite for food was equal to his appetite for life. She had just met him and she already liked him. Brooklyn's mother, too. Brooklyn looked so much like both of them there was no mistaking her parentage. Santana could tell where Brooklyn got her striking good looks as well as her often biting sense of humor.

The jury was still out on whether Brooklyn's parents were as fond of her as she was of them. She expected to hear the verdict by the time they parted ways on Sunday. When it came down, she hoped it would be in her favor.

"We're all adults here," Mr. DiVincenzo said. "You don't have to keep calling me 'sir' or 'Mr. DiVincenzo.' I'm just Sal, okay?"

She recalled having a similar conversation with Harry. It felt weird taking part in it from the opposite perspective.

"Sorry, sir, but I can't do that. Where I was raised, it's disrespectful to call someone who's older than you are by their first name unless you call them Uncle or Auntie at the same time."

He chuckled. "It would feel weird for you to call me Uncle when I might end up being your father-in-law one day, wouldn't it?"

"Yes, sir, I guess it would."

"So bite the bullet and call me Sal, okay?"

"I'll do my best."

"That's all we can do." He tilted his floppy hat, which was so threadbare in spots she could practically see through it. "Brooklyn says you're originally from the Philippines. Is that true?"

"Yes, I was born in Manila."

"Her grandfather on her mother's side was stationed in the Philippines during World War II. He said it was a beautiful country when enemy soldiers weren't shooting at him. He always longed to go back but never made it. Is it as nice there as he made it out to be?"

"It depends on where you go. Parts of the country are so beautiful there are no words to describe them. Other parts of it leave you speechless, too, but for much different reasons."

"That's the case just about everywhere you go, isn't it? You seem to be doing okay for yourself now, though. What is it you do again?"

"I'm a venture capitalist."

"Like that Elton Musk guy?"

"Elon."

"Yeah, him."

"I don't have nearly as many controversies swirling around me as he does, but we perform the same functions, yes."

"You must make a decent living then."

"To put it mildly, yes."

"Good. Brooklyn's fortunate enough that she doesn't need anyone to provide for her, but I don't want her to get stuck with someone who can't provide for herself. She's sweet, but she doesn't need to be anyone's sugar mama."

"Definitely not an issue in our case."

"I'm happy to hear that."

"What do you do?"

"I'm in construction. I used to pound a jackhammer for a living. That's how I got these huge guns of mine." He patted one of his massive forearms before he stopped and rubbed his belly. "But I'm a foreman now so that's how I got this. I spend my days telling the younger guys which concrete to break up rather than doing it myself. It's not rocket science, but it's an honest living, and it's helped me keep a roof over my family's heads so I can't complain about it. Hey, let me see your hands."

Confused, Santana set her rod down and held out her hands, palms up. Instead of reading her future, Sal read her past.

"You might be living in a penthouse now," he said, "but I can see you know a thing or two about hard work. Brooklyn said you had it rough coming up. Don't look so surprised. She and her mother tell each other everything. Connie likes to tease me about not being able to keep a secret, but she can't keep anything under her hat either.

So if you've got something you don't want the rest of the world to know about, you'd best keep it to yourself."

His comment made her question if she could be as forthcoming with Brooklyn as she planned to be. "I'll keep that in mind, thanks."

❖

Brooklyn sipped her wine as she and her mother sat on the back deck and pretended not to be watching what was going on by the lake.

"How do you think they're doing out there?" her mother asked.

"I haven't seen them catch anything yet, which means we'll get to hear one story after another about the one that got away."

"I wasn't talking about the fishing. I was talking about the two of them. How do you think they're getting along?"

Brooklyn took a long look at Vilma and her father, but their body language didn't give anything away. Her father sat slouched in his chair like he was ready for a nap and Vilma sat ramrod straight as if she were ready to snap to attention. Standard behavior for both of them. Her father was so relaxed she often wondered if he even had a pulse, and there was a coiled intensity about Vilma that never seemed to dissipate, no matter if she was on the move or, like now, sitting perfectly still.

"I can't tell. Can you?"

Her mother flashed an indulgent smile. "He likes her. If he didn't, he and I would be on our way back to Queens by now. Remember when you were nine and you invited one of your classmates to the house for a sleepover?"

"Are you talking about Gillian?"

"Yeah, that was her name."

"When she asked me to partner up with her in our science class, I thought that meant she liked me. It turned out she was just trying to suck up to me because she thought I could help her get an easy A without having to put in the work."

"Sal saw through her act right away. He made the poor girl so miserable she was ready to go home even before we'd sat down for dinner."

"God, I was so upset that night. I remember telling him I hated him and locking myself in my room after Gillian's parents came to pick her up. Did I ever apologize to him?"

"You didn't have to because he knew you didn't mean what you said." Her mother rested a hand on her arm. "No matter how old you get, he's always going to look out for you. We both are. That's the reason you invited us up here this weekend, isn't it?"

"I wanted you to meet Vilma."

"Yes, because you wanted us to give you our blessing."

"Do I have it?"

"I like what I see." Her mother held up a cautionary finger. "So far. Ask me again when I have less of a buzz. As the kids say, this wine is on freak."

Brooklyn couldn't help but laugh at her mother's valiant attempt to be hip. "I love you, Mom. Don't ever change."

"If I did, how would you and the rest of the family be able to recognize me? Oops, we've got action."

Brooklyn returned her attention to the lake, where Vilma was out of her chair and running toward the water. "What is she doing?"

"I think she lost her fishing pole."

After Brooklyn lowered her gaze, she spotted Vilma's fishing rod snaking across the ground. The reel was spinning crazily as the rod made a beeline for the water. Vilma obviously had a fish on the line. Instead of taking the hook and a few inches of broken line, the creature seemed determined to take the rod and reel, too.

Vilma dove for the rod just as the tip of it disappeared into the water. She scrambled to her feet soaking wet but reel in hand.

"That's it, kid," Brooklyn heard her father say. "Now reel him in."

Vilma braced the end of the rod against her thigh as she cranked the reel for all she was worth. The returning line thrummed against the water as the slack slowly disappeared. The rod bent at a precarious angle when the line became taut.

Brooklyn and her mother rose to their feet as they continued to watch the spectacle play out.

"Oh, she's got a big one," her mother said.

Brooklyn knew better than to judge a fish's size by how much of a fight it put up before giving in. Some fish she had caught had felt like whales when she had them on the line only to turn out to be minnows once she pulled them out of the water.

She pulled her mother back when she tried to move closer. "Let's stay here until she reels it in. Pop's superstitious. If the fish breaks the line after we show up, he'll blame us for ruining his luck."

"He's the same way whenever one of his favorite teams is playing. If someone leaves the room before the team goes on a hot streak, they aren't allowed to come back until the team starts messing up again."

"It used to drive Stefano mad when he'd get up for snacks and wouldn't be able to reclaim his seat until halftime. No wonder he spends so much of his time in the basement. He's probably waiting for some team's hot streak to end."

"In a sense, we're all waiting for something."

As she watched Vilma and her father share high fives over the huge fish Vilma had caught, Brooklyn had a feeling her wait might have come to an end.

Santana raised the largemouth bass over her head to acknowledge Brooklyn and Connie cheering her on from their perch on the back deck.

"That's a nice one, kid," Sal said as she carefully took the hook out of the fish's mouth and placed her catch in a lidded basket. "A ten-pounder, at least. One more like that and we'll be set for tonight *and* tomorrow. Your technique needs some work," he added, pointing at the dirt and leaves clinging to her wet clothes, "but I can't argue with the results."

"I'll let you catch the next one," she said as she handed him another beer.

"Sure thing. Just don't expect me to do a belly flop, too. I'm liable to displace a whole lot more water than you did. You should come to dinner next Sunday. You could use a big plate of Connie's manicotti."

"I'm looking forward to it already."

He gave her a pat on the back and she was surprised by how good it felt. Not only to be acknowledged but to be accepted as well. The good vibes didn't last long, though, because what he said next made her tense up all over again.

"I've heard you don't have a relationship with your father. I'm sorry to hear that. I truly am."

She waited to hear what point he was trying to make before she allowed herself to react.

"Connie and I live in a close-knit neighborhood. Brooklyn's friends have always felt like my kids, too. I know you and I don't know each other very well. Hell, we barely know each other at all. But if it's all right with you, I'd like to add you to the list. If you need someone to shoot the breeze with while we drink a few beers and dip some worms in the water, I'm your guy. Unless you break Brooklyn's heart. Then I'll be obligated to respond by breaking every bone in your body."

"I wouldn't expect anything less."

"I'm glad we understand each other. Don't expect me to give you an official welcome to the family, though. That's Connie's job. I'm the first line of defense. She's a much more difficult obstacle to overcome."

"Do you have any words of wisdom for me?"

"Just three." He crooked his finger at her, beckoning her closer. She leaned toward him, anxious to hear what he was about to impart. "Don't fuck up."

## Chapter Twenty-nine

That wasn't such a bad first day," Brooklyn said as she and Vilma sipped glasses of whiskey on the front porch after dinner. "You and my dad did a great job grilling the fish."

"I didn't have to do much. I just had to pass him the appropriate tool when he asked for it and hold the serving tray when he was done."

"Both very important jobs." She tapped her glass against Vilma's. "To the sexiest sous chef ever."

Vilma set the swing they were sitting in into motion as they watched the moonlight shining on the still water. She started when she heard a twig snap under the weight of something heavy. "Remind me to call my travel agent. She said we were supposed to be alone up here."

"Relax," Brooklyn said. "It's probably just a squirrel searching for a lost nut."

"Or a bear looking to make a meal out of one of us."

"Bears usually hang out close to the campsites because that's where most of the free food's found. Cabin owners are usually a lot better about policing their trash cans."

"You've been up here before?"

"The first summer camp I ever attended was held a few miles from here. The first few days, I didn't want to be there. By the time camp ended, I didn't want to leave."

"I've never done anything like this before."

Brooklyn often forgot how different Vilma's backstory was from hers. "You've never gone camping or swum in a lake?"

"I used to sleep outside every night when I didn't have a place to call home. As for swimming in a lake, this afternoon is as close as I want to get for a while. Your father was right. The water *is* cold enough to make your ass pucker."

"Oh, my God, he said that? Sometimes, I think he doesn't realize words are coming out of his mouth rather than rattling around inside his head."

"At least you always know where you stand with him. Kind of like you. Now I know where you inherited the trait."

"I'm trying to get better at hiding my feelings."

"Don't," Vilma said earnestly. "I like the fact that you're an open book."

"Being easy to read works in my personal life. Not so much in my professional one. I often have to be diplomatic with my employees, and sometimes I have to flat out lie to my competitors. That's hard to do when my true thoughts are written all over my face."

"But your vivid expressions make making love with you even more of a rush."

Brooklyn buried her face in her hands. "You make me sound like an adult film actress. A bad one, at that."

"Speaking of a porn movie, are you hearing what I'm hearing?"

At first, Brooklyn didn't hear anything other than a group of bullfrogs reciting the lines from an old beer commercial. Then she heard the distinctive sounds of a couple having sex. Not just any couple. Her parents.

"I guess they weren't as tired as they said they were," Vilma said. "There must be something in the air up here."

Brooklyn didn't want to be reminded that, a few hours earlier, she and Vilma had spent some serious quality time doing exactly what her parents were doing now. She felt like crawling under one of the rocks the croaking bullfrogs were perched on. She was living proof that her parents had always had a healthy sex life, but this was the first time she'd been an earwitness to it.

"Look on the bright side," Vilma said.

"Is there one?" she asked as the intimate act they were listening to seemed to approach its anxiously awaited conclusion. "Because from where I'm sitting, the light at the end of the tunnel is a locomotive bearing down on me."

"An unfortunate analogy, given our current circumstances, don't you think?"

Brooklyn groaned as the phallic imagery of what she had described hit home. "Just give me something positive I can glean from all this."

"When we sit down for breakfast in the morning and you ask your parents if they enjoyed themselves tonight, you'll know they won't be lying when they respond in the affirmative." Vilma ducked away from Brooklyn's attempt to punch her in the arm. "Too soon?"

"Much too soon. Now shut up and pass the whiskey." She started giggling when she finally began to view the situation as humorous rather than cringe-inducing. "And slip my parents a couple of cigarettes while you're at it."

"Given the audio evidence, I think they deserve a whole pack."

Brooklyn wiped her streaming eyes as her laughter continued unabated. "I'm not going to be able to look either one of them in the eye tomorrow without turning several shades of red. Are we supposed to sit across from them and pretend we don't know they were hooking up tonight?"

"You said you wanted to work on your poker face. This seems like the perfect opportunity for you to do just that."

Brooklyn took a deep breath and slowly released it. "You know what? If this is the worst thing that happens this weekend, I'll take it."

"Thank you for finally lightening up. Life is only as serious as you make it out to be."

Brooklyn rested her head in Vilma's lap as the swing continued to slowly sway back and forth. She wished she could bottle this moment and save it for when she was having a bad day because she had never felt luckier—or more loved.

❖

Santana woke early and decided to go for a run. She slipped out of bed without rousing Brooklyn and changed from her pajamas into her workout gear. She was trying to find the right mix of songs to play during her run when she heard someone raising a racket in the kitchen. She kissed Brooklyn on the cheek and closed the door behind her as she headed out of the room to investigate.

"Do you need some help?"

"Yes, please," Connie said with an exasperated sigh. "I'm dying for a cup of coffee, but I can't figure out how to make this machine work. My coffeemaker at home is a lot simpler than this. I fill it with water, spoon some grounds into the filter, and wait for the carafe to fill. I don't even know where to start with this thing."

"No worries. I've got you covered. First of all, what flavor would you like?"

"I get a choice?"

Santana tried not to smile as she opened one of the cabinets to reveal a selection of coffee pods designed to fit the single-serve coffeemaker. "Just pretend you're at Starbucks."

"Oh, I don't want to do that. Then I'll have to make up a name to give the barista and add in all sorts of fancy extras I really don't want."

Santana reached for one of the small plastic pods. "Basic black, it is. Let me show you how this works. First you place the pod in here and close the lid."

"Uh-huh. I'm with you so far."

"Then you fill the chamber with water and select your preferred serving size. Would you like a small cup or an extra large one?"

"Small's fine. I slept really well last night for some reason. It must be the mountain air."

"I told Brooklyn the same thing."

"Great minds think alike. Sal might need the extra caffeine, though. He's never been much of an early riser. He and Brooklyn could sleep all day if you let them."

"So I've noticed." Santana punched the appropriate buttons and waited for the coffee to brew. "Here you go."

"Bless you." Connie took the cup and blew on the steaming beverage before she took a tentative sip. "Perfect. Aren't you having any?"

"Actually, I was about to go for a run on one of the trails."

"I was planning on exploring those today. If you don't mind waiting or moving at a slower pace, I'd love to go with you."

Santana had been looking forward to having some time to herself, but she didn't know how to refuse Connie's invitation without being rude. "Sure. That sounds great." She pulled out a chair and waited for Connie to claim it before she sat across from her. "How is your room? Did you and Sal have any problems getting to sleep?"

"Oh, gosh, no. We didn't realize how much the drive took out of us until we finished dinner. Both of us slept like rocks. We fell asleep as soon as our heads hit the pillow. Did you and Brooklyn rest well?"

Santana fought to maintain her composure. "She was startled by a few things she heard, but once she got to sleep, she slept like a log."

"That's always been the case with her. The rest of my kids, they'd fall asleep as soon as they closed their eyes. Brooklyn would fight it as hard as she could. It was like she was afraid she'd miss something."

"What was she like as a child?"

"Just like she is now: funny, curious, and way too smart for her own good. I swear I don't know where she gets her brains from. Sal and I both did okay when we were in school, but if you add our IQs together, I doubt they'd equal hers. Don't get me wrong. I'm proud of all of my kids. Each one has something different to offer. But Brooklyn is something special. I realized that the moment I held her in my arms the first time. When she looked at me, there was such awareness in her eyes. Like she already knew who she was and what she wanted to do with her life. I hope she feels that kind of connection one day. She's always said she's too much of a kid to have one of her own, but she has time to change her mind. Would you like to be a mother someday?"

"It's not something I've ever considered, no."

"Why not?"

"I don't have nurturing instincts."

"I beg to differ."

"Do you know something I don't?"

"I know you made Brooklyn feel safe when no one else could."

Santana felt a pang of guilt at the unintentional reminder that she might have been the one who had exposed Brooklyn to danger in the first place. She couldn't take credit for helping Brooklyn deal with a situation she might have helped bring about. "I didn't do anything special."

"No, you didn't. You did something extraordinary. You did far more than you're willing to admit. I appreciate your modesty, but I appreciate your actions even more. Charlie was Brooklyn's best friend. I don't know where she'd be right now if you hadn't stepped in to help her deal with the loss."

"How are Charlie's parents coping?"

"It's been understandably hard on both of them. Pete's okay, but Gail's still struggling. Charlie was their only child. In a way, she was their miracle baby. Gail had her later in life. When she was forty, she thought she was experiencing early menopause. Her doctor was even more surprised than she was when he saw the results of the ultrasound."

Santana examined the grain in the wood tabletop because she couldn't bring herself to look Connie in the eye. "I wish I could have met Charlie."

"She was a firecracker, that's for sure."

"So I've heard. No wonder Brooklyn misses her so much."

"Yes," Connie said with a heavy sigh, "but, like it or not, life goes on. Are you ready for that walk?"

"Ready when you are."

"Give me a few minutes to change and we can head out." Connie placed her empty mug in the sink but didn't leave the room. Instead, she returned to the table and cupped Santana's face in her hands. "You have such kind eyes. That's the first thing I noticed when I met you yesterday. And I don't care what you say. You would make an excellent mother someday. You know why? Because you have a lot of love to give. Thank you for choosing to share it with my daughter."

Santana's eyes filled with tears. The feelings she had always held at bay threatened to overwhelm her.

Brooklyn shuffled into the kitchen, rubbing her eyes and barely awake. "I smelled coffee," she said in a voice thick with sleep. "Did I miss something? Vilma, why are you crying? What's wrong?"

"Just a little girl talk. Nothing that concerns you." Connie discreetly slipped Santana a napkin so she could dry her eyes and blow her nose. "Come be my guinea pig," she said as she steered Brooklyn away from the table. "Vilma showed me how to use the coffeemaker, and I'm anxious to try it out. What kind of coffee would you like, the one I can't pronounce or the one I can't spell?"

Santana excused herself before she broke down again. She felt like a fraud. With the right disguise, the proper paperwork, and a few plausible lies thrown in, she could be anyone she wanted. But no amount of prosthetics could turn her into the person she truly wanted to be: the woman who deserved Brooklyn's heart.

She wanted to be with Brooklyn. She wanted to give her the kind of life they both dreamed about. But she couldn't. Not until she left her old life behind. Maybe then she could start fresh. Maybe then she could be the woman Connie had claimed to see when she had looked into her eyes.

Brooklyn was shaken by what she had witnessed in the kitchen. She had never seen Vilma cry. Not even when they had watched a tearjerker Brooklyn could never manage to get through without emptying half a box of Kleenex in the process.

Neither Vilma nor her mother would tell her what had caused the scene. Now they were off wandering the woods together like they were besties. She didn't know whether to feel happy that they seemed to be getting along so well or jealous because they were bonding without her.

"You've never been a micromanager before. Don't start now."

She pulled on jeans, sneakers, and a comfy sweatshirt, then grabbed a rod and headed to the lake. "Morning, Pop," she said, briefly resting a hand on his shoulder. "Mind if I join you?"

"That depends."

"On?"

"Whether you're here to talk or whether you're here to fish. Fishing's free. Talking will cost you."

"Free works for me."

"Good choice."

Brooklyn sat in the chair next to him and took a peek in the fishing basket. Three largemouth bass of varying sizes flopped inside. "Are you planning on taking those back to Gianni and Angie?"

"If they want fish, they know where the store is. Those are heading to my freezer. The bait's in the bucket. Grab a couple of worms and see if you remember how this works. Where's my sidekick this morning?"

She waited until she had completed her task to answer his question so she wouldn't end up sticking the rusty hook through her finger. She didn't want to spend the penultimate day of her weekend getting a tetanus shot in the local ER. "She and Mom went for a walk."

"I hope Vilma has a better sense of direction than Connie does. Otherwise, they'll never find their way back."

Brooklyn flicked her wrist and tossed her line in the water. Then she reeled it in a few feet, hoping the subtle movement would capture a fish's attention. She tightened her grip when she felt a gentle tug on the hook.

"Careful," her father said. "You don't want to spook him."

She relaxed her fingers. "I thought you weren't in the mood to talk."

"I'm not in the mood for *you* to talk. I never said anything about me."

Her father teased all his kids, but he had always seemed to save his best jibes for her. Probably because they shared the same sense of humor—dark, biting, and just this side of sarcastic.

"Are you having fun?" he asked.

"This weekend has been a blast."

"I wasn't asking about this weekend. I was asking about Vilma. Are you serious about her or are you just having fun?"

Her line jerked suddenly. She reeled it in to see what she had caught. "Not bad, huh?" she asked, holding up a five-pound bass.

"She's a keeper, that one. And I'm not talking about the fish."

She followed his line of sight. Across the lake, her mother and Vilma were tossing pieces of bread to a family of ducks. Vilma must have said something her mother found hilarious because her laughter carried clear across the water. Even from a distance, Brooklyn could see the broad smile on Vilma's face. Seeing two women who meant so much to her getting along so well made her heart swell.

"You did good, honey," her father said.

"I think so, too, Pop. I think so, too."

## CHAPTER THIRTY

For Santana, the trip to the Catskills was the best and the worst thing that had ever happened to her. The idyllic weekend had given her a glimpse of everything she had to gain, but it had also showed her how much she had to lose.

She imagined spending holidays and special occasions with Brooklyn and her raucous family. She imagined the two of them starting a family of their own. Not the kind of thoughts she should be having when she was preparing to carry out an assignment, but for the past few weeks, she hadn't been able to think about anything else.

She had been in Reykjavik for two days now. Just enough time for her to settle in and reacclimatize to her surroundings without overstaying her welcome. Jusuf Mladić's party was scheduled for tonight. Tomorrow morning, she would be on a plane back to New York City. When she landed, she planned to take Brooklyn to Little Manila so they could have dinner in the restaurant they had visited the night they'd had sex for the first time. They would share a big platter of food, then they'd each have two—no, three— scoops of dirty ice cream for dessert. Afterward, they would go to her apartment, where she would present Brooklyn with a key and ask her to move in with her. The key would be symbolic since she would probably be forced to vacate her current apartment when her relationship with Winslow officially ended. The request wouldn't amount to a marriage proposal, but it would mark the first step on her and Brooklyn's path to the future. A shared future.

She had it all planned. The only mystery that remained was what the topic of conversation would be before and after they made love that night.

She was dragging her feet on telling Brooklyn the complete truth about herself. If she was honest from this point forward, why should it matter what she had lied about in the past? Because in a few hours, that part of her life would be over. In a few hours, it wouldn't matter who she used to be. What mattered was who she would be tomorrow and all the days that followed. Because in a few hours, she would be free.

Two hours before the party was supposed to start, she headed to the Midnight Sun so she could pick up her uniform and sit through the mandatory training session. Aron Einarsson, the restaurant's owner, looked more like a conductor than a chef as he put the kitchen and wait staffs through their paces. When he wasn't waving his arms back and forth like Leonard Bernstein, he was up to his elbows in a big pot of something gelatinous that was probably a delicacy but she wasn't very eager to try.

"Who are you, and what are you doing in my kitchen?" he asked when he spotted her standing in the doorway.

"I'm Delphine Durand. Sigrun recommended me."

"Oh, yes. I didn't recognize you without the crazy hair."

After she had submitted her job application, he had set up a Skype call so he could conduct a face-to-face interview. The questions he had asked had been relatively routine so she hadn't been forced to think too hard to come up with the answers. He had seemed more interested in her appearance than her ability to balance trays of watered-down drinks anyway. "I want people who can do the job without drawing attention to themselves," he had said. She had promised to switch to a more conservative hairstyle and, just as Sigrun had promised, the job was hers.

Today, she had ditched the spiky platinum blond wig she usually wore when she was Delphine in favor of a reddish-brown one that had been shaped into a stylish bob.

"Better," Aron said.

"What would you like me to do?"

"Look for a small woman carrying a big clipboard. That's Margret. She'll give you your job assignment and direct you where to get changed. Now get out of here. This sheep's head jelly is refusing to set and I'm running out of time to get it right."

His description of Margret turned out to be an accurate one. She was decidedly small in stature—barely five feet tall, if that—and the checklist in her hands seemed a mile long. She was just as busy as Aron but seemed far less harried. Santana wouldn't have been surprised to discover she had a military background because she was straight to the point and worked with uncanny efficiency.

"Delphine?" Margret skimmed through a list of names and drew a line through one. "Nine down, one to go. If Alexander doesn't show, you'll be doing double-duty. Right now, I've got you on canapés. Can you handle cocktails, too?"

"I can do whatever you need me to do." Especially if it afforded her a chance to sneak into Mladić's bathroom. She would need less than five minutes to make the switch, but five minutes was an eternity when there were a slew of armed guards around.

"Your uniform's right over there. It's yours to keep whether this turns out to be your first job with us or your last. The price will be deducted from your pay."

"Speaking of pay, do I get that now or later?" Santana didn't care about the pittance she would make for working the event—an amount that would be even smaller after the price of her uniform was deducted from it—but Delphine lived from paycheck to paycheck and she had to be true to the character she was playing.

Margret must have been used to fielding such questions. Her cool, professional demeanor never wavered, even though she probably found the question annoying as well as ridiculous. Santana admired her ability to remain calm under pressure.

"We can't have you walking out halfway through the party," Margret said. "The promise of a paycheck should provide you the proper incentive to stay. Now, I selected the sizes you provided, but make sure the clothes fit. Before you do that, though, help the rest of the team get the prepped food packed and loaded in the van. We'll be leaving in thirty minutes to transfer everything from our kitchen to the client's. While Aron completes his final preparations, I will accompany you and the rest of the wait staff on a walkthrough of the property. It's a private home so certain areas are understandably off-limits. The head of our client's security team will let us know what those are."

"Are there any other rules I need to be aware of?"

"Just two. The food and drinks are for the guests, not the staff, so don't even think of helping yourself to any free samples. And no cameras, telephones, or recording devices of any kind will be allowed inside the house. You will be searched when you arrive to make sure you comply with the request so if you have any of those things on you, leave them here. There's a locker in the changing room. You can store your belongings there for the time being and collect them after your shift ends."

"Can I leave them in one of the vans? You have two, don't you? One for the food and one for the staff?"

If she had to make a hasty retreat, she didn't want to be forced to make any pit stops along the way. She also didn't want to leave any belongings behind. When the job was over, she planned to burn all her identities one by one.

She had been pretending to be other people for so long she had almost forgotten how to be herself. She knew there would be some missteps along the way, but she was looking forward to embarking on the journey.

"The vehicles are less secure than the restaurant," Margret said. "Many people will have access to them, and the management team, myself included, will be far too busy to keep an eye on what's inside. Mr. Magnusson is a stern taskmaster. The staff's primary duty will be making sure the event goes well, not guarding the parking lot."

"As you said, there'll be a security team onsite."

"And they will be focused on the goings-on inside the house, not out."

"Even so, I'll take my chances."

"As you wish. I hope I've answered all your questions. If not, I'm sure another member of the wait staff will be able to. Right now, I have another matter that demands my attention. Good luck."

"Thanks," she said after Margret left to take care of the next item on her list. "I think I'll need it."

She had anticipated being searched so she had made contingency plans for that. The pills she planned to use to poison Mladić were hidden in a secret compartment in her travel mug rather than on her. She had hoped that, after the security team cleared them, the wait staff would have free rein of the house as they wandered around serving guests. If you couldn't trust someone carrying a tray of toast points smeared with sheep's head jelly, who could you trust?

As she helped load the delivery van, she tried to figure out how she was supposed to switch out Mladić's erectile dysfunction medication if, as she expected, his living quarters had a virtual Keep Out sign posted on them. Nothing like a last-minute wrinkle to keep her on her toes. She would find a way somehow. She always did.

One of the other cater-waiters introduced himself. "I'm Matthias." He had bright red hair and a beard to match. His long hair was pulled back into a man bun and his luxurious beard nearly touched his chest. So much for blending in rather than standing out.

"Delphine. It's nice to meet you."

"You, too," he said before he went back to loading boxes. "Is this your first time doing one of these parties?"

"For this guy, yes. What about you?"

"This is my third. Magnusson's a bit of a dick and his friends are, too, so don't expect any tips. A pinch on the ass, maybe, but no tips."

"Then why do you do it? The pay's not that great, is it?"

"No, but every little bit helps. Just between you and me, I exact a bit of revenge when I can." He looked around to make sure no one was listening in on their conversation. "For the guests that go too far, I serve them a side order of DNA with their fancy food and drinks. They're so caught up in themselves they don't even notice, but I do, and it's freaking awesome. Try it if you get a chance. You won't believe how good it feels."

She told him she'd give it a shot if someone crossed the line, but she had no intention of doing so. In her profession, leaving DNA at a crime scene was something to be avoided at all costs.

If everything went according to plan, Mladić's death would look like natural causes. Only she and whoever had ordered the hit would know any different. If her plan went awry or someone grew suspicious and requested an autopsy, she didn't want to be a suspect in the subsequent investigation when poison was found in Mladić's system. If she didn't leave any trace evidence behind, his cronies would most likely point fingers at each other, leaving no one to take the reins of Mladić's empire. Not the kind of regime change she normally helped bring about, but the principle was the same.

Aron had insisted each of the servers wear white gloves tonight because he liked the look. His eccentricity played in Santana's favor. If her hands were covered at all times, all the glasses and serving trays she touched would contain only the guests' fingerprints, not hers. And she wouldn't have to don latex gloves before she entered Mladić's room. Provided she found an opportunity to slip inside in the first place.

"Details."

This was her last job. There was no way she would leave without seeing it through to the end. Because like all the other jobs that had preceded it, she didn't have a choice.

## Chapter Thirty-one

F our beefy security guards with handheld metal detectors stood outside the entrances to Mladić's compound, two at the front and two at the back. After the vans parked near the rear entrance, the guards waved everyone out. One searched inside the vans and used a mirror on a telescoping pole to check the undercarriages, undoubtedly looking for explosives.

"Do they go through this routine every time they have visitors?" Santana asked.

"They take security seriously around here," Matthias said with a shrug. "Don't sneeze too loud or you might get shot."

He was joking, but if one of the guards had a hair trigger, he might not be too far from the truth. Something to keep in mind when she made a move on their boss.

While the first guard continued to inspect the vehicles, the second waved the staff forward. "Arms up."

Santana spread her arms. "I'm ticklish," she said when the guard rubbed the metal detector against her breasts rather than waving it in front of her body. "If you keep that up, you're going to make me spill my coffee all over you."

She shook the travel mug in her hand to let him know it was still half full. After weighing the cost of copping a free feel against the price of having his suit dry cleaned, he waved her through.

"Good choice."

She stepped into the entryway and looked around the kitchen. The room was even more spacious than the kitchen in Aron's restaurant and filled with nearly as much high-tech equipment.

"Are you going to give us a hand," Matthias asked, "or are you going to stand around and gawk all night?"

"Just looking for a place to put my mug so it doesn't get lost in the shuffle."

"Good luck with that."

After Matthias turned his back, she unscrewed the bottom of the stainless steel tumbler, removed the plastic bag of pills from the hidden compartment, and slipped the bag into her pocket.

"Step one complete," she said to herself. "Let's do this."

She emptied the mug, gave it a thorough rinse, and placed it in her backpack, which contained a change of clothes but no valuables. Everything she needed to make a quick escape—money, passport, plane ticket—was on her. After the party broke up, she would spend the night in the airport rather than returning to the rented house. If someone had been tracking her movements as she had been tracking Mladić's, the change of scenery would throw them off her tail and provide her a secure environment in the process.

"So glad you could join us," Matthias said when she reached for a case of champagne.

"Are you always this grouchy before an event, or did you save your bad mood for me?"

"Sorry," he said after they set their burdens in the kitchen and headed back to the van for more. "I always get a little anxious when I come here. This guy—Magnusson—he gives me the creeps."

"Why?"

He lowered his voice to a conspiratorial whisper. "Don't you know who he used to be?"

"I've heard rumors. Are you saying those rumors are true?"

"I'm saying watch yourself tonight. He's dangerous. So are the rest of his friends. They act like the rules don't apply to them because they don't."

Matthias maneuvered an oversized food pan carrier toward the ramp leading from the van to the ground. They moved slowly so they wouldn't spill any of Aron's culinary creations.

"Then it's a good thing they don't apply to me, either."

"With an attitude like that, you're going to fit in just fine."

"With the killers or everyone else? On second thought, don't tell me. I don't want to know."

❖

While the kitchen staff unpacked and prepped the food, Kristjan Isaacson, the head of Mladić's security team, took the wait staff on a tour of the house. Margret, clipboard in hand, tagged along.

"The party will primarily take place here on the first floor," Kristjan said, "but it will by no means be limited to this location. Guests will wander throughout the common areas in the house and on the surrounding property."

He beckoned for the group to follow him upstairs. The tour stopped in front of a door that seemed to be made of wood but was probably reinforced with steel inserts to prevent an assassin's bullets from reaching the occupants inside.

"All the rooms on this floor will be open to guests except this one," Kristjan said. "This is Mr. Magnusson's room. I humbly ask you as well as the guests to respect his privacy. Understood?" He waited for everyone to give some form of verbal or visual assent before he continued the tour. "Good. Now let's go take a look at the garden. The stone walkway can be slippery once night falls so you will want to watch your footing."

"I would advise you to be careful," Margret said. "Broken glasses pose a hazard to the guests and the expense will be deducted from your salary."

At this rate, Santana could end up owing Margret at the end of the night instead of the other way around. If that happened, she felt confident it wouldn't take her nearly as long to repay that debt as it had taken her to pay the one she owed Winslow Townsend. She still couldn't believe the day she had dreamed about since she was fifteen years old was finally here. But she couldn't afford to think too far ahead. If she did, she wouldn't make it out of here alive.

"Now what?" she asked after the tour ended.

"We sit back and wait for the fun to begin." Matthias held up a pack of cigarettes in one hand and a flask in the other. "A or B?"

"I don't smoke, and I prefer to keep a clear head tonight."

"You're not getting nervous, are you?"

"Now that you mention it." She held a hand over her stomach as if she were trying to prevent the contents from making a sudden appearance. "Where are the bathrooms? The good ones, not the cramped half-bath Kristjan said we were supposed to use."

"There's one across from the library on the first floor and there are two more upstairs, but I doubt you'll be able to talk your way past the guard posted there."

"We'll see about that."

She headed upstairs and walked toward Mladić's room. The guard held out his hand as she approached the door. "No."

"What's wrong? Is he in there with someone?"

"No, Mr. Magnusson not here," the guard said in heavily accented English.

"Good. Because I need to use the bathroom."

She took a step toward the door, but the guard blocked her path.

"No," he said again. "You use bathrooms downstairs."

"They're full." She rubbed her stomach and grimaced as if she were in severe discomfort. "Something in one of the dishes Aron fed us during the staff meal must have been off because three of us have the runs." She ramped up the pressure before he could contact another member of the security team to verify her claims. "I can take a dump right here if you want, but you'll be the one stuck with cleaning up the mess."

The guard screwed up his face in disgust and moved out of the way. "You have five minutes, and I will be standing outside door the whole time."

"Whatever works for you."

After the guard let her into Mladić's bedroom, she ran toward the bathroom and locked the door behind her. Moving quickly, she took Mladić's pill bottle out of the medicine cabinet and dumped the contents in the toilet. Then she took the plastic bag from her pocket and slowly poured the pills into the bottle, holding her hand over the opening to muffle the sound. She jumped when the guard banged on the door.

"Are you done yet?" he asked.

"Almost," she said with a melodramatic grunt. "Just give me… two more minutes. Oh, God, that's better."

She put the pill bottle back in the cabinet, positioning it exactly as she had found it. She used a camera app on her smartwatch to photograph the scene, then she flushed the toilet and watched carefully to make sure all the pills washed away. Satisfied, she picked up a can of lemon-scented air freshener and sprayed half of it into the air. She wished she had something else to add to the olfactory illusion. A rind of *Epoisses de Bourgogne* would have been perfect. The cheese was so smelly that lawmakers in its native France had made it illegal to carry it on public transportation.

"What took so long?" the guard asked after she opened the door.

"I wanted to make sure I wouldn't need a second trip. I wouldn't go in there for a good thirty minutes if I were you." The guard put his hands over his face and recoiled from the cloud of air freshener drifting toward him. "And whatever you do," she said as she strode toward the hallway, "stay away from the sheep's head jelly. That stuff will kill you."

She sighed with relief as she headed down the stairs. She was tempted to walk out the door and never look back, but she knew her absence would be sure to draw attention. First by the short-handed staff. Then, after Mladić's death, by his frantic staff.

"The most difficult part of the job is over," she said to herself. "Now it's just a waiting game."

No matter how short, the wait would undoubtedly feel like the longest of her life.

"Big crowd tonight," Matthias said after he and Santana returned to the kitchen to refill their respective serving trays. "If they keep drinking like this, we're going to run out of champagne before the party's over. That's a scene I'm not looking forward to."

"What's the special occasion anyway?" she asked as she waited for a member of the kitchen staff to give her a fresh batch of hors d'oeuvres.

"Because it's Saturday? Any excuse to party." He hoisted a tray of filled champagne flutes to shoulder level. "See you out there."

"Right behind you."

She picked up her tray and followed him out the door. She tried not to sneeze when the pungent scent of marinated herring with juniper berries reached her nose. She hadn't screwed up once tonight and she didn't want to start now.

She slowly circled the room, pausing near each cluster of guests to give them a chance to sample one of the appetizers on her tray. A few, as Matthias had warned her, tried to sample her as well. She avoided their wandering hands as best she could when she would have preferred to dump the vinegar-soaked fish on their heads or drive her fist into their stomach and follow up with a knee to the face when they doubled over in pain.

She headed toward a pair of new arrivals who were acting as if they had crashed the party rather than being invited to it. They pointed and gasped each time they saw someone sporting an expensive piece of jewelry, and they giggled into their glasses of champagne whenever Mladić or one of his cronies looked their way.

Even though the party was held in his house, Mladić had been fashionably late. He had finally made an appearance nearly an hour after most of the guests did. His arrival had been greeted with a "spontaneous" burst of applause followed by a series of toasts. He had made a short speech to welcome everyone, then he had ordered several of his minions to set up a huge projection screen TV tuned to a KR game. In short, he had spent well over five figures to throw a watch party for his favorite soccer team, and he didn't seem to notice—or care—that he was the only person in the room who was interested in the game or its eventual outcome. Everyone else, the newcomers included, was there for the free food and drinks.

"May I offer you a—"

The words died in her throat when the women turned to face her. She didn't know the blonde in the too-short cocktail dress, but she recognized the woman with her. Hekla.

"Does your mother know you're here?"

"No, she thinks Katrin and I went to the movies." Hekla did her best to look defiant, but she looked more like a kid playing dress up.

"You shouldn't be here."

"You could have had a say in where I go and who I choose to go with, but you lost that opportunity when you walked away without an explanation."

"Is she the one you told me about?" Katrin's words were slurred, signaling the glass of champagne in her hand wasn't her first drink of the evening. "You were right. She *is* cute. I would offer to take her off your hands, but I have my eye on someone else tonight."

She made a wobbly beeline for Mladić, who was holding court with a bunch of his former lieutenants and an assortment of hangers-on as the announcers on TV droned on about what KR needed to do in the second half to recover from a two-goal deficit. She wasn't the only woman who was trying to get Mladić's attention tonight, but she certainly seemed to be the most determined. She pushed herself through the adoring crowd and pressed herself against him. Whatever she said must have been to his liking because he took her by the hand and led her upstairs.

"At least one of us got what we came here for," Hekla said.

"And what did you come here for? Did you want to be some stranger's easy lay, too?"

"No."

"Then please tell me what you're doing here."

"Coming here was Katrin's idea. She said it would be fun, and I believed her. I'm primarily here because I wanted to make sure she had someone to look after her if she had too much to drink, but I'm here for me, too. I've been working across from this house for years. I've always wondered what went on inside. I wanted a firsthand view of the danger. The excitement. Things I'm not going to get if I'm waiting tables for the rest of my life."

"And Sigrun—"

"She wants me to take over for her when she retires, but the restaurant has always been her dream, not mine," Hekla said hotly. "I want to watch the sun set from the top of the Eiffel Tower. I want to watch it rise on a beach in Australia. I want to walk along the Great Wall in China. I want to ride a donkey down the Grand

Canyon in America. I want to see the world. When you walked into the restaurant the first time, I thought you were the one. I thought you and I would see the world together. Is that why my mother told you not to see me anymore? Because she thought you would take me away from her?"

"She didn't want you to get hurt and she knew that, whether I intended to or not, I would do just that."

"Are you involved with someone else?"

Santana didn't want to bring Brooklyn into the conversation—into this part of her life—but Hekla insisted on doing just that.

"You are, aren't you?"

Hekla's raised voice drew a few stares so Santana lowered hers to make sure they didn't become the center of attention. "Yes, I am."

"The whole time?"

"That doesn't matter."

"It matters to me." Hekla's chin quivered as she fought back tears.

"I know, and I'm sorry for leading you on, but it proves I'm not right for you. Your mother didn't have to point that out to me. I already knew it. If you're lucky, you'll find a way to do all the things you've dreamed of. And you'll find the right person to do them with. Just promise me you won't look for either here."

"Katrin did. It turned out well for her. If he marries her—"

"He won't marry her."

"How do you know?"

A piercing scream brought all conversations to a halt. The only sound was the play-by-play announcer's excited chatter on the TV after KR scored to pull to within a goal. Katrin, naked except for a sheet loosely wrapped around her body, stood at the top of the stairs. She was crying hysterically and repeating something in her native language.

"What is she saying?"

Hekla's face was pale. "She's saying, 'He's dead.' Do you think she means—"

"Grab her," Kristjan said, pointing at Katrin. "Don't let anyone leave, and make sure no one calls the police. We will handle this situation ourselves."

The security guard who had allowed Santana to use Mladić's bathroom wrapped Katrin in a bear hug. The guests began to panic as one set of security guards raced up the stairs and another moved to block the exits.

"What's going on?" Hekla asked.

Santana found it ironic that even though she had promised Sigrun she would protect Hekla from danger, Hekla had still found herself right in the middle of it. Was Brooklyn doomed to suffer the same fate if she remained in Brooklyn's life? She pushed thoughts of future scenarios out of her head as she tried to manage the current one. "You'll be fine. Just stay calm."

Kristjan ran into Mladić's room and back out again. "We need a doctor. Is there a doctor here? You," he said, pointing to a man who timidly raised his hand, "come with me."

The man handed his drink to his date and quickly made his way up the stairs. Hekla tried to follow him.

"Don't." Not caring about the fine Margret might assess her, Santana dropped the tray of appetizers she was holding and grabbed Hekla by the arm.

"Katrin's my friend," Hekla said, trying to pull away. "She needs me."

"She needs you to keep your head and not do anything stupid. If you go up those stairs right now, those guards might think you had something to do with whatever happened in that room. You can comfort her later. Let's get through the next few minutes first. Is this the kind of excitement you were hoping for?"

"You were right. I should have left when I had the chance."

Santana held Hekla in her arms to take the sting out of her words. "It's okay. You'll be okay."

But she wondered if Katrin would ever be the same again, especially after the doctor came out of the room and shook his head.

"Are you sure?" Kristjan asked.

"It was his heart," the doctor said. "I'm sure of it."

"He survived a war and escaped a tribunal but dies trying to fuck a twenty-year-old? That's not how his story should end."

"What do you want me to say? Facts are facts."

Kristjan poked the doctor in the chest. "Those are your facts. Leave it to me to come up with better ones."

"What do you want me to do with her?" asked the guard who was holding Katrin captive.

"Let her go." Kristjan tossed Katrin's dress, purse, and shoes on the floor. "Let them all go. The party's over."

The guard released his grip, and Katrin slumped to the floor, her belongings strewn all around her. The doctor hurried down the stairs and joined the crowd of guests rushing for the door.

"I can go to her now?" Hekla asked.

"Come on. I'll go with you."

Santana steered Hekla through the throng and accompanied her up the stairs. She tried to be unobtrusive so the squeamish guard she had conned earlier wouldn't see her and possibly tie her to Mladić's death. As he, Kristjan, and the other guards huddled to decide their next move, she discreetly snapped a picture of Mladić's naked body slumped across the bed. His eyes were open and his jaw was slack. He had red marks on his chest, probably caused by someone's desperate attempt to perform CPR.

"Take her somewhere and help her get dressed," she said, turning back to Hekla. "I'll take you home."

Hekla's eyes were wide as she cradled Katrin in her arms. "I can't go home. Not like this. My mother will never let me hear the end of it."

"Trust me. She'll be too busy celebrating the fact that you're still alive to care."

And if she was lucky, Brooklyn would care more about the woman she was now than the one she used to be.

## Chapter Thirty-Two

Vilma was being mysterious. More so than usual. Not that Brooklyn minded. After a long stretch of twelve-hour days, she liked having something to look forward to other than the next pitch meeting or conference call.

Vilma asked her to meet her at Brgy for dinner so they could talk. Naturally, Brooklyn had asked her what she wanted to talk about, but Vilma had only told her to be prepared to be surprised. That could mean anything from a kiss-off to a proposal.

God, what would she do if Vilma asked her to marry her? What would she say? It felt too soon to even be considering the question, but it felt right, too. Vilma had spent quality time with her parents and had sat down for dinner with her family more than once and she hadn't run for the hills yet. Perhaps the future she often dreamed about was closer than she thought.

She was about to shut down her computer and head home to change for dinner when her office phone rang. Her corporate attorney's name was displayed on the caller ID. "What's up, Scott? Please tell me you're calling with good news rather than bad."

"That depends on your perspective. Are you working on a new search engine?"

"Yes, but it's still in the developmental stage and isn't ready to go to market. How did you hear about it?"

"I got a call from a company that's extremely interested in the finished product. They want to buy it and, if they like what they see, they're willing to add BDV Enterprises to the deal. I haven't asked the accounting team to crunch the numbers yet, but I think we should be able to set an asking price of eight figures. Nine if you don't add any crazy contingencies to the contract."

"Like insisting on one hundred percent retention of my current employees after I sign on the dotted line?"

"This is business, Brooklyn. Everything is negotiable."

"Not for me. These people are more than employees. They're my family. I'm not going to pad my pockets if it means throwing them under the bus in the process. When I think of companies that have the capital to make a deal of that magnitude, two come to mind. But Apple gets three billion dollars a year to use Google as the default search engine for its products and Microsoft created Bing for the same purpose. So who's left?"

"TechSass."

Scott named one of the companies that had caught Brooklyn's eye during the tech conference she had attended in Tokyo. TechSass's market share was growing by leaps and bounds and their business philosophy mirrored hers. It didn't hurt that the company's founder and board members were all female. She had spent several hours chatting with them during the conference. She had taken copious notes on their successes and failures. Apparently, they had been taking notes on her, too.

She liked the idea that her company had drawn the attention of one of the heavyweights in the game, but it saddened her a little, too. She didn't want to see her company become part of a tech giant. She wanted to build it into one.

"What if I say no?" she asked.

"I doubt you're the only company on their list. They'll probably move on to the next entry. Luke Ridley is constantly testing the market. His company is the same size as yours and some of the product offerings are comparable."

Brooklyn's competitive instincts kicked in. "Mine are better."

"Shall I set up a meeting?"

"Not yet. Give me some time to think it over first."

"I'll reach out to my point of contact and ask her to circle back in a couple of weeks. Is that good?"

Two weeks was the perfect duration for a vacation, but it didn't feel like nearly enough time to make a life-altering decision that could affect her future as well as everyone who worked for her.

"No, but I suppose it'll have to do."

Brooklyn stopped by her apartment to shower and change. She ditched her work attire in favor of the little black dress she had worn the night she had met Vilma. She hadn't worn it since then. Tonight, it felt appropriate somehow. Though she had no idea what Vilma had in store for her, it felt like they were going back to the beginning. When they had spent a night flirting shamelessly with each other without revealing their real names.

Olaf? What had she been thinking? She wished she had come up with something sexier, but she had never been very good at thinking on her feet. She needed time to plan her quips. Too bad snappy comebacks worked best in the moment, not several hours later.

Still, Vilma seemed to care for her despite her faults. Or perhaps it was because of them. Brooklyn still cringed when she thought about the time she had fallen asleep while Vilma was making her dinner. She had tried to sneak out before Vilma could see her, only to be caught red-handed. Thankfully, Vilma had made her feel comfortable rather than embarrassed. She seemed to have a knack for doing that.

From the beginning, she had felt safe in Vilma's presence. Protected. Like nothing and no one could touch her. AJ had expressed doubts about Vilma. For a while, she had allowed those thoughts to hold sway with her, too. Then she had convinced herself to rely on her own instincts rather than other people's opinions. She might not know all the aspects of Vilma's life—all the terrible things she had witnessed while she was growing up—but she knew her heart. There was no doubt about that.

She arrived at Brgy in a daze, her mind swirling with thoughts of what she could do if she accepted TechSass's offer. After a lifetime of watching her family struggle to make ends meet, neither she nor they would have to worry about money again. If TechSass agreed to her terms, her employees would be cared for, too. Most importantly, she and Vilma would be on relatively equal footing, financially speaking. She could finally quash the lingering feeling that she was out of her element.

When she walked into Brgy, Vilma's smile was nothing but welcoming. "You look incredible," Vilma said as she rose from the table she had already claimed.

"So do you." Vilma was wearing a sleek tailored suit that fit her like a glove. The outfit was striking. Her expression even more so. She was practically glowing. "What's put that smile on your face?" Brooklyn asked as she spread a napkin in her lap. "Did you make the deal?"

Vilma poured two glasses of *arrack*. "I did, but that's not the reason I'm smiling."

"What is?"

"You are. You make me happy."

"Not the answer I was expecting, but I like where this is headed. Please continue."

Vilma's eyes twinkled as she smiled. Something was different. There was a lightness about her Brooklyn had never seen before. As if a weight had been lifted off her shoulders. She had been so busy stressing over her own business affairs she hadn't stopped to think that Vilma might be having similar issues.

"Tell me about Zurich," she said after they placed their orders. "I want to hear every detail."

"You didn't come here to be bored, did you?"

"Trust me. Nothing about you is boring."

"You might change your mind after the bloom is off the rose. Constant exposure tends to have that effect."

Vilma reached into the inside pocket of her jacket. Brooklyn's breath caught when she pulled out a small velvet box. "Is—Is that—" She was so shocked she couldn't get the words out. Other people had moments like this, not her.

Vilma remained in her seat rather than dropping to one knee. Then she flipped the box open. A key rather than a ring was nestled inside. "A few weeks ago, we agreed to take our relationship to the next level. I don't know where we'll eventually end up, but I'm ready to take the next step if you are. Brooklyn DiVincenzo, would you do me the honor of—"

"Santana?"

Vilma turned at the sound of an inquisitive voice. Brooklyn looked up to see a slight man in his late fifties standing next to their table. The man was dressed like a busboy—black tennis shoes, black pants, and a white T-shirt—and had a large plastic bucket tucked under one arm.

"It really is you." His slight shoulders were rounded. Like he had spent his life fending off a series of disappointments. "I saw you when you walked in, but it took me this long to convince myself I wasn't seeing things."

Vilma didn't say anything. Brooklyn couldn't read the expression on her face, but it didn't seem to be one of recognition.

The man moved closer. "It's me. Benjie. I'm living here now. My friend Danilo helped me get a work visa. He's letting me stay at his place until I get on my feet. At this rate, that could take a while. You seem to have done well for yourself, though."

The pride on his face was almost paternal. Brooklyn knew it couldn't be because Vilma had said her father was American, and, by his own admission, Benjie had only recently arrived.

"Nice threads." He jerked a thumb in Brooklyn's direction. "She's not half-bad either. I should introduce myself." He wiped his hand on his shirt, then held it out to Brooklyn. "I'm Benjie. Benjie Aquino. I taught Santana everything she knows. How to lie, how to cheat, and how to steal. She was a quick study, too. I guess you could call her my apprentice. I used to call her LC, short for Little Criminal, but she's definitely a big fish now."

He turned back to Vilma. Except why did he keep calling her Santana?

"I never thought I would see you again." Vilma's continued silence seemed to unnerve him. "I know this must be a shock. It is for me, too. When Winslow took you, I—" He stopped and shook his head. "It doesn't matter now. I didn't mean to disturb you. I just wanted to say hello."

He turned to leave but lingered when Vilma called his name. She drew him into a tight hug and whispered something in his ear. Brooklyn heard the words but couldn't understand them. Waray, Vilma had called it the first time they had come here. One of the nearly two hundred languages native to the Philippines.

Vilma reached into her pocket and slipped a wad of bills into Benjie's hand. There were tears in his eyes as he walked away. Vilma's, too.

"You know him?" Brooklyn asked.

Part of her had hoped he was confused. That he had simply mistaken Vilma for someone else and she had given him money to help him maintain his delusion. That way, she wouldn't have to accept the fact that the things Benjie had said about Vilma and her past were true. The look on Vilma's face paired with the aura of defeat in her body language said otherwise.

"Yes." When Vilma looked at her, the light had gone out of her eyes. "And it's time you got to know me, too."

## CHAPTER THIRTY-THREE

Santana didn't want to do this. She didn't want to hurt Brooklyn, or watch the relationship they were building crumble before her eyes. As hard as she had tried to outrun the truth, it had finally caught up to her. If she didn't keep pace, she would get trampled in its wake.

"Who was that man?" Brooklyn asked after they got to her apartment.

"His name is Benjie Aquino. I met him when I was just a kid. I was poor, and he taught me how to make money. Real money, not the scraps I could earn picking through garbage at the landfill. I didn't care that his methods weren't legal. I just wanted to put a smile on my mother's face and find a way to do my part so she wouldn't have to work her fingers to the bone trying to keep food on the table and a roof over our heads. She didn't approve of what I was doing, we argued about it, and she kicked me out."

"He's the reason for your estrangement?"

"No, the fault is mine. Benjie was kind enough to take me in, but he didn't force me to stay with him. I did that on my own."

"Little Criminal. Isn't that what he called you?"

Santana briefly closed her eyes. Before tonight, she hadn't heard that nickname in years. Benjie used to say it with such pride she eventually took pride in it, too. Now it only served as a painful reminder of a life she used to live—and one she might be about to lose.

"I'm not that person anymore."

"Who are you then?" Brooklyn asked as the tears she had been holding back finally began to fall. "Is Vilma Bautista even your real name?"

"No, my name is Santana. Santana Masters."

"Santana. That fits." The sadness in Brooklyn's smile broke Santana's heart.

"What do you mean?"

"The first time you invited me here—the night I invited myself here, really—you stood next to that window and formally introduced yourself to me. We'd been playing the cutesy nickname thing for a while, and I was so excited to hear what your real name was. When you told me, my initial thought was your name didn't seem to fit. I didn't know how right I was. You've been lying to me from the beginning. From the night we met until this moment, none of it has been real."

"It's been real to me. I love you, Brooklyn, and I know you love me, too."

"Love you? I don't even know you. Logic says you're not a venture capitalist either. What's your actual profession?"

Santana hesitated. This was the part she had been hoping to avoid. "I don't have one. I suppose you could say I'm retired."

"That implies that you once did something for a living. What might that something be?"

"You wouldn't believe me if I told you."

"I fell for your lies, didn't I? Why should it be so hard for me to believe the truth?"

Santana got up and poured two double shots of whiskey, even though chances were high she might end up wearing one of them. She set one glass in front of Brooklyn, then resumed her seat opposite her.

"Please stop dragging this out. Just tell me what is it that—"

"I was an assassin, okay?" Santana said in a rush. "I killed people for a living."

"People like who?" Brooklyn's voice was so quiet Santana had to strain to hear her. "People like Charlie?"

"I was there the night she died, but I wasn't the one who pulled the trigger. I had been ordered to, but when the time came, I couldn't pull the trigger."

Brooklyn rocked back as if she had been struck. "Ordered to? You sound like you didn't have a choice."

"Because I didn't. Not if I wanted my mother to live. I didn't choose this line of work. I was forced to do it to keep my mother safe."

"So, what? Someone threatened to kill her if you didn't do what they say?"

"Yes, his name is Winslow Townsend. He took me against my will and slowly bent me to his. Everything you see around you is his, not mine. For all intents and purposes, I was one of his possessions, too, but that's over now. I know the things I'm saying sound far-fetched, but I swear every word is true."

"Truth," Brooklyn said bitterly. "Are you even remotely familiar with the term? God, I feel like such a fool."

Santana reached out to comfort her, but Brooklyn shrank from her attempted embrace.

"Don't touch me!" Brooklyn said.

It wasn't the rebuff that hurt the most. It was the fear she saw in Brooklyn's eyes. She would have felt better if she had seen hate reflected there instead. Then she would have felt like she still had a chance, not like she had lost Brooklyn for good.

"I didn't do it, Brooklyn. I didn't kill Charlie."

"But you said you were there that night. Did you see who did?"

"From a distance, yes, but I didn't get a good look at the shooter's face. I couldn't pick them out of a lineup."

"Can't or won't?"

"What do you mean?"

"There's allegedly loyalty amongst thieves. Does that code apply to killers, too?"

"I'm not a killer," Santana said fiercely. "Not anymore. I did what I had to do to survive. To—"

"Keep your mother safe. I heard you the first time, though I'm still not quite sure if I believe you. If you didn't kill Charlie, why did you stick around? So you could take pleasure in everyone's collective grief like some sort of sadist?"

"I wanted to make sure no one in your inner circle posed a threat to you. I wanted to make sure you weren't in danger, too."

"How were you supposed to do that?" Before Santana could respond, Brooklyn answered her own question. "You followed me, didn't you? That *was* you I saw in the cemetery. The one with the lavender flowers."

Santana nodded in affirmation.

"Why aren't I surprised to hear you lied about that, too?" Brooklyn's tears began to stream even faster. "Where were you last week? You obviously weren't closing some nonexistent deal in Zurich. So where were you?"

"I was in Reykjavik."

"Were you 'ordered' to kill someone there, too?" Brooklyn used air quotes to show how much contempt she felt for the word.

"Yes."

"Was it anyone I know?"

"Brooklyn—"

"Well, was it?"

Santana sighed as she came to terms with her fate. She had known Brooklyn wouldn't understand, but she deserved a right to know. Everything.

"Jusuf Mladić. He was the former warlord who—"

"I know who he was. He was an evil man who deserved to pay for the many atrocities he committed back in the day, but who gave you the right to decide his fate?"

Santana felt her body slowly begin to go numb. "I didn't make the decisions. I just carried them out."

Brooklyn looked at her as if she didn't recognize her. "I defended you." She angrily dried her eyes. "Every time someone said something negative about you, I told myself that they didn't know you like I did. I told myself that I was the one person who knew the real you."

"Because you do."

"Bullshit. I know who you were pretending to be, not who you are."

"The only time I wasn't pretending was when I was with you."

Brooklyn's face crumpled as her resolve finally broke. "How I wish I could believe that."

Brooklyn gathered her things and prepared to walk out of Santana's life for what felt like the last time. Santana longed to go to her, but Brooklyn already felt like part of her past. When Brooklyn opened the door and walked out without looking back. Santana could do nothing but let her go.

❖

Brooklyn felt lost and didn't know where to turn. She normally relied on her family and friends whenever she had a crisis, but she couldn't go to them now. Not this time. This was a problem she needed to solve on her own.

She headed home after she left Vilma's apartment. Not Vilma. Santana. How could she possibly have allowed herself to fall for someone who had lied to her about something as fundamental as her name?

After she let herself into her apartment, she locked the door behind her, then dropped her purse and coat on the floor. She sat in the dark rather than risk catching a glimpse of her own reflection. She didn't think she could take seeing the pain she felt reflected on her face. Experiencing it was bad enough.

Her day had started out so well. She had received an unexpected but generous offer to purchase her company, then the woman she loved had asked her to move in with her. At least, that's what Vilma—*Santana*, damn it—had been leading up to before she had been interrupted by someone from her past. Someone who had introduced her to a life of crime. The life she had lived before she and Brooklyn had crossed paths in a bar in Tokyo.

She had told herself that their meeting had felt like fate. Now it felt more like the premise of a supremely bad joke. And she was the butt of it.

She held her head in her hands and tried not to cry. She had done more than enough of that already, yet it seemed like she was just getting started.

She still had Detective Barnett's card. If she told him what Santana had confided in her, perhaps he could use the information to find Charlie's killer. Of course, that was contingent upon him believing her story and Santana remaining in the country long enough to corroborate it. Both were long shots. Winslow Townsend was a tech billionaire, not a criminal mastermind, and now that their relationship was over, Santana had no reason to remain so close to the scene of the crime. Especially if there was a chance she might end up in prison if she did.

Brooklyn didn't reach for her phone because she had no idea what to say.

And what was she supposed to tell her parents? She needed to think of a plausible excuse when they asked why she and Santana had stopped seeing each other. They genuinely liked Santana. She didn't want to taint their opinion of her, but some secrets were too big to keep.

Initially, she couldn't reconcile the person Santana had appeared to be with the person she actually was. Then she remembered the circumstances under which they had met. When Santana had nearly broken a man's wrist simply for coming on too strong. By her own admission, she was not only capable of violence, she was capable of murder. Charlie's murder?

Santana had admitted witnessing Charlie's death, but she had denied being involved in it. Was it possible that Brooklyn had allowed herself to fall for the woman who had killed her best friend? She had made love with her. Slept in the same bed with her. Dreamed of sharing a life with her. She was sickened by the realization that she had been at her most vulnerable with someone so dangerous. Or had that been part of the attraction?

It didn't matter now. None of it did. Because she and Vilma or Santana or whatever the hell her name was were done.

Now all she needed to do was get her heart to buy into the mantra. Because every time she closed her eyes, she couldn't stop reliving all the good times they'd had. The bad ones, too. She remembered the sound of her voice, the tenderness of her touch, the taste of her skin, the wistful look in her eyes she got when she thought no one was watching. She remembered laughing with her. Talking with her. Just being with her. Those moments had felt so real. Now it appeared they had only been an elaborate illusion.

She didn't want to love Santana, but how was she supposed to stop?

A few weeks ago, her life had been perfect. She and Santana had sat in a porch swing in the middle of nowhere, serenaded by the sounds of nature on one side and the sound of her parents having sex on the other. What she wouldn't give to have that moment back. What she wouldn't give to feel that carefree—that loved—again.

"Who needs love? I've got a company to run."

## CHAPTER THIRTY-FOUR

Santana had burned all of her identities except one. Vilma Bautista was the only alias that remained. She had a few more loose ends she needed to tie up while she waited for Winslow Townsend to finalize their separation, then she would be able to get rid of that one, too.

Saying good-bye to Delphine Durand had been somewhat bittersweet. She had always enjoyed embodying her. Someone with no ambitions and no responsibilities. Someone so unlike herself. Before she had shredded Delphine's identification documents and smashed her phone, she had reached out to Hekla one last time. Not directly, of course. She hadn't wanted to risk reopening any old wounds.

She had sent her some money. Not enough to draw anyone's attention but enough to help Hekla fulfill some of the dreams she had spoken about. Santana wondered which dream she would chase first. Would she watch the sun rise on a beach in Australia or ride a donkey down the Grand Canyon? No matter which she chose, at least she would be living her life instead of sleepwalking through it.

"Good morning, Harry," Santana said after she walked into the flower shop. "I need you to make one last delivery for me, so let's make it a good one, okay?"

Harry tossed his floppy hair out of his eyes. "What do you mean 'last'? You haven't found another florist you like better, have you?"

"Like that could ever happen."

"Then what gives?"

"I'm going to be putting my apartment on the market soon. I'll be heading home to put my feet up for a while until I decide my next step."

"That's too bad. I mean, I'm happy for you if you're doing something you truly want to do, but my dads and I are going to miss having you around."

She felt a surge of melancholy after he came around the counter and gave her a hug. She had literally watched him grow. The first time she had met him, he was in middle school. Now he was preparing to go off to college. "I'm going to miss you, too."

"Are these for your girlfriend?" he asked. "I don't want to assume this time."

"Yes, they're for Brooklyn, but she's not my girlfriend anymore."

"Really? The two of you didn't break up because I put my foot in my mouth, did you?"

"No, we broke up because I did. Now I need your help saying good-bye."

"I'm all over it. What kind of theme would you like?"

She thought about the time she had spent with Brooklyn and her parents in the Catskills. A time she would always treasure, even though her time with Brooklyn had come to an end. "Something sophisticated but rustic."

"Choice of flowers?"

"Something that won't die if she forgets to water them after spending too many hours hunched over her computer."

"She sounds like a real character," Harry said with a laugh. "I'm sorry you guys parted ways."

"Yeah, so am I."

"Last but not least, would you like a cut flower arrangement or a potted one?"

"Potted. I want it to last a while."

"Aww. That's sweet." Harry stuck his pencil behind his ear as she scanned the notes he had made. "I'll need a few minutes to create something fabulous. Do you want to wait or come back later?"

"Work your magic. I've got nothing but time."

While he ran around pulling the items he needed to create the perfect arrangement, she grabbed a note card and tried to figure out how to cram all the things she wanted to say into such limited space.

It had been just over a week since she and Brooklyn had broken up. One of the longest weeks of her life. She had spent the first few days waiting for her phone to ring. Waiting for Brooklyn to reach out to her and say she wanted to talk. But the call hadn't come. She didn't know if she and Brooklyn would ever be on speaking terms again, but she did know she couldn't leave without saying good-bye.

She knew Brooklyn wouldn't want to see her—she would feel the same way if she were in her shoes—so she had to find another way. This was the one she had chosen.

"Does this work?" Harry asked as he added raffia handles to a wooden crate he had filled with a variety of succulents.

"That's perfect." She sealed the note in an envelope and handed it, along with a small gift box, to Harry. "Could you make sure she gets this, too?"

"I'll put it in her hands myself." He gave her another hug.

Her cell phone rang. "Finally," she said when she saw Winslow's number printed on the display. "Excuse me, Harry, but I have to take this."

"No biggie. I want to add a few more finishing touches to your order anyway."

She moved to the other side of the shop so she could have a bit of privacy.

"I apologize for the delay in reaching out to you," Winslow said. "Let me start off by offering you my overdue congratulations on completing your most recent assignment."

She didn't want to be thanked for taking a man's life, even a man as malicious as Jusuf Mladić, so she quickly changed the subject. "How would you like to handle the sale of the apartment? If you have a buyer in mind, I can call a lawyer and arrange a title transfer. If not, I can contact a real estate agent so they can place it on the market."

"No need."

"Is everything already arranged? If so, I can leave by the end of the week."

"No, I need you to stay right where you are."

Santana didn't like the direction the conversation was heading.

Winslow sighed. "We've had a good run, you and I. A very prosperous one, I might add."

He had benefited from their one-sided partnership far more than she had, but she didn't want to argue with him when he was this close to finally freeing her from their unwritten contract.

"That's why I have chosen to extend our arrangement rather than terminate it."

Winslow liked to boast he was a man of his word, yet she couldn't remember the last time he had followed through on any of the guarantees he had made to her. "But you promised to—"

"Promises, like bad business deals, are made to be broken. And you, my dear, are one of the best business deals I have ever made. Your recent exploits showed me that you're capable of much more than I gave you credit for. I'm willing to increase the amount of your compensation, but there's no way I'm willing to release you from my employ."

"But I thought—"

"Do yourself a favor and leave the thinking to me. You will work for me until the day you die. Or until your mother does, whichever comes first. The sooner you accept that fact, the better. This conversation is becoming quite tedious, and I have a meeting to attend. I will forward your next assignment as soon as I am presented with one worthy of your skills."

"Are you okay?" Harry asked after she ended the call. "You look like you've seen a ghost."

She hadn't seen one, but she definitely felt like she had become one. "I'm fine," she said, even though she was anything but.

"I'm sure my dads will want to have you over for dinner one last time before you go. You're not leaving right away, are you?"

"No, I've got a few things I need to take care of first."

What she was about to do wouldn't make up for all the wrongs she had committed in her life, but she had to start somewhere.

❖

Time was running out for Brooklyn to respond to TechSass's offer. She was tasked with the most important business decision she had ever been asked to make, but she hadn't been able to give the matter any serious thought since Santana had told her the truth about herself. She hadn't been able to concentrate on anything other than work, and she was doing a piss-poor job at that, too. If not for the quality control team checking behind her, there was no telling how many bugs would have ended up in the software she had worked on during the past two weeks.

"Hey, boss."

Brooklyn looked up after AJ knocked on her door. "What's up?"

"Do you have a sec to talk?"

Brooklyn waved her inside. "As long as you promise not to tell me you're about to put in your two weeks' notice."

AJ closed the door, cluing Brooklyn in that the conversation they were about to have was not for public consumption. "Did Vilma tell you?"

"Tell me what?"

AJ grimaced as she took a seat in one of the chairs in front of Brooklyn's desk. "That Luke tried to poach me. He invited me to meet him for lunch a few weeks ago, and she saw us together in the lobby downstairs. The receptionist just forwarded me a call from her."

"What did she want?"

"To know how my meeting with Luke went."

Brooklyn was flabbergasted. "I almost don't know where to begin. With her, you, or him. Let's start with you. Are you staying or going?"

"Like I told her, I'm not going anywhere," AJ said firmly. "I felt I owed it to myself to hear what Luke had to say, but I didn't like the terms of his offer. Plus he seemed a lot more interested in hearing about our past projects than telling me about his current or future ones. After I reminded him that all of our software is proprietary and wouldn't be coming with me if I decided to join his company, he seemed to lose all interest in our conversation. The whole thing was a bust. That's why I didn't mention it to you."

Brooklyn decided to deal with Luke after she'd had time to rein in her temper. She couldn't blame him for going after one of her best employees. She only wished he had given her a heads-up about it. As for trying to steal her software, that deserved more than a disapproving finger wag.

"Thank you for telling me. Did Vilma say why she picked now to follow up with you?"

"I think she's worried about you. We all are."

"Worried? Why?"

"You're off your game. I'm not the only one who's noticed it. I'm simply the one who pulled the short straw when the time came to tell you so."

When Brooklyn glanced out her office window, nearly a dozen heads suddenly snapped in the opposite direction. "Wow. Okay."

"Based on your reaction when I said her name, I assume you and Vilma broke up."

Brooklyn wanted to tell AJ that her personal life wasn't her concern, but it had become just that the moment she had allowed her personal life to affect her professional one. "Yeah. She was—I was—It didn't work out."

"Relax. I wasn't planning on saying, 'I told you so.' I admit I had some issues with her, but I can tell she truly cared about you. If she didn't, she wouldn't have asked me to look out for you if something ever happened to her."

"When did she do that?"

"The day she saw me and Luke downstairs. I thought she was kidding at first. When she bit my head off after I didn't give her an immediate answer, I realized she was serious. I don't know what was going on with her, but she sounded like she was more worried about you than herself."

Brooklyn thought back to that day. During lunch, Santana had told her about her upcoming business trip and they had made a date to talk about their future when she returned. Santana had said she was going to Switzerland, but she had actually traveled to Iceland, where she had come face-to-face with a man who was responsible for the deaths of hundreds of thousands of innocent men, women, and children. There had been no guarantee Santana would survive the encounter. It was telling that in the days leading up to it, she had been more concerned about Brooklyn's safety than her own.

"She's fine," Brooklyn said. "So am I. It just—"

AJ finished her sentence for her. "Didn't work out. I heard you the first time. Whose idea was it to end things, yours or hers?"

"The decision was mutual."

"Do you have any regrets?"

"Plenty."

"But if given a choice," AJ said gently, "would you do it all again?"

"My head says no, but my heart says yes."

And when she saw Harry standing outside her office with a box of flowers in his hands, she knew she needed to figure out which one was lying.

She tried to tip him after he set the flowers on her desk, but he wouldn't accept her money. "Ms. Bautista already took care of it."

"Of course she did. She always had a thing for details."

At first, Brooklyn had thought it was by choice. Now she realized it was by necessity. One of the requirements of Santana's job. The real one, not the one she had pretended to have. If she hadn't been such a stickler for details, she wouldn't have been able to pull the wool over Brooklyn's eyes. Brooklyn's and all the other people she had conned over the years. She wondered if hers was the only broken heart Santana had left in her wake or simply the most recent.

"Oh, I almost forgot." He pulled a rectangular gift box from his pocket and set it next to the flowers. "She wanted you to have this, too. I hope I see you around sometime."

"Thanks, Harry. You, too."

After Harry left, AJ seemed to sense Brooklyn wanted some time alone. "I'll leave you to it."

"Thanks for the pep talk. And thanks for letting me know about Luke, too."

"Does this mean I'm not fired?"

"Ask me after I review the results from the next round of product testing on your app."

"You got it, boss. Would you like the door open or closed?"

"Closed, please."

Brooklyn eyed the flowers. Six succulents planted in a wooden crate that had been distressed to look much older than it actually was. The crate was lined to protect the wood from water damage, and colorful pebbles had been added to provide visual appeal as well as drainage. The arrangement was gorgeous, but she could barely bring herself to look at it.

She picked up the note card and gift box that had come with the flowers. She opened the box first because she figured its contents would hurt less than the card's.

The box was simple. Understated. So was what lay inside. A silver ID bracelet with "WWBD" engraved on the plate. She ran her fingers over the letters.

"What Would Brooke Do?"

She remembered telling Santana about the alter ego she had created to help her get through challenges she didn't think she could face on her own. She remembered telling her about wanting to get a T-shirt with the letters she was staring at now printed on the front. She remembered telling her so many things. Things Santana had not only taken in but taken to heart.

She took a deep breath before she opened the card, steeling herself to read what Santana had written. Flowing cursive script filled the inside of the card as well as the back. Tears sprang to her eyes before she got past the first word.

*Olaf,*

*The first time we met, it was by chance. If we're fortunate enough to meet again, I hope it will be by choice. If you ever find yourself in 'Ohe Sojukokoro, there's a barstool in the Kon-Tiki Grill with your name on it. The first round's on me.*

*TDH*

*P.S. I hope you like the bracelet. In case you're wondering, the letters mean What Would Brooklyn Do because it's always been you, not Brooke, the whole time.*

Brooklyn covered her mouth with her hands to hold back the sobs that were welling up inside her. She would never be able to forget how Santana had deceived her. There was no denying that. The real question was would she ever be able to forgive her?

She had some serious decisions to make. Both personally and professionally. If she made the wrong ones, forgiving Santana wouldn't be an issue. Forgiving herself would.

## CHAPTER THIRTY-FIVE

The receptionist stationed behind the desk in the lobby of the building where Luke Ridley's company was housed looked up from the Sudoku puzzle she was struggling to solve when Santana approached her. "May I help you?" she asked after she removed the half-moon reading glasses perched on the tip of her nose.

"Good afternoon, Dana," Santana said after she took a quick peek at the receptionist's name tag. "I would like to see Luke Ridley."

"Do you have an appointment?"

"No, I don't."

Dana referred to the digital calendar displayed on her computer. "Mr. Ridley's schedule is quite full today. Tomorrow doesn't look very promising either. Would you like me to try to squeeze you in next week?"

"I'm sure he'll be able to carve out some time for me today. Tell him Winslow Townsend sent me."

"Winslow?" Dana dragged out the name as if she were unfamiliar with it.

"Townsend. Don't worry. I'll wait."

Santana looked around while Dana put a call through to Luke's private secretary. Luke's schedule might have been crowded, but the lobby certainly wasn't. Most of the chairs in the lobby were empty and the occupants appeared to be waiting to visit other companies. No wonder Luke had sought out Winslow's services. At least that's what Santana's instincts told her. Along with all the clues that had pointed her in his direction. In a few minutes, she hoped to gather the evidence she needed to support her theory that he was the person who had hired a professional assassin to kill Charlotte Evans.

If he called Winslow to confirm someone was supposed to be meeting with him today, she was screwed. She was counting on the fact that he, like most of the people in Winslow's orbit, had a healthy fear of the man and would automatically approve her unscheduled visit rather than risk Winslow's ire.

On some level, she supposed she had known Winslow wouldn't grant her her freedom. She couldn't believe she had been foolish enough to believe he would. But foolish she had been. Foolish when she had allowed herself to fall in love with Brooklyn, and foolish to allow herself to dream of being able to have a life with her. That dream had been dashed and she had no one to blame but herself.

She might not be able to have the future she had dreamed of, but there was still a chance she could have one she could live with. As long as she was willing to make a few sacrifices along the way.

Dana cleared her throat to get her attention. "Mr. Ridley will see you now," she said, handing her a laminated visitor's pass. "Pin that to your lapel and head up to the fifteenth floor."

"Thanks for your help."

"My pleasure."

Santana rode the elevator to the appropriate floor. Luke was waiting for her as soon as the doors slid open. His eyes were wide and filled with panic. He calmed a bit when he recognized who she was. "You're the woman AJ introduced me to a few weeks ago. The one Brooklyn's been dating. Vilma something, isn't it?"

"Yes, that's me."

He peered behind her to see if someone else had ridden in the elevator with her. "I don't know what Brooklyn's told you, but she's already called to rip me a new asshole. I don't need her girlfriend to do it, too. My meeting with AJ was strictly business. Nothing personal."

"What about trying to steal BDV's software? Was that strictly business, too?"

"I don't have time for this shit," he said with a melodramatic eye roll. He led her to his office. "Let's make this quick, okay? I'm actually expecting someone else."

"The person you're expecting," she said after he closed the door behind them, "is me."

"Wait." He didn't so much sit in his desk chair as collapse into it. "*You're* the person Winslow sent to see me?"

"I'm here to talk about the job I was hired to perform for you."

"Does Brooklyn know you work for Winslow?" He lowered his voice to a conspiratorial whisper, even though no one was in earshot. "Does she know what you did?"

"I came here to ask questions, Luke, not answer them. What Brooklyn does or doesn't know isn't your concern. And I said I was *hired* to perform a job for you. I never said I carried it out."

"If you didn't do it, someone certainly did." The color drained from his face. "There isn't a problem with the payment, is there? Charlie's as dead as a doornail and the funds for the wire cleared my account weeks ago. Winslow should have the money. I have the email confirmation to prove it."

"Show me," she said with the most menacing look she could muster.

His hands shook as he reached for his cell phone. "See? It's right here."

She read the message, forwarded it to her email address, and tossed the phone on the desk.

"I told you," he said, regaining a bit of his bravado. "Not that it did me any good to spend the two hundred fifty thou. When I went to see Brooklyn the night of the hit, she told me she had opted to pull the plug on the software I was trying to prevent her from perfecting. My team's closer to working out the kinks than they were before, but they're not where I want them to be yet. That's why I tried to convince AJ to jump ship."

"Because she was Charlie's protégée?"

Luke nodded. "Logic says she and Charlie shared work product. I thought if I waved enough money in her face, she might be able to give me the intel I needed to solve our bug problem."

"But she turned you down."

"A temporary setback, I promise you. I know I'm late delivering the product by the original agreed-upon date, but when you speak to Winslow, please assure him I'm on track to meet the revised deadline."

"You can tell him yourself if you're lucky enough to share the same prison cell." Santana pointed to the buttonhole camera attached to her shirt. She removed the tiny two-way radio in her left ear and held it up to her mouth. "Do you have everything you need, Detective Barnett?"

Detective Barnett pushed the office door open. "Everything and then some. Take him away, boys."

One of the two uniformed police officers flanking Barnett pulled out a pair of handcuffs. "Lucas Ridley, you're under arrest for conspiracy to commit murder."

"I want a lawyer," Luke said.

"If I were in your shoes, buddy, I would, too." The arresting officer began to read Luke his rights.

"This wasn't my idea," Luke said, ignoring the part about his right to remain silent. "It was Lee Townsend's. One of his business associates hit on Brooklyn in Tokyo. She turned him down hard and some chick named Santana put him in his place. Lee suggested the hit as a way to save face for his friend, give my team a chance to take the lead on the software, and get back at Santana at the same time. He was so gung-ho about the idea, he probably pulled the trigger himself."

Luke's confession explained so much. The hastily assigned hit. The discounted fee. The "insurance policy" Winslow said Lee had insisted on instituting.

Santana felt the missing pieces of the puzzle finally snap into place. Even though she and Brooklyn had originally met by chance, their second encounter had been carefully orchestrated. Lee Townsend had set it up. And he had set her up to fail. Even if she had succeeded in carrying out the hit, she would have lost any chance she might have had of being with Brooklyn.

Lee had placed a second shooter onsite because he had wanted to guarantee that nothing would go wrong. Because he resented her prominent place in his father's life so much that he was determined to see her hurt.

If she carried out the hit, she would be responsible for killing a potential lover's best friend. If she didn't, she would displease Winslow. She would lose either way, and Lee would get what he wanted.

He had always harbored the delusion that Winslow was grooming her to become his eventual replacement. He seemed to notice only the occasional pats on the head Winslow gave her, not the much more common figurative kicks in the teeth. She had always known Lee didn't like her, but she hadn't realized just how much he truly hated her. Until now.

"Do you want to call Ms. DiVincenzo," Detective Barnett said after the uniformed officers dragged Luke away, "or shall I?"

"I'm sure she'd much rather hear from you than me."

Santana handed him the hidden camera a technician had affixed to her shirt a few hours ago. She had headed for his precinct after she left the flower shop the day before. He had initially been skeptical of her story when she had informed him of her suspicions about Luke's involvement in Charlotte Evans's murder, but she had been able to provide him enough details to convince him to allow her to visit Luke's office the next day while wearing a wire. Since New York was a one-party consent state, officials wouldn't need Luke's permission for her to make the recording and any statements he uttered on it could be used against him in court.

"I'll take that, too," he said as she dropped her cell phone into a plastic bag. The emails on it, including the one she had forwarded to herself from Luke's account, would soon be marked as evidence.

"What happens next?" she asked. "Are you going to arrest me, too?"

"Not right now, but the district attorney's office will definitely have some questions for you. They'll be the first to come calling, but they probably won't be the last. The information you could provide might help bring down Winslow Townsend's entire criminal network. You might be able to cut a deal with the authorities for past misdeeds if you're willing to testify against Winslow and forfeit your assets, but I can't guarantee you won't end up doing some time yourself. Do yourself a favor and don't leave town until someone from the DA's office gets in touch with you."

"You've got my passport so I couldn't possibly get very far until you return it to me. What about my mother? Does someone have eyes on her to make sure nothing happens to her?"

"Relax," he said, patting the air with his hands. "She's safe. We'll be sure to tell her you're the reason why."

"I don't want credit, Detective. Just confirmation. Is Winslow in custody, too?"

"Someone from Interpol should be picking up him and his son as we speak. Townsend's employees and business associates won't be happy about the steps you've taken today. We'll do our best to keep your identity a secret for as long as we can, but how do you know one of those people won't come after you?"

"I don't." Some of the people who'd had similar arrangements with Winslow as she had might be glad to see their jobs come to an abrupt end, but she was well aware that others might not share the same opinion. She felt destined to spend the rest of her life, however long that turned out to be, looking over her shoulder.

"Then why did you come forward?"

"Because some things are worth the risk."

And Brooklyn was one of them.

"Come on," he said, taking her by the arm. "Let's get you someplace safe."

"What the fuck?" Brooklyn said after AJ burst into her office, grabbed her by the hand, and dragged her to the conference room. The employees who weren't huddled over their laptops were staring at the TV screen. "What's going on?"

"Don't talk," AJ said. "Just watch."

The TV was tuned to one of the twenty-four hour news channels. The coverage on it was split in half. Luke Ridley was being led on a perp walk on one side of the screen, Winslow Townsend on the other.

"If you're just joining us," the news anchor said, "Lucas Simon Ridley, the CEO of Riddle Me This Technologies; reclusive tech mogul Winslow Townsend; and Townsend's son, Lee, are all in police custody. Ridley is charged with hiring a contract killer employed by the Townsends to kill Charlotte Denise Evans, a computer programmer employed by one of Ridley's stiffest competitors. Details are still coming in at this hour, but sources say the motive behind the hit was to prevent BDV Enterprises, the company Evans worked for, from taking a particular software program to market before Ridley and the Townsends could perfect it first."

"Asshole," Trevor said as he threw half of a cream cheese-laden bagel at Luke's image on the TV screen.

"Easy, Trev." AJ held him back before he could reach for something heavier. "He'll be someone's prison bitch soon enough."

"Though police sources are taking care to protect the identity of certain individuals involved," the anchor continued, "authorities have confirmed that they were tipped off by someone inside Winslow Townsend's organization."

"Jesus," Brooklyn said under her breath.

Santana had been honest with her after all. She hadn't willingly performed any of the heinous acts she had committed. She had been compelled to. She was like a child soldier who had been taken from her home and given the "choice" of fighting for her oppressors or watching her loved ones die.

Not only had Santana been telling the truth, the actions she had apparently taken today showed she was willing to risk her life to make sure the truth came to light. Instead of the monster Brooklyn had made her out to be, she was just as much a victim of Winslow Townsend's cruelty as Charlie had been.

Brooklyn dialed Santana's cell number, but the call went straight to voice mail.

"Who are you trying to reach?" AJ asked.

"The bravest woman I've ever met," Brooklyn said.

And one she feared she might never see again.

# CHAPTER THIRTY-SIX

*Six Months Later*

Santana pressed two fingers against the side of her neck to check her pulse after she finished her run. It was slightly higher than normal, but that was to be expected. Today was an especially hot day and she had pushed herself more than she had since she'd returned home. Home. Funny how such a small word could provide such tremendous comfort.

She went through her cool down routine, then decided to grab a late lunch to restore some of the calories she had just burned off. Even though the Kon-Tiki Grill had a casual vibe and featured plenty of outdoor seating, she figured the customers might appreciate it if she showed up in something other than sweat-drenched workout gear. She took a shower and swapped her sports bra, nylon shorts, and running shoes for a T-shirt, cargo shorts, and flip-flops.

The Tiki, as most people called it, was located just steps away from the beach. It was a place locals loved and tourists made a beeline for as soon as they made their way through 'Ohe Sojukokoro's lone airport. Santana couldn't count the number of surfers and divers she had shared pitchers of beer with over the years. If the local governing bodies received permission to lengthen the airport to accommodate larger planes, that number could grow exponentially as more and more people discovered what was still something of a hidden gem.

"I'd better enjoy this while I can."

"*Pehea 'oe*, my sistah," David Kahale said as he wiped down the bar.

He reached out to give her a fist bump. Santana tapped her knuckles against his. His hand was twice the size of hers. Then again, so was he. His personality was even more outsized than his body. Whether he knew them or not, he treated everyone who walked into his bar like family. He treated her that way as well. When her house had been seized by one of the many law enforcement agencies to whom she owed restitution, he had allowed her to convert the tiny space above the bar into an apartment. He had also given her a job helping the cooks run the line. The job didn't pay much, but it was honest work and that was all that mattered.

She felt like she had come full circle. She had started out broke and she was broke once more. But she had something now that she hadn't possessed back then: the wisdom to realize that she didn't need money to feel rich. Even though she barely had a dime to her name, she had something that was priceless. Her freedom.

"I'm good, my brother. How's your day going so far?"

He pointed to the spectacular view behind him. "Just another shitty day in paradise." He placed a sun-bleached paper coaster in front of her. "Are you eating or just drinking?"

"Why can't I do both?"

"I knew I liked you for a reason." He picked up one of the laminated menus but didn't hand it to her. "You don't need this, do you?"

"Nah, I've got it memorized by now."

He punched a code on a touch screen as he prepared to take her order. "What'll it be then?"

"I'll have a Tusker and a couple of fish tacos."

"Just two today? You know my mahi-mahi's the best in town."

"Fine. You talked me into it. Make it three."

He unleashed a loud belly laugh. "I didn't have to twist your arm too hard." He turned to the kitchen and repeated the food order he had just entered into the computer. "Three mahi-mahi tacos with the works."

"Three all day," Bishme, the lead cook said. "Coming right up, brah."

Even though he wasn't classically trained, Bishme was good at his job. He was a patient instructor, too. She was grateful for his tutelage. She made mistakes from time to time, but at least she was finally able to make a meal without resorting to throwing something frozen into the microwave.

Santana pointed to the touch screen. "Why do you even bother using that when you still insist on taking orders the old-fashioned way?"

David winked as he opened the bottle of Kenyan lager she had ordered. "The computer keeps track of customers' tabs better than I do, but I give a better floor show." He set the bottle on the coaster and tossed the cap in the trash. "Don't look now, but I think the *wahine* who just walked in is checking you out."

Santana sipped her beer but didn't turn around. "Not interested."

"You've been saying that for a while now. How long have you been back? Four months?"

"Three months, two weeks, four days, seventeen hours, and twenty-six minutes. But who's counting?"

"It sounds like you are. Isn't it time you had a little company?"

"You're all the company I need."

He laughed as he draped a bar towel over his shoulder. "I won't tell Kalani if you won't."

"My lips are sealed."

"Let me check on those tacos. Hang tight. I'll be right back."

"Don't look. Don't look. Don't look," she told herself after he went to the kitchen. Eventually, her curiosity got the best of her.

Acting as nonchalantly as she could, she turned around and pretended to check out the local scenery. The white sand beach and turquoise water mere feet from the Tiki's patio were beautiful, but the woman standing just inside the front door took her breath away.

Brooklyn.

She looked away, convinced she was seeing things. When she looked back, she realized what she was seeing was real. This was really happening. Brooklyn DiVincenzo, the woman she had watched walk out of her life five months, two weeks, four days, and twenty-nine minutes ago had just sauntered back into it.

Santana hadn't even allowed herself to dream that this could happen. Now that it was, she didn't know how to react.

Brooklyn walked toward her. She was wearing strappy sandals and a floral print sundress that flowed like water as she moved. The two bodyguards stationed at each end of the bar moved to intercept her, but Santana shook her head to let them know it was okay for them to let Brooklyn pass. The men nodded and returned to their seats.

"Friends of yours?" Brooklyn asked.

"Something like that."

The pair were her constant shadows. They came courtesy of one of the alphabet soup of federal agencies she was assisting.

"You're a hard woman to find," Brooklyn said.

"I've been keeping a low profile."

She had been in something akin to the witness protection program for a good three months while she helped the attorneys assigned to prosecute Luke's, Winslow's, and Lee's cases. She had been allowed to return home until the trials began, but she had no idea when that would be since Winslow's and Lee's defense lawyers were doing everything they could to drag things out.

Santana tried to think of something witty to say when Brooklyn joined her at the bar, but what came out sounded lame even to her own ears. "You got my note."

Brooklyn peered at the seats on either side of her. Both were empty since the midday rush had already come and gone. "You said there was a barstool with my name on it, but I can't tell which one it is."

"Take your pick."

Brooklyn claimed the seat to her right. "Nice one," she said after she settled onto it. "I think I'll keep it."

Santana tried not to read too much into the comment—or the fact that Brooklyn was wearing the bracelet she had bought her. Brooklyn was here. Why and for how long didn't matter.

Brooklyn looked her up and down. "I don't think I've ever seen you look this…"

"Casual?" She no longer owned any designer clothes, so she usually resorted to what she was wearing today—shorts and a T-shirt. Here, she didn't need to dress to impress. Here, she could just be herself.

"I was going to say 'relaxed,' but casual works, too."

"I'm an island girl. I'm in my element."

"I can tell. It looks good on you."

The way Brooklyn was looking at her reminded her of how they used to be. How they could be again? Not in this lifetime. She handed her a menu. "Are you hungry?"

"Starved. Thirsty, too. The only things they fed us on the flight from Hong Kong were pretzels and peanuts. The inside of my mouth feels like a salt lick."

"I'll bet." Santana grabbed a glass from behind the bar and filled it with water. "I just ordered some fish tacos. We can share them if you like."

Their fingers touched when Santana handed her the glass of water. "Yes," Brooklyn said, holding her gaze. "I'd like that."

Santana tried not to stare at Brooklyn's mouth as she took a sip of her water. It had only been a few months since she had kissed those lips, but it felt like forever. So much had happened since the last time they had seen each other. And once Winslow's and Lee's trials finally got underway, so much was still to come.

"I heard about the deal you made with TechSass," she said. "How did you manage to talk them into entering a partnership with your company rather than purchasing it?"

"Before I met with them, I read your note for inspiration. Then I gave the presentation of my life. My knees were knocking the whole time, but I did it. And the best part is I didn't have to pretend to be someone else to get myself through it. I went in there telling myself that who I am was good enough. Then I proved myself right."

All the doubts Brooklyn had in her abilities were gone. For the first time, she truly seemed to believe in herself. No wonder she had never looked more beautiful.

"Sorry about the wait, my sistah," David said when he came out of the kitchen. "Here's your lunch." He set a plate containing a trio of tacos and a couple of lime wedges on the bar. "Can I get you anything else?"

"An extra plate and two more beers would be great. Thanks, David."

He arched his eyebrows when he saw Brooklyn sitting next to her, but he didn't say anything except, "Coming right up."

Santana slid the food toward Brooklyn. "Go ahead. It's probably been a lot longer since you ate than I have."

There were no nonstop flights to 'Ohe Sojukokoro. From New York, the trip took a good twenty-four hours. Sometimes more, depending on how many connecting flights you were willing to endure in order to lower the price of your ticket.

Brooklyn offered a mild protest, then inhaled one of the tacos in less than thirty seconds. "Sexy, right?" she asked after Santana wiped a blob of spicy aioli off her lip.

"Very."

They shared a laugh, then fell into an uncomfortable silence, uncertain how to move past the small talk and get to the heavy lifting.

"Detective Barnett refused to name names, but I know what you did," Brooklyn said. It was so like her to skip straight to the point. "You took quite a risk by coming forward."

"If you're trying to make me out to be a hero, don't. I didn't do what I did for the glory. I did it because it needed to be done."

"Is your mother safe?"

"For now." Santana had sobbed like a baby when they had finally been reunited. They were still working on repairing their broken relationship. She could only hope they would have time to make all the pieces fit.

"And what about you?" Brooklyn asked. "Will you have to spend the rest of your life looking over your shoulder?"

Santana indicated the burly bookends on each end of the bar. "Not as long as I have them around."

"Was the risk worth the reward?"

"That remains to be seen."

Luke, Winslow, and Lee had made numerous preliminary court appearances since they had been taken into custody. In light of his impromptu confession, Luke had chosen to cooperate and plead guilty in exchange for a lighter sentence. Winslow and Lee, on the other hand, had decided to contest their respective charges. Santana hoped the prosecutors' expertise and the testimony she and the other witnesses had agreed to provide would be enough to convince the juries in the Townsends's trials to return favorable verdicts.

"What about us?" Brooklyn asked. "Were we worth it?"

The question hit Santana like a punch to the gut. "Of course we were. Do you even have to ask?"

"No, but I need to hear you say it."

Though the doubts Brooklyn had once harbored about herself were gone, the doubts she had about her—about them—seemed to remain. Yet she had flown thousands of miles to be here. Her willingness to do that spoke volumes. Santana resolved to make sure she hadn't traveled all this way in vain.

"Yes," she said, "we were worth it."

Brooklyn must have been feeling the same kinds of emotions that were roiling inside her body because her hands shook when she took them in hers. Santana tried to offer her the stability she needed. The kind she had only been able to pay lip service to before. She wanted to show she was ready to do it right this time. That she was ready to go all in, not just far enough to keep her cover story intact.

"You were the best thing that ever happened to me, Brooklyn. Meeting you didn't just change my life. It gave me life. I was numb before I met you, but you sparked something in me I didn't even know was there. Like you, I've lived my life hiding behind different personas, but I've never felt more like myself than I was when I was with you. I don't expect you to take me back. I don't expect you to ever forgive me. I just want you to know that I never lied about my feelings for you."

"My parents ask about you all the time. They still adore you. When he talks about you, Pop always refers to you as 'the one that got away.'"

"Did you tell them who I am or what I used to do?"

Brooklyn shook her head. "It's your story, not mine. You should be the one who gets to share it."

"Thank you for that. I'll tell them everything as soon as I can. Charlie's parents, too. I know how much they mean to you. I won't allow myself to become a wedge that comes between you. I wouldn't be able to live with myself if I did. I'll willingly accept the consequences, no matter what they turn out to be."

"You'd do that?"

Santana could tell how much of a toll the situation had taken on her. She caressed her cheek. "For you, I'd do anything. Even if it means staying as far away from you as I can."

"What? Why?"

"It's not safe for you to be around me. As much as I want to be with you, I won't let you risk your life by—"

Brooklyn didn't let her finish. "You've spent so many years worrying about the ones you love. Give us a chance to return the favor."

Santana remembered the conversation she'd had with Brooklyn's father about his hope for Brooklyn to find a partner who wasn't seeking to leech off of her. "I'm flat broke and practically homeless. I have nothing to give you."

"All I want is your heart."

"You've had that from the beginning."

Brooklyn slid off the barstool and threw herself into Santana's arms. Santana held on tight. She didn't plan on letting her go. Not this time. Not ever again. When Brooklyn kissed her, the vast empty space inside her began to fill. Then it—and her heart—began to overflow.

"I love you, Brooklyn," she said when they finally broke the kiss.

"I love you, too, Santana." It was the first time she had ever heard Brooklyn call her by her real name. She couldn't wait to hear it again. "I do have a question for you, though."

"Ask me anything." From now on, her life would be an open book. Because she would be able to spend it with the woman she loved.

Brooklyn pointed to the tacos. "Are you going to eat those? Because I am really, really hungry."

Santana felt the laughter bubble up from inside her. Laughter that always seemed to come so easily whenever Brooklyn was around. "Take them. They're all yours."

And so was she.

# Epilogue

B rooklyn's heart was full. So was her stomach. Santana and her father had grilled enough fish to feed an army. They had been so proud of themselves and their catch that she and her mother had felt obligated to treat themselves to not only a second helping but a third. Now she was paying the price.

"I really should have skipped dessert." She rubbed her stomach as Santana sat next to her on the porch swing.

"Isn't it a sin to say 'no' to tiramisu?"

"If it isn't, it certainly should be."

"Drink this." Santana handed her a highball glass filled with two fingers of Scotch. "It will make you feel better."

Brooklyn took a sip and sighed as she felt warmth slowly permeate her body. "Good whiskey makes the best digestif."

"I couldn't agree more."

Santana draped her arm across her shoulders. Brooklyn curled up against her side. "For an island girl, you certainly seem to enjoy the country."

"What can I say? I like it here."

They were back in the Catskills. Back in the cabin Santana had rented more than a year ago when she had met Brooklyn's parents for the first time. Now they were practically family. Not practically. Now they were family.

Naturally, her parents had been shocked when Santana told them the unvarnished truth about herself. Like her, they had eventually been able to separate who she was from what she had been forced to do. Santana had vowed to spend the rest of her life making amends, and the role she had played in bringing the ones responsible for Charlie's death to justice proved she was a woman of her word. Her bond with Brooklyn's parents had grown stronger in the ensuing months. Brooklyn was looking forward to watching it deepen as well as forging her own ties with Santana's mother.

"This place holds special memories for me," Santana continued. "For us."

"I can't help but smile every time I remember you doing a header in the lake after you lost your grip on your fishing rod during that first trip. I can't help but tear up each time I remember you making my mother laugh during your walk through the woods."

"I noticed you didn't mention the part about us sitting here listening to your parents have sex."

"The less said about that, the better."

"Did you remember to pack the earplugs? It's almost that time, you know."

"Got them right here." Brooklyn patted her pocket. Her parents' sexual shenanigans were nothing if not predictable.

Though they joked about them now, Brooklyn considered herself lucky every time she watched Santana and her parents interact. It was like they had known each other all their lives. Something she was immensely grateful for since she planned to have Santana in her life for the rest of her life.

She sighed again. She wished she could replicate the contentment she felt being here in this place with this woman by her side. No matter what a series of advertising campaigns once proclaimed, there wasn't an app for that.

"What's on tap for tomorrow?" she asked.

Santana turned to her. "Making more memories?"

Brooklyn pressed a kiss to her lips. "I can't wait."

# About the Author

Yolanda Wallace is not a professional writer, but she plays one in her spare time. Her love of travel and adventure has helped her pen numerous globe-spanning novels, including the Lambda Award-winning *Month of Sundays* and *Tailor-Made*. Her short stories have appeared in multiple anthologies including *Romantic Interludes 2: Secrets* and *Women of the Dark Streets*. She and her wife live in beautiful coastal Georgia, where they are parents to two children of the four-legged variety.

# Books Available from Bold Strokes Books

**30 Dates in 30 Days** by Elle Spencer. A busy lawyer tries to find love the fast way—thirty dates in thirty days. (978-1-63555-498-4)

**Finding Sky** by Cass Sellars. Skylar Addison's search for a career intersects with her new boss's search for butterflies, but Skylar can't forgive Jess's intrusion into her life. (978-1-63555-521-9)

**Hammers, Strings, and Beautiful Things** by Morgan Lee Miller. While on tour with the biggest pop star in the world, rising musician Blair Bennett falls in love for the first time while coping with loss and depression. (978-1-63555-538-7)

**Heart of a Killer** by Yolanda Wallace. Contract killer Santana Masters's only interest is her next assignment—until a chance meeting with a beautiful stranger tempts her to change her ways. (978-1-63555-547-9)

**Leading the Witness** by Carsen Taite. When defense attorney Catherine Landauer reluctantly becomes the key witness in prosecutor Starr Rio's latest criminal trial, their hearts, careers, and lives may be at risk. (978-1-63555-512-7)

**No Experience Required** by Kimberly Cooper Griffin. Izzy Treadway has resigned herself to a life without romance because of her bipolar illness but wonders what she's gotten herself into when she agrees to write a book about love. (978-1-63555-561-5)

**One Walk in Winter** by Georgia Beers. Olivia Santini and Hayley Boyd Markham might be rivals at work, but they discover that lonely hearts often find company in the most unexpected of places. (978-1-63555-541-7)

**The Inn at Netherfield Green** by Aurora Rey. Advertising executive Lauren Montgomery and gin distiller Camden Crawley don't agree on anything except saving the Rose & Crown, the old English pub that's brought them together. (978-1-63555-445-8)

**Top of Her Game** by M. Ullrich. When it comes to life on the field and matters of the heart, losing isn't an option for pro athletes Kenzie Shaw and Sutton Flores. (978-1-63555-500-4)

**Vanished** by Eden Darry. A storm is coming, and Ellery and Loveday must find the chosen one or humanity won't survive it. (978-1-63555-437-3)

**All She Wants** by Larkin Rose. Marci Jones and Tessa Dalton get more than they bargained for when their plans for a one-night stand turn into an opportunity for love. (978-1-63555-476-2)

**Beautiful Accidents** by Erin Zak. Stevie Adams and Bernadette Thompson discover that sometimes the best things in life happen purely by accident. (978-1-63555-497-7)

**Before Now** by Joy Argento. Can Delany and Jade overcome the betrayal that spans the centuries to reignite a love that can't be broken? (978-1-63555-525-7)

**Breathe** by Cari Hunter. Paramedic Jemima Pardon's chronic bad luck seems to be improving when she meets police officer Rosie Jones. But they face a battle to survive before they can find love. (978-1-63555-523-3)

**Double-Crossed** by Ali Vali. Hired thief and killer Reed Gable finds something in her scope that will change her life forever when she gets a contract to end casino accountant Brinley Myers's life. (978-1-63555-302-4)

**False Horizons** by CJ Birch. Jordan and Ash struggle with different views on the alien agenda and must find their way back to each other before they're swallowed up by a centuries-old war. (978-1-63555-519-6)

**Legacy** by Charlotte Greene. When five women hike to a remote cabin deep inside a national park, unsettling events suggest that they should have stayed home. (978-1-63555-490-8)

**Royal Street Reveillon** by Greg Herren. Someone is killing the stars of a reality show, and it's up to Scotty Bradley and the boys to find out who. (978-1-63555-545-5)

**Somewhere Along the Way** by Kathleen Knowles. When Maxine Cooper moves to San Francisco during the summer of 1981, she learns that wherever you run, you cannot escape yourself. (978-1-63555-383-3)

**Blood of the Pack** by Jenny Frame. When Alpha of the Scottish pack Kenrick Wulver visits the Wolfgangs, she falls for Zaria Lupa, a wolf on the run. (978-1-63555-431-1)

**Cause of Death** by Sheri Lewis Wohl. Medical student Vi Akiak and K9 Search and Rescue officer Kate Renard must work together to find a killer before they end up the next targets. In the race for survival, they discover that love may be the biggest risk of all. (978-1-63555-441-0)

**Chasing Sunset** by Missouri Vaun. Hijinks and mishaps ensue as Iris and Finn set off on a road trip adventure, chasing the sunset, and falling in love along the way. (978-1-63555-454-0)

**Double Down** by MB Austin. When an unlikely friendship with Spanish pop star Erlea turns deeper, Celeste, in-house physician for the hotel hosting Erlea's show, has a choice to make—run or double down on love. (978-1-63555-423-6)

**Party of Three** by Sandy Lowe. Three friends are in for a wild night at billionaire heiress Eleanor McGregor's twenty-fifth birthday party. Love, lust, and doing the right thing, even when it hurts, turn the evening into one that will change their lives forever. (978-1-63555-246-1)

**Sit. Stay. Love.** by Karis Walsh. City girl Alana Brendt and country vet Tegan Evans both know they don't belong together. Only problem is, they're falling in love. (978-1-63555-439-7)

**Where the Lies Hide** by Renee Roman. As P.I. Camdyn Stark gets closer to solving the case, will her dark secrets and the lies she's buried jeopardize her future with the quietly beautiful Sarah Peters? (978-1-63555-371-0)

**Beautiful Dreamer** by Melissa Brayden. With love on the line, can Devyn Winters find it in her heart to stay in the small town of Dreamer's Bay, the one place she swore she'd never remain? (978-1-63555-305-5)

**Create a Life to Love** by Erin Zak. When sixteen-year-old Beth shows up at her birth mother's door, three lives will change forever. (978-1-63555-425-0)

**Deadeye** by Meredith Doench. Stranded while hunting the serial predator Deadeye, Special Agent Luce Hansen fights for survival while her lover, forensic pathologist Harper Bennett, hunts for clues to Hansen's disappearance along the killer's trail. (978-1-63555-253-9)

**Death Takes a Bow** by David S. Pederson. Alan Keys takes part in a local stage production, but when the leading man is murdered, his partner Detective Heath Barrington is thrust into the limelight to find the killer. (978-1-63555-472-4)

**Endangered** by Michelle Larkin. Shapeshifters Officer Aspen Wolfe and Dr. Tora Madigan fight their growing attraction as they work together to destroy a secret government agency that exterminates their kind. (978-1-63555-377-2)

**Incognito** by VK Powell. The only thing Evan Spears is focused on is capturing a fleeing murder suspect until wild card Frankie Strong is added to her team and causes chaos on and off the job. (978-1-63555-389-5)

**Insult to Injury** by Gun Brooke. After losing everything, Gail Owen withdraws to her old farmhouse and finds a destitute young woman, Romi Shepherd, living in a secret room. (978-1-63555-323-9)

**Just One Moment** by Dena Blake. If you were given the chance to have the love of your life back, could you ignore everything that went wrong and start over again? (978-1-63555-387-1)

**Scene of the Crime** by MJ Williamz. Cullen Mathew finds herself caught between the woman she thinks she loves but can no longer trust and a beautiful detective she can't stop thinking about who will stop at nothing to find the truth. (978-1-63555-405-2)

**Accidental Prophet** by Bud Gundy. Days after his grandmother dies, Drew Morten learns his true identity and finds himself racing against time to save civilization from the apocalypse. (978-1-63555-452-6)

**Daughter of No One** by Sam Ledel. When their worlds are threatened, a princess and a village outcast must overcome their differences and embrace a budding attraction if they want to survive. (978-1-63555-427-4)

**Fear of Falling** by Georgia Beers. Singer Sophie James is ready to shake up her career, but her new manager, the gorgeous Dana Landon, has other ideas. (978-1-63555-443-4)

**In Case You Forgot** by Fredrick Smith and Chaz Lamar. Zaire and Kenny, two newly single, Black, queer, and socially aware men, start again—in love, career, and life—in the West Hollywood neighborhood of LA. (978-1-63555-493-9)

**Playing with Fire** by Lesley Davis. When Takira Lathan and Dante Groves meet at Takira's restaurant, love may find its way onto the menu. (978-1-63555-433-5)

**Practice Makes Perfect** by Carsen Taite. Meet law school friends Campbell, Abby, and Grace, law partners at Austin's premier boutique legal firm for young, hip entrepreneurs. Legal Affairs: one law firm, three best friends, three chances to fall in love. (978-1-63555-357-4)

**The Last Seduction** by Ronica Black. When you allow true love to elude you once and you desperately regret it, are you brave enough to grab it when it comes around again? (978-1-63555-211-9)

**Wavering Convictions** by Erin Dutton. After a traumatic event, Maggie has vowed to regain her strength and independence. So how can Ally be both the woman who makes her feel safe and a constant reminder of the person who took her security away? (978-1-63555-403-8)